Meant

to be

Different

Meant to Be Series
Book Two

By AMELIA FOSTER

Meant to be Different

Limitless Publishing, LLC
Kailua, HI 96734
www.limitlesspublishing.com

Formatting: Limitless Publishing

ISBN-13: 978-1-64034-844-8
ISBN-10: 1-64034-844-1

Chapter One

Wyatt

Present Day

"I'm retiring."

Just as Wyatt had anticipated, Jim's jaw dropped and his pale complexion mottled. "Now son, this is a bit unreasonable. We don't need to be hasty. Let's just talk about this first. You're only thirty years old—"

Wyatt held his hand up, cutting off his manager's bluster. "Thirty is damn near geriatric in this business. And I don't want to wait until my body is broken and useless and my brain has turned to mush."

The older man tapped his pen on the desk several times in rapid succession, regarding Wyatt solemnly. "And what are you going to do with yourself? Write a book? Go on that celebrity dance competition show and learn the cha-cha?"

He snorted and crossed his leg, resting his ankle on the opposite knee. "I'm not that desperate for attention. Although some of those girls are pretty hot."

He tilted his head back and forth a few times in mock consideration before giving it a definitive shake. "Nah, I'm done with being in the spotlight."

Jim leaned back in his office chair and folded his hands over his plump midsection, the whitening of his knuckles belying his relaxed posture. "So you're going to work some middle management job and go home to your PTA wife and two-point-five kids at the end of the day and mow your picket fence-lined yard on the weekends? You're just going to fade into oblivion in suburbia?"

The confident smile Wyatt had walked in with slipped. His agent's derisive questions were hitting a little too close to home. He wanted more than two kids and the only woman he'd ever considered marrying could be called a lot of things, but an average PTA mom wasn't one of them.

But everything else? Hell yeah. Jim had unwittingly described Wyatt's version of perfect.

He held no disillusions about the man's motivations. While Jim had proven himself competent and capable over the years they'd worked together—despite all the warnings Wyatt had been given about the man from other competitors—Wyatt knew he was one of Jim's highest-grossing clients. Which translated into a nice, fat percentage landing squarely in Jim's bank account. He couldn't care less if Wyatt would be bored by a career change, only that his influx of money would drop considerably.

"My mind is made up. Five more competitions and then I'm done." He stood and straightened the legs of his jeans. "Run whatever ads and promotions you need to run. Create whatever hype you can."

He pinned his manager with a knowing stare Wyatt had made most of his important life decisions by trusting his gut and ignoring rumors, including the ones that Jim had some personal issues that were bleeding into his professional career, but lately his manager was making him uneasy. "And, by all means, get as many endorsements lined up as you can to pad your wallet with that fifteen percent you take off the top of all my deals."

With that parting shot, he grabbed the cowboy hat he was never without and jammed it on his head. He pointedly ignored the sputtering from Jim behind him, scrambling for another excuse as to why Wyatt shouldn't retire.

For more than a decade, his life had been a series of nondescript hotel rooms and nearly never-ending aches and pairs. Not to mention interviews, flights, buses and...perpetual exhaustion.

It was an unpleasant and sometimes irritating lifestyle, but it was also familiar and comfortable. And Wyatt's new career path, hell, his new life, was uncertain, risky, and could easily fail long before he even had a chance to get off the ground.

A slow smile spread across his face as he stepped out of the tall, gray office building and into the hot Houston sun. Yeah, he was taking a big chance. Sure, it was damn near terrifying to think of doing something new, something that required more thought than any endeavor before in his life, and something that could possibly end up as the second biggest mistake of his life.

But it was also far more thrilling than eight seconds on any bull he'd ridden in his career.

Once his plan began to take shape, he could finally correct the one thing that had been haunting him for nearly a dozen years. That was possibly the biggest draw of all.

He slid into his truck, blasting the AC as high as it would go, and pulled his cell phone from the breast pocket of his black western shirt, his finger landing on the familiar name. Three rings later, a groggy hello greeted him.

"Tanner, what the hell are you doing asleep?" He shot his arm out straight to view the time on the thick, stainless steel watch. "It's almost nine o'clock on a Thursday morning!"

"Remember, brother," Tanner's sleep-roughened voice came over the line. "I've got a new work schedule now."

Wyatt was just about to remind him that Tanner Carlisle wasn't the kind of guy to put off work when he heard a giggle in the background that made him roll his eyes. "Yeah, and I'm sure my hot sister-in-law has absolutely nothing to do with it."

"You need to stop saying that." Tanner practically growled, exactly the reaction Wyatt was hoping for, and he couldn't help the laugh that spilled out.

Before he could say anything else, a soft whisper from Izzy and Tanner's nausea-inducing enamored response trickled through the phone, and Wyatt's gut clenched. He'd always made fun of Tanner for the kind of relationship he had with his wife, but now Wyatt found himself wanting the same thing. Missing something he'd never had.

If he were to be completely honest—something he usually avoided at all costs—he'd admit that he was jealous. Not of Izzy herself, although taunting his brother by shamelessly flirting with her was a favorite pastime. No, his green-eyed monster flared at everything she represented. Everything he could have had years ago.

"I need a favor, big brother." He took a deep breath. "Can you find me some property? A lot of it. Think three hundred acres."

He heard some rustling, and Tanner's voice suddenly cleared. "What for?"

"I'm moving home." The words felt even better to say out loud than to play on repeat in his head. He plunged ahead, laying out all his plans. "I'm going to open a training facility for kids who want to follow in my impressive footsteps, so I need a lot of acreage to build a house and a barn and a paddock and—"

Tanner coughed dramatically. "Yeah, got it. Give you land, lots of land, under starry skies above. Listen, I'll look around and call you back later, little brother, okay?"

And without waiting for a response, Tanner ended the phone call and Wyatt was met with only silence. Yeah, they really were disgusting.

But lately he found himself wishing he had a little of their kind of disgusting in his life.

***

Georgia

Present Day

11:34 a.m.

The daily alarm on her phone sounded, pulling Georgia from her frustrated musings over the latest design panel her team had delivered. She uncrossed her legs and stood, pausing just a moment to steady herself on the red-soled, spindly heels she had a love/hate relationship with. She walked to the door, closing it with a soft click, just as she did every day at this time.

As soon as she was settled in her black leather office chair, she picked up the nameplate from the front of her desk and ran a finger over the gold script engraved into the dark wood.

Georgia Marsh
Marketing Director

Being a marketing executive at thirty years old was practically unheard of, but adding in the fact that she was a woman, the title, the nameplate, and everything they represented were nearly impossible achievements.

Every day she put all the clambering demands on hold to commemorate the moment Elias Joseph shook her hand after she'd accepted the position. She cradled the seemingly innocuous rectangle in her hand with reverence befitting the achievement. A moment to appreciate her position. And just a moment to wish her mom could see what she'd done with her life.

Georgia's gaze fell on the boards strewn across her desk once again, and she sighed. Her name carried weight, and she certainly wasn't going to allow it to be attached to these fashion disasters.

Joseph Boots and Apparel was built on creating family-friendly western-style clothing at affordable prices, offering choices that defied the cheesy clothes from other companies that looked better suited for an off-Broadway production of *Oklahoma!* than a retailer.

The designs her team sent were neither chic nor family friendly. She frowned, gingerly replacing her nameplate, and threw the sketches in the trash. A few clicks on her keyboard cued up a blank email.

To: Apparel Design Team
Subject: Try Again
While your attempts at creating something unique are appreciated, I feel you've all forgotten some of the cornerstones of this company. Mr. Joseph wants the image to be family friendly but still trendy. The sketches you've sent are completely opposite to both of these precepts. You have forty-eight hours to bring me something new and please keep these two things in mind:

1. If it can double as a costume for a stripper, it is not family friendly.

2. If Granny Clampett was your inspiration, it is not trendy.

– Georgia

Her finger hovered over the send button for several long minutes. She didn't want to be that boss. The unreasonable, unapproachable, unlikable dictator.

P.S. ~ Food is fuel. To get good out, we must put good in. Bagels, fruit, and coffee on me tomorrow morning and we'll review the designs over pizza Thursday night.

Not allowing herself to question or change her mind, she quickly sent it off just as her phone rang.

"Georgia Marsh," she answered absently as she scrolled through the emails in her inbox. It wasn't even noon yet. How could she possibly have this many messages?

"Georgia."

The deep voice booming across the line immediately made her sit up straighter in her seat, grab a pen and paper, and bring her mind into laser-sharp focus. "Yes, Mr. Joseph. How are you, sir?"

If it were physically possible, she was certain the receiver in her hand would shake from his rumbling laughter. "Georgia, Georgia, when are you going to start callin' me Elias?"

She smiled at his thick Texas drawl that hadn't lessened in all the years since he'd moved to North Carolina. "What can I do for you, Elias?"

"I met a young man recently. Fine young man. He's plannin' on openin' a business here soon, and I think if we could partner with him, help back his endeavor, well, I think it would be one of those win/win things you're always lecturin' me about."

Georgia scribbled out some notes on the blank page. Partner? New business? WTH??? "I'm sure it's a great idea, but maybe you can give me just a little more information…"

Elias' booming laughter greeted her suggestion. "Georgia, I'll do ya one better. We're meetin' this fella for lunch today."

Her eyes flicked over to the clock on her computer screen. 11:50 am. "Lunch? Today? Wouldn't it be better if I had time to prepare? To pull together some ideas and suggestions and—"

"Nope. We're meetin' him at 12:30 in the conference room. I've already ordered the food from Monte Cello's. Just trust me, Georgia. I got a gut feelin' about this guy."

A wry grin tugged at her lips, and she closed her eyes. Her boss was kind, generous, and gave her far more leeway than anyone else probably would, but then he'd make decisions based on a whim or a gut feeling…

And she'd quickly learned to just go with it. She owed Elias a debt she could never repay. He gambled when he offered her a position that was more than just the golden door, but an opportunity to take care of her family. Again. "All right, Elias. Let me wrap up a couple of things and I'll be right over."

Twenty minutes later, the tapping of Georgia's heels echoed on the tiled surface as she walked down the hall. She paused for a moment outside the door of the conference room to tuck a strand of her straight auburn hair behind her ear, take a deep breath, and put on her most charming smile.

Which promptly disappeared as soon as she pushed open the door and spied her boss' guest.

"Oh, hell no." The words tumbled out of her mouth before she could stop them, followed quickly by a flood of memories she thought she'd banished to the furthest reaches of her mind, never to be heard from again. Wyatt Carlisle, her first love, sat at the same table as her boss, stupid, cocky, lopsided grin firmly in place.

Chapter Two

Wyatt

Twenty Years Earlier

Wyatt blinked several times, but the view didn't change. He was certain his dad hadn't taken a word he'd said seriously until this very moment.

"Come on, son." Mike Carlisle's mammoth-sized hand clapped onto Wyatt's much smaller shoulder, and he directed him up the bleachers to their seats.

He didn't know where to look first. His eyes darted from the half dozen jean-clad men lined up along the metal railing to the one racing the horse around the perimeter of the dusty oval that seemed only feet away. Every sound, sight, and even smell made the blood in Wyatt's veins hum with pleasure.

Thirty minutes later, they announced the bull-riding competition would start and Wyatt sat up straighter in his seat. He took in everything that happened in the six seconds the cowboy lasted. Immediately his little brain tried to figure out exactly what the older man

11

had done wrong and what he would do better if he'd been the rider.

"Daddy," he finally said when he found the voice to speak. "I-I really wanna do this...really." He turned his head and looked up at the man he saw as an indestructible giant. His father was his hero in every way, even more so after their excursion, but there was no way he'd be like his older brother and follow in Michael Carlisle's intimidating footsteps.

Mike smiled, wrinkles forming at the corners of the blue eyes that were identical to his two oldest boys. "I know, son. But you're only nine. You've got a lot of years ahead of you to make those kind of decisions."

Wyatt shook his head vigorously. "No, Daddy. I wanna do this forever. I'm gonna start practicing and training and—"

His father tilted his head and chuckled. "All right, son, we'll talk about this more at home. But first how about we get something to eat?" He inclined his head down to the arena below them. "I think they are going to take a break for a little bit."

Standing in line, discussing lunch options listed on the white board hanging on the side of the food truck with his dad, Wyatt's eyes kept getting pulled to the dirt-filled oval that was practically sacred. He couldn't find the words to describe how right every part of this felt to him.

On the way back to their seats, Wyatt couldn't stop himself. "I mean it, Daddy. This is what I'm gonna do when I grow up."

His proclamation was met with a bark of laughter to his right. His eyes traveled up the walking, talking epitome of everything he wanted from life. Every bit, from the cracked leather boots to his oversized buckle and well-worn cowboy hat, was Wyatt's vision of the future. Wyatt couldn't speak, think, or remember how to blink in the presence of the older man.

"What's your name, cowpoke?" His idol had a gravelly voice and weathered face, but his genuine smile encouraged Wyatt to answer.

He took a deep gulp. "W-Wy-Wyatt, sir. Wyatt Carlisle."

When the older man crouched down to his level, Wyatt tore his eyes away for long enough to meet his father's encouraging smile.

"Well, Wyatt, I think with a name like that you were practically born to be a cowboy." He held out a calloused, giant paw. "I'll be mighty pleased to see ya on tour with us in a few years."

The short interaction replayed through Wyatt's mind the rest of the evening, even as he greedily devoured every different event at the rodeo, committing it all to his memory. When they reached his father's car, he impulsively wrapped his arms around Mike's waist. "Thank you, Daddy."

Mike squeezed him and patted his back. "I'm glad you had fun today, son."

He pulled away and offered a wide grin. "I'll give you my first buckle, Daddy."

***

Georgia

Fourteen Years Earlier

Her chest heaved with labored breathing as she pushed herself to run just a little faster, her flip-flops slapping against the sidewalk with each step. She needed to get as far from her house as fast as she could. She needed to get to the beach. The air rolling off the ocean would soothe her soul and calm her fears, just as it always did.

As soon as the concrete ended, Georgia kicked her shoes off and raced over the dunes, falling to her knees a few feet from where the wave lapped against the shore. She licked her dry lips, sucking air into her burning lungs and trying desperately to slow her speeding heart.

Her fingers dug into the coarse sand. She closed her eyes and focused her mind on the sound of the waves and the gulls in the distance. Her nostrils flared as she inhaled the blend of saltwater and earthy vegetation unique to the one place that could make any problem in her life feel minor and easy to overcome.

Stage Four.

Metastasis.

Comfort measures.

Words no sixteen year old should know circled through her mind on a scratchy repeat like a broken record player.

Georgia had no idea how long she sat there, the outer picture of total peace, as the storm inside slowly settled. She jumped when a hand landed on her shoulder, and her eyes lifted from the swelling tides in front of her to meet the weary eyes of her father.

"Daddy, I don't want to go."

His shoulders sagged and he dropped to the ground beside her. "It's what your mom wants."

"Do you really think the doctors in North Carolina are going to be better than the ones here in Tampa?" she scoffed.

Barry Marsh's gaze fixed out on the horizon, and he rested his forearms on his raised knees, not answering for several minutes. "Pumpkin." Her father's pet name for her since infancy was barely more than a whisper. "It doesn't matter how many or what kind of doctors your mom goes to. Not anymore."

A lump the size of a grapefruit lodged in Georgia's throat. "Wha-what do you mean, Daddy?"

He turned his bloodshot eyes to her and offered a haunted smile. "Mom…well, Mom didn't want to tell you, Georgia, but she…" He sighed heavily, a deep crease forming between his brows. "She isn't taking any more treatments. The chemotherapy makes her sick and weak. She doesn't want to live the rest of her life that way. It's not helping anyway. The spots keep growing—"

Georgia clapped a hand over her mouth and choked out a sob.

"She wants to go home, Pumpkin." Matching tears streamed down his face. "She wants to be home and be close to Grandma and Grandpa. She wants you to have them." His hand waved, encompassing the water in front of them, glowing orange in the light of the setting sun. "The mountains are for her what the ocean

15

is for you."

She swiped the moisture creating trails down her cheeks. She swallowed back the anger, bitterness, fear, and every other emotion crashing against her battered heart like a wave from the gulf. "Then I guess we're moving to North Carolina."

Chapter Three

Wyatt

Present Day

The urge to laugh, throw his hat in the air, do an incredibly embarrassing victory dance, or some strange combination of the three was overwhelming. What were the chances the one person who made moving home to Asheville more appealing than any other option would be having lunch with him this soon?

God bless his lucky hat. Six championship buckles couldn't be wrong.

The way the black pencil skirt hugged the curve of hips that were imprinted on his memory made his mouth go dry. His eyes trailed up over the pale pink satin blouse that she left unbuttoned at the neck, exposing just enough to make his fingers itch to open it the rest of the way and discover if her skin was still as soft as he remembered.

The stormy expression on her face made his smile

falter. Yeah, he remembered her temper too.

Wyatt stood and swiped his hat from his head. "Hey there, Gigi."

Her full lips parted and her hand popped up on her hip, but before a word came out, her eyes fell on the older gentleman seated at the head of the long table. Her mouth snapped closed and twisted at the corner. "Good afternoon, Wyatt."

The ice that dripped from each syllable made it pretty damn clear that she didn't mean a word of it, but the sound of his name on her lips still called his body to attention. He pulled the chair he'd been sitting in out a little farther and gestured for her to sit down in his place.

Without a word, she ignored the proffered seat and crossed behind Elias Joseph sitting to his left, directly across the smooth, wooden surface from Wyatt. She set her tablet on the table and knit her hands together in front of her. His mouth jerked into an involuntarily grin. Damn, she was adorable when she was mad.

Elias raised a bushy gray brow, and his eyes darted between the two of them as Wyatt resumed his seat. "You two know each other?"

"You could—"

"We went to high school together a million years ago," Gigi smoothly cut in with a dismissive flick of her wrist before shooting him a fiery glance. "That's all."

Wyatt's smile completely evaporated. He wasn't an idiot; he'd known a dozen years ago when he left if he ever had a chance to see her again she wouldn't fall into his arms. She couldn't. She still never knew... "Yeah." He confirmed her downplaying of their relationship with a definitive nod. "Gigi and I went to high school together."

We also went to the movies. And dinner. And down by the lake where we—

A vibration against his thigh cut through the haze of irritation, and he slid the phone from his pocket. He immediately regretted it when he saw his manager's—former manager's—name flash across the screen. Again. Undoubtedly another desperate attempt at getting Wyatt to change his mind.

"Georgia. My name is Georgia." She folded her arms across her chest and pinned him with an irritated glare, bringing his mind back to their present reality, which was far less exciting than the memories teasing him.

He slid the phone back into place and rested his forearms on the long wooden table, leaning forward slightly. "I've never called you Georgia."

Her head tilted to the side, and straight, shining strands of her auburn hair fell over one shoulder. "You just never called."

Their eyes locked in silent battle. Damn, this wasn't how he'd planned his first meeting with her going. He caught the worried look on Elias Joseph's face in his peripheral vision as the man's gaze darted back and forth between the two younger people seated on either side of him. He had definitely never expected an audience.

The door behind Wyatt's left shoulder opened again, and he held his breath, halfway afraid of who could possibly walk in next. The fourth grade teacher that he tormented by shooting spitballs into her frizzy, bleached blonde hair? The band director he pranked throughout high school? His life was turning into a bad reality show.

When the waitress, clad in the black pants and crisp white shirt uniform of Monte Cello's, quietly stepped through the door and immediately began setting up dishes, he released an audible sigh of relief.

But his disobedient gaze couldn't be held by the Caesar salad placed in front of him. His eyes devoured all things Gigi from the tapping of her French tip nails on the smooth veneer of the table to the gentle tilt of her lips when she smiled at something Elias said.

Everything about her had changed.

And everything about her was exactly the same.

He watched her slide the forkful of leafy greens into her mouth and thought he'd explode in his seat. Since when had a woman eating a salad been sexy? The answer quickly followed the question. Since Gigi.

She moved her stylus over the tablet as she chewed. When her tongue darted out to lick a drop of the creamy dressing from the corner of her mouth, Wyatt hurried to shove a pile of lettuce in his own to silence the groan.

"Elias, I think we should discuss the wisdom of aligning the company with Wy-Mr. Carlisle." Her arctic stare caught his for a second before she turned to her boss, the polar ice caps in the hazel depths melting into puddles of warmth. "Privately."

Wyatt rolled his eyes. Mr. Carlisle? Really? Yeah, she deserved to be pissed. He earned that. Expected it. But Mr. Carlisle was so ridiculous it was damn near funny more than insulting. "Now, Gigi, you know my name pretty damn well." He winked, knowing it would infuriate her more. "You've said it plenty of times. And if you have any thoughts or…concerns about Joseph Boots and Apparel and my ranch coming to a mutually beneficial arrangement, I think it's only fair that I'm here to listen and ease your worries."

Elias raised his brows and inclined his head. "He's got a point there, Georgia. Man has a right to speak for himself."

Her nostrils flared, and her gaze narrowed at him. Damn. Pushing her buttons never got old, although the fun he had teasing her when they were kids might be better suited for after she forgave him. There wasn't an "if" she did in his mind because failure wasn't an option for Wyatt Carlisle. Especially not where Gigi was concerned.

"Fine." The word had never sounded so much like an epithet as it did through her clenched teeth. "JBA prides itself on being a family friendly company. We choose the athletes we sponsor and the retailers we partner with based on that principle."

Elias' thinning gray head nodded along, and the admiration radiating from his eyes toward Gigi was evident. Wyatt couldn't blame him in the slightest. When she squared her shoulders and began to speak, she commanded attention. And he was pretty damn proud of her.

The corner of her mouth quirked up again with the agreement from her boss. "I will grant you that Mr. Carlisle has been an incredibly successful bull rider, won countless championships, and even set several records."

She paused, looking for all the world like she was filled with regret at the words she was about to speak. But Wyatt didn't miss the flame of retribution that flashed in her eyes. "However, he also is photographed with a different supermodel at every event he attends, and his drunken antics have been the subject of more than one social media firestorm. I think those reasons are good enough to keep our name from being linked with his."

Hell and damnation. So that's the card she was going to play. A small part of him was smug knowing she'd easily rattled off several very accurate and complimentary facts about him. There wasn't a doubt in his mind she had been following his career carefully to know these things.

But she wasn't right about his dating life. Well, not totally. It was so much more complicated than that. Every aspect of his life was carefully orchestrated from which companies he endorsed to which woman he dated. A fact he'd failed to realize until he'd stepped into the spotlight and everyone started begging for a piece of Wyatt Carlisle.

He straightened in his seat just as the server set the chicken Marsala in front of him. "First of all, Ms. Marsh," he paused and his eyes dropped to her left hand, fearful for a moment that she'd...but the bare finger forced air back into his empty lungs, "thank you for the compliments. While my championships are impressive, they aren't countless. I'm afraid you've been sucked into the same falsehoods about my personal life every celebrity gossip magazine wants the world to believe. It isn't half as exciting as it's been portrayed. Even if it were, I've retired now. Mr. Joseph and I are working on a private venture separate from my former career."

Gigi's mouth fell open, and Wyatt had to control

his laughter. The green and gold eyes that he'd dreamed about more times than he would admit widened with a combination of shock and confusion.

"Then why the hell are you here?" As soon as the words left her mouth, all the color drained from her face. "I'm so sorry for my language, Mr. Joseph. That was highly inappropriate—"

The older man threw his head back with a loud chuckle. "Georgia, you gotta stop saying that Mr. Joseph stuff, and for cryin' out loud, girl, don't be afraid to speak your mind. You've more than proven your competency and natural talent."

A rosy blush blossomed on her cheeks, and Wyatt's heart sped at the sight. His voice softened when he answered her. "I'm opening a training facility here. Teaching the next generation all the tricks of the trade from bull riding to lassoing and barrel racing. I'm going to have a competition to kick off the grand opening and Mr. Joseph—" The older man coughed, and Wyatt grinned. "I mean, Elias wants to be a sponsor of the competition and my supplier for merchandise for the ranch."

She lifted her fork to her lips and slowly chewed. Dammit, first the salad, now the chicken. He wouldn't be able to make it through a meal with this woman.

After several long moments of silence punctuated only by the occasional sound of the silverware against the china dishes, she nodded while shooting daggers at him with her eyes, unbeknownst to her boss. "I'll have my team work on a marketing strategy. Perhaps some exclusive clothing only available at your training facility?"

Wyatt grinned at her clipped tone and stiff posture

and congratulated himself. Maybe he should've moved back a hell of a long time ago.

***

Georgia

Present Day

The sun glinting off the deep plum-colored Jeep in her driveway caught Georgia's attention as soon as she turned onto her street. A small bit of the tension in her shoulders eased as she pulled her red Infiniti next to it. She gave herself a moment to breathe before collecting the files she brought home with her and her cumbersome red snakeskin laptop case.

If she were still living in Tampa, she'd have simply spent a few extra hours at the office so she could keep her home the stress-free sanctuary she loved. She bit her bottom lip as she crossed the threshold and groaned in relief as she kicked off her heels.

A messy bun of strawberry blonde curls bopped around in the kitchen, and Georgia couldn't help but grin. One that melted into uncontainable laughter as her best friend jumped ten feet in the air when Georgia tapped her shoulder.

Paige pressed a hand to her heart and popped one of the earbuds free. "Dammit, Georgie, you scared the shit out of me."

She pointed at the bottle sitting on the island. "Is that a Vinho Verde?"

Paige rolled her emerald eyes. "Did we just meet?"

"I have had a day from hell. My vote will firmly be

that we set our goal for the evening to polish off this and the bottle of red I'm sure you tucked away somewhere." She crossed into the living room, grabbing the glass of white wine her best friend held out to her on the way, and sank into the couch.

Georgia took a long sip of the wine, savoring the peach and green apple flavors. She stared sightlessly at the blank screen of the fifty-four-inch television hanging on the wall across the room, barely registering when Paige sat down close to her. "How has she been today?"

An impish grin curled Paige's lips. "Same as always. Sassy as hell and ready to blow this popsicle stand to join a circus somewhere."

The first genuine laugh in her tumultuous day escaped Georgia's mouth, and she tilted her head on the firm back of the sofa. She held her glass midair, knowing her best friend wouldn't fail to clink against it in a sardonic toast. "Here's to feisty patients and ex-boyfriends coming back from the depths they were banished to."

"So…" Her friend drew out the single word. "He isn't fat and bald with bad BO, is he?"

"Nope." She popped her lips on the "P" with extra emphasis. Breaking every self-imposed rule, Georgia stretched her legs out and rested her feet on the coffee table, crossing them at the ankles. "Not fat. Not bald. He smelled like cedar wood. And musk." Her head hit the back couch. "And dirty, dirty thoughts."

"Asshole."

Georgia snorted and emptied most of her glass with one deep gulp. "No kidding."

Paige took a smaller sip, angled her knee onto the

cushion, and turned to face Georgia. "What are we going to do about this?"

Not certain she wanted to discuss the stupid freaking cowboy who had lurked in the back of her mind and heart for twelve years and now had been brought violently to the forefront, she twirled the stem between her thumb and forefinger. "I don't think we need to do anything. The fair just ended and I can't imagine her Googling to find the nearest circus."

The other woman's lips twisted to the side, and she blinked slowly three times. "You're hysterical. I can handle her. It's him we need to discuss. Specifically what are we going to do about him?"

One simple sentence summed up everything Georgia loved about her best friend. They were in this together, and she knew Paige would keep her from doing anything stupid. Like falling into Wyatt's arms and begging him to hold her and make the past twelve years disappear. Or at least the last two. Definitely the last two.

An involuntary grin spread across her face that dissolved into a slightly hysterical bubble of laughter. If Wyatt had been in the picture when everything exploded, there was a very good chance Bruce would be walking with a permanent limp. Damn, why did he have to pop back up two years too late?

Paige plucked the empty glass from her hand. "Okay, clearly you need food before more wine." She carried it into the kitchen and began rattling around in Georgia's cabinets. "Go take a shower and change. I'll make something."

She popped up from the couch just a little too fast, and the glass of wine her friend had filled to the brim hit her hard, making her sway slightly. Only a few bites of the salad and a quarter of the chicken had managed to make it in her rolling stomach during the uncomfortable lunch. "I can cook."

After a momentary look of shock, Paige doubled over with laughter. She filled a stainless steel pot with water and set it on the stove. "That's a good one, Georgie girl."

Georgia fixed her hands on her hips and opened her mouth to argue. Until she remembered the birthday dinner she attempted to make Paige that ended with smoke alarms blaring and a tear-filled call for pizza delivery. "Fine."

She walked into the bathroom, stripped off her clothes, and stepped beneath the nearly scalding spray. As she skimmed the soapy loofah over her skin, her thoughts involuntarily went back to Wyatt. Prickles of heat that had nothing to do with the water cascading against her body raced across her flesh. She hated the way that man could affect her after so many years. And after shattering her eighteen-year-old heart.

But she wasn't that girl anymore. She'd pieced herself back together after he left and somehow managed to build a life she was proud of and one she rabidly protected.

From almost everyone except the only other man she'd allowed as close as Wyatt.

She turned the knobs, the shiver that passed through her as she stepped out of the shower had less to do with the cool air in the room and more with the onslaught of memories she'd battled all afternoon. Georgia grabbed the giant blue towel from the rack and dried off before slipping on yoga pants and an oversized USF sweatshirt.

Georgia was led to the kitchen by her nose like in the old cartoons. Paige was plating some creamy pasta dish with mushrooms, spinach, and tomatoes.

She sat in one of the oak chairs and moaned at the first bite. "Marry me, Paige."

The other woman placed a refilled glass of wine in front of her and took the seat on the other side of the table. "I think Jonah might fight you over that."

Georgia dismissed her concern with a wave of her fork. "You can still have sex with him. I just want you to cook for me."

They ate in silence, but Georgia could practically see the concern rolling off her best friend in waves. "Go ahead. Say it."

Paige quirked an eyebrow. "You're handing this off to the minions, right? Georgia, you can't do this."

She pushed the empty plate away and downed a mouthful of wine. "I have to be hands on with all the designs and make sure Wyatt is happy. This is a bigger deal than I thought. He's going to have a training camp for basically every rodeo event imaginable, but he's also putting on his own competition."

Leafing through his business plan this afternoon had impressed Georgia. She had no idea Wyatt could be such a visionary and turn a few hundred acres of nothing into a massive complex that would undoubtedly be a draw. And that served to annoy her even further. Why couldn't he just be a stupid cowboy?

The infuriating corner of her heart that still loved Wyatt, the one she'd spent so many years trying to exorcise, chose that particular moment to speak up. To remind her Wyatt had always been so much more than a stupid cowboy. He'd been her first ally in North Carolina and her single strongest source of comfort when she needed it most.

Paige gathered the dishes and began to load Georgia's dishwasher. "Just because you need to micromanage all the planning doesn't mean you have to meet with him. Make one of your underlings deal with big bad Wyatt Carlisle one-on-one."

Georgia drained her second glass of wine, carried it into the kitchen, and added it to the rest of the load in the dishwasher. She wrapped her arms around her best friend's waist and rested her head on her shoulder blade. "Thanks for being my best friend."

Closing the dishwasher door, Paige turned and squeezed Georgia. "Nowhere else I'd rather be. I'll just buy Vinho by the case to get us through this project."

Chapter Four

Wyatt

Thirteen Years Earlier

"Oof." Wyatt's backside hit the dusty ground once again with a resounding thud. This time he remembered to land in a way that didn't end with a crack on the back of his skull. Only took doing that three times before he finally learned his lesson.

He shook his head and glanced around for his hat. He'd worn it practically every day for five years. More than once he'd done battle with teachers and school administration over wearing the cowboy hat to school, often resulting in phone calls home and some added chores for him.

Wyatt slapped the hat back on his head and stood gingerly. The echoing laughter at his back forced him to make sure his gait was as natural as possible despite the screaming muscles from his neck to his knees.

He leaned his forearm on the wooden railing with a wide grin. "All right, boys, which one of y'all is next?" All of the six men lined along the other side of the fence were a good decade or more older than Wyatt, but affecting obnoxious levels of confidence was something he did easily.

Three hours and several more falls later, his dad pulled up in his enormous blue truck. Just in time to see Wyatt's longest ride at six seconds. Followed by his most epic throw.

His hat skidded across the ring, his head bounced off the ground, and every molecule of air disappeared from his lungs. He lay on the dirt for several long moments, blinking rapidly as the clouds doubled and began swirling in the sky above him. Wyatt forced himself to slowly breathe again, refusing to give in to the panic wanting to rise.

"Wyatt!"

Before he had a chance to command his aching back or shaking legs to hold him, his father had skidded to a halt beside him. Clouds of dust swirled around and clung to Wyatt's clothes. Mike dropped to his knees next to Wyatt. He wanted to groan at the look of panic on his father's face, but he was too afraid his dad would attribute it to pain rather than sheer embarrassment.

Embarrassment and a tinge of fear his parents wouldn't let him train anymore.

Ignoring every screaming muscle, he offered his father a cocky grin and climbed to his feet. "It's all right, Dad. That was nothing."

Mike put a hand on his son's shoulder, and Wyatt clenched his teeth, refusing to allow his body to react to the stab radiating from the sure to be bruised flesh.

"That didn't look like nothing. That looked like my

son got thrown six feet in the air from an eight hundred pound animal and landed on the ground with a force that could have broken his back or given him a concussion."

Wyatt climbed in the cab of the truck as gingerly as possible without giving away how much it hurt. Which it did. It hurt like a bitch.

They drove in silence for several miles. Just as Wyatt started to relax, Mike cleared his throat. "Are you sure about this, son? Are you sure this is what you want to do with the rest of your life?"

He rubbed some of the residual dirt from his eyes. "Not a doubt in my mind, Dad."

"All right then." Mike propped his elbow on the window ledge. "We...are gonna need to ease your mom into this."

***

Georgia

Georgia grabbed the kohl eyeliner from her dresser top and swiped another thick line across her lid, already heavily coated, for good measure. She raked a hand through her choppy shoulder length hair with a frown.

When she started to wear dark, heavy makeup, her parents hadn't said a word. When her entire back to school wardrobe consisted of varying shades of charcoal and gray, her mother smiled but remained silent. But when she came home with a bottle of black hair dye, they finally drew the line.

She stuck her bottom lip out. She still thought it

was ridiculous. It was just hair.

Her pout turned into a full-fledged frown. First day at Podunk High. She missed her school. She missed her friends. She missed Tampa. She missed...

She missed having a healthy mom who would watch movies and eat popcorn with her when her dad had to work late.

Georgia shook her head to dispel the thought. She buckled a wide leather belt over the black plaid skirt and adjusted the jagged horizontal slashes in the long sleeves of her tight ebony shirt. She liked this new look, and she couldn't care less what Jethro and Billy Bob would think of her.

Asheville was a temporary stop. Either her mom would get better and they could move back to Tampa or—

No matter what the outcome, she was moving back to Tampa. She'd go to USF and have the life she planned for herself.

She hated North Carolina, she hated the accent, and she hated the stupid fake smile she pasted on her face every day to make her mom think she was happy.

Georgia hiked her backpack higher on her shoulder and walked down the hall. She poked her head in her mother's room, not surprised to find her sleeping.

Luckily she managed to escape the house without having to speak to her father. She loved him dearly, but seeing the deep sadness in his eyes day after day made her feel darker than the matte lipstick stain she wore.

Georgia walked the half mile to the high school, staring at the sidewalk and counting the lines. The toes of her new knee boots pinched already. She'd be riding the bus if they still lived in Tampa. Walking was stupid.

She turned to the left and followed the sidewalk up the slight incline. She lifted her gaze to figure out which door would lead her to her Southern fried fate when she stopped dead in her tracks and her jaw hit the concrete.

A freaking cowboy.

A pack of giggling girls surrounded the periphery of his small group, doe-eyed wonder radiating in their worshipful gazes. A couple of other guys dressed much more casually flanked him on each side but paid far more attention to the entourage of females twirling their hair and toeing the ground. Georgia closed her eyes slowly and then opened them again, but the sight in front of her didn't disappear.

Part of her—if she were honest a large part of her—wanted to erupt into a violent fit of laughter. He was the personification of the stereotypical good ole southern boy. He probably drove here in some beat-up pickup truck blaring country music.

Instead of laughing, or mocking him anywhere but in her head, Georgia pushed her way through what she hoped was the right door. It's like pulling off a bandage, get this day done quickly…and hopefully the other one hundred seventy-nine would follow suit.

She forgot all about the freaking cowboy until she went to her locker after lunch to collect her books for the afternoon classes. Before she could finish, one of the girls clinging to him bumped her skintight jean-clad hip into Georgia's back as they pushed through the hall. She snarled as she slammed the locker shut. "Who the hell do they think they are?"

"You're not from around here, are you?" the cynical voice from the locker to her right piped up.

Georgia turned to face the strawberry blonde who didn't look old enough to be in high school. She leaned her back against the cold metal. "Hell no, I'm not from around here." A twinge of guilt churned her gut at the expletive. Her mother would correct her coarse language if she'd heard her. Or if she were feeling well enough to stay awake.

The other girl tugged at the curls erupting around her head before pushing her cat-eye frame glasses up on her nose. "That's Wyatt Carlisle. His family's loaded, but he's planning to walk away from it all and join the rodeo. He's like a legend in the making."

Mirthless laughter bubbled up, cracking the pale makeup she'd applied to her cheeks that morning. "You've got to be kidding me with this. So some moron wants to hop on an animal big enough to kill him and ride it for a few seconds before said beast throws his sorry ass off and gives him a concussion...and this is what is legendary around here?"

The bell rang just then, and the girl scurried off to her class. Georgia pushed off the row of lockers and trudged off as well. She made a mental note to once again search the web tonight for specialists in her mother's type of cancer. Someone, somewhere had to be able to treat her—to cure her—so they could move home. "My time in Mayberry can't be up soon enough."

Chapter Five

Wyatt

Present Day

Clouds of dust swirled around the sleek, red Infiniti as it sped up his driveway. Who in the blue hell decided it was a good idea to use his property as a racetrack?

Wyatt threw the saddle over the rack, tugged off his gloves, and marched out of the largest of the several barns dotting his land, determined to find out. Apparently no one respected "Private Property" signs anymore. As an afterthought, he grabbed his discarded faded green t-shirt off the railing on his way through the wide door.

He didn't know who he'd thought the occupant of the undeniably gorgeous luxury car was, but he certainly wasn't expecting Gigi. Nothing on the face of this earth could have prepared him for the sight of two long legs exiting the vehicle first, balancing precariously in spindly heels on the rocky terrain surrounding the barn.

Damn, he'd always loved her sexy legs, but they looked even more delectable than he remembered. He snorted to himself. Too many head traumas. He couldn't stop himself from grinning when she slammed the door and folded her arms in front of her. Gigi mad was a thing of beauty.

"There something I can do for ya there, Gigi?"

Her hands fell to her sides for a brief moment before she stalked over to him, pointing an accusatory finger. "Why in the world do you have to be so difficult? I've sent three of my most qualified people out here to review some of the best designs we've created this year and you refuse to even speak to them." She stopped a few feet in front of him. "For crying out loud, Wyatt, the last girl came back in tears."

He swiped the shirt he still held in his hand across his sweat-soaked face. "Did she tell you why she was crying?"

Georgia crossed her arms again. "She said she tried to review the portfolio with you and you told her you didn't want to see a damn thing."

Wyatt slung the cotton over his right shoulder. "Well, now, Gigi, that's only about half right. Your meek little mousey 'person' wanted to show me a hell of a lot more than pictures in some portfolio." He matched her stance, hoping if he kept his arms folded it would prevent him from doing air quotes again. How ridiculous. Who the hell was he turning into? "But she's right, I did tell her I didn't want to see a damn thing she thought I needed to look at."

"You." Her shoulders slumped as she sighed out

the word. "You manage to drive perfectly sane and reasonable people to madness."

His gaze had fixed on her full, red, glossy lips as she spoke, but now he raked his eyes over her body. From the creamy shoulders peeking out of the black sleeveless dress, to the crimson leather belt, all the way to her matching pointy shoes. "Well, now, looks like my Dark Angel has added a bit of color to her wardrobe." He winked. "A little, at least."

He couldn't resist poking the bear. Every move she made stole his breath, but the fiery passion that raged through her, whether it was in anger or excitement, was a work of art.

But his Angel never played by anyone's rules. As always she managed to turn the tables and offer the exact opposite of the reaction he had prepared for. Gigi doubled over with laughter, one hand on her chest, the other waving in his direction. The smug smile he wore when he had her good and irate turned into a frown.

"There...there..." She swiped a tear from her eye, gasping to catch her breath. "There is so much wrong with that sentence." She straightened her posture, a few light giggles still lingering. "First of all, I outgrew the goth phase about a decade ago. Second, black is sleek, slimming, and very professional." Her gaze hardened a fraction. "And finally, I am not yours."

They stood locked in a silent standoff under the hot summer sun long enough a fresh trail of sweat rolled down Wyatt's back. How she could possibly stand before him looking cool as a cucumber he had no idea.

"Why can't you just let my people do their jobs?"

He ran the shirt over his chest and the back of his

neck. "This is a big deal, Gigi. This is going to be the biggest training facility in the area, and my competition is going to be a World Championship qualifier. You might not understand, hell, you might not care, but this entire thing deserves the marketing director's attention. Not some little peon."

His temperature shot up a thousand degrees when her eyes fell on his chest and then trailed over to his bicep. "You got tattoos?"

The corner of his mouth kicked up. "Yeah, a few." The more her laser-sharp gaze focused in on his body, the more uncomfortable his jeans became. He shrugged his shoulders and tried to think of anything other than the flames he saw in her hazel depths. "The first time was after a long-ass night on some really tough broncs, more beers than I care to remember, and a stupid bet with the guy who beat me in that competition."

She took two hesitant steps toward him and tilted her head, glistening strands of auburn hair falling over her shoulder. "Which one was your first?"

Damn. This wasn't how he wanted to tell her. He tapped his smallest tattoo, the one on his left pec. "This one."

Gigi swallowed then ran her tongue over the crimson lips Wyatt hadn't been able to look away from for more than a few seconds. The lips begging to be kissed. By him. "What…I-I mean, why? D-does it mean anything?"

He chuckled lightly, closed the gap between them, and gently laced his fingers through hers where they dangled limply beside her hip. "It's a pair of black wings. What could it possibly mean other than I was thinking of my Dark Angel?"

Her entire being was completely still other than the infinitesimal tightening of her grip on his. She didn't blink, move, hell, he wasn't even sure if she was breathing. Wyatt dropped his voice to a whisper, the raucous noise from the machines finishing the work on the various outbuildings of his ranch fell away, and a cocoon of silence enveloped them. "I'm sorry I left the way I did, but I never stopped thinking about you."

Gigi tugged her hand from his, and he was certain she'd hop in the sexy little car that fit her so well and fly away faster than he could blink. But before he could utter a single word, before he could beg her to stay, her hand was behind his neck, tugging his mouth against hers. His hands grabbed her hips and pulled her tight against him.

Desperation drove his lips to devour her, his tongue skating along the seam. Georgia answered with her own demand as she both held him closer and sealed her mouth more firmly against his. The battle for control raged between them until he rubbed the front of his increasingly tight jeans against her.

She moaned against him, and he took advantage of her parted lips to stroke her tongue with the tip of his. Fire ignited in his veins.

She broke the kiss long before he was ready for it to end and took two stumbling steps backwards. One hand clapped over her swollen mouth and the other landed on her stomach.

"No. No, I cannot do that again. I cannot fall into the same damn trap."

Before Wyatt could ask what the hell she was talking about, she put an invisible divider between them as she opened her car door and sobered her face. "I'll have someone call you. We'll set up a date. No, not a date. A time. A meeting. At my office." Not waiting for a response, she quickly got in her car and raced out of his driveway.

Without any help from his brain, his tongue ran over his lips. Damn, he'd missed the taste of Gigi.

***

Georgia

The scent of decadent amounts of butter combined with the tinny sound of kernels ricocheting off the stovetop popper relaxed some of the tension holding Georgia's face taut as she stepped from the shower. "I thought you were off duty today." She finished pulling her damp hair back into a ponytail as she padded into the kitchen, assessing the scene before her. "Five bottles?"

Paige dumped the contents of the popper into the already half full chocolate-colored glass bowl. "I told you I'd buy Vinho by the case." She nodded toward the empty living room. "And your dad asked me to come in because he had some dinner plans come up with a company wanting to switch to him for their insurance or some such thing." She shrugged sheepishly. "I adore your dad, but I tend to zone out when he goes into his 'shop talk' routine."

Georgia nodded then stretched her arms across the cool granite countertop of her island and pressed her forehead against the stone. "I kissed him," she whined into the solid surface.

41

"I figured that out when you called me hyperventilating on the way back to the office."

She lifted her head from the counter and fixed her best friend with a withering stare. "I need support, not sarcasm, Paige."

Paige tossed a handful of popcorn in her mouth with a little laugh. "Those go hand in hand, Georgie girl. You know that."

A silence descended over them weighted enough to draw Georgia's gaze up as she propped her chin on her folded hands on the granite. "What?"

With barely more than a whisper, Paige managed to speak to Georgia's biggest fear. "He isn't Bruce."

Georgia closed her eyes against the burn of unshed tears. "No, he isn't. He's Wyatt. That is so much worse. I can't go there with him. Not again."

A shuddering sigh and deep groan accompanied her move into an upright position. She waved over to the butterfly tote bag Paige brought with her. "What kind of magic do you have in there to make me forget this horrible, awful, no good, very bad day?" Rustling behind her interrupted her thoughts and her back stiffened at the sound. She waged a familiar battle with wanting to check on her grandmother to make sure she didn't get hurt and letting her be to go back to sleep. Sometimes going in calmed her, sometimes it agitated her. Hell, every moment with Gram was a crapshoot.

She and Paige exchanged a meaningful look, and Georgia held her breath for several minutes with only the ticking of the clock to fill the silence between them.

Finally Paige nodded. "She's just restless with the

new medication."

Georgia pressed her lips together tightly, swallowing several times past the lump of emotion clogging her throat. "I think it's working though. Most of the time." She lifted a shoulder. "During the day at least. Sometimes I catch a glimpse of…Gram."

Her friend leaned forward and covered Georgia's hand with her own. "It is. It definitely is."

Somewhat confident the older woman had settled back down for the night, Georgia grabbed the open wine bottle and generously filled a glass. "Did I mention that Jenny *flirted* with him? I mean that girl barely says two words to anyone in the office but she manages to flirt with Wyatt freaking Carlisle?"

"You mentioned that in between breathing into a paper bag because you sucked face with that very same Wyatt freaking Carlisle." Paige quirked up an eyebrow with a half grin. "Jealous much?"

Georgia made a choking sound in the back of her throat, grabbed the overflowing bowl of popcorn with one hand, and drained her glass with the other. She held the bottle near the rim to refill her glass before deciding to just take the entire bottle along with the buttery snack into the next room. "Definitely not. Even if I was jealous—which I am not—it certainly wouldn't be of some backwards little intern who doesn't know the difference between a fashion sketch and a caricature."

Paige trailed behind Georgia into the living room with her colorful bag in hand. "Oh, good. I am so glad you aren't jealous."

Heat rose in Georgia's cheeks as she collapsed onto the couch and stuffed a handful of crunchy, butter-coated goodness in her mouth to prevent the laughter from spilling out. She wasn't sure if she was more annoyed with her employee for flirting with a client or herself for caring.

The answer was swift and decisive. Both. It was both.

Paige pulled two DVD cases from her bag and held them up. "Whatcha in the mood for, Georgie girl? Action or romance?"

Georgia's gaze narrowed in on the one in her best friend's left hand. "That's a joke, right?" She took a long swig from the bottle of wine.

Her mouth dropped open in shock, and Paige clutched the movie to her chest. "I do not kid about romances starring Scott Eastwood." She closed her eyes and bit her lower lip. "Especially not Scott Eastwood in the shower."

"I've had one ridiculously sexy cowboy drive me crazy today. I don't need a second one." Georgia would never admit, even to Paige, that her lips still tingled at the memory of their kiss. "Put in the action. And Taron Egerton is hella hot too."

Paige popped the movie into the DVD player and bounced as she took her seat next to Georgia on the couch. "Can't argue with your taste in man candy. You did land...he who must not be named." Her eyebrows jumped three times in rapid succession, and Georgia laughed.

Twenty minutes and an empty bottle of wine into the movie, Paige laid her temple on Georgia's shoulder. "It'll be okay."

Georgia sighed and tilted her head to rest against Paige's. "As long as I've got my best friend and a good bottle of Vinho, I'm certain it will."

Three quick raps on the front door made them both jump and look at each other in confusion. "You expecting someone, Georgie girl?"

Georgia uncurled her legs and stood up. "Nope. Maybe Jonah has come to look for his fiancée?"

"Not possible." Her curls bounced as she shook her head. "He's got four back to back flights scheduled and won't be home for three days."

She crossed the room, flipped the lock, and slowly opened the front door. Before she had a chance to think, speak, or deliver a well-placed knee between his legs, Wyatt pushed through and grabbed her around the waist.

Her mouth opened in shock just as his lips crashed against hers. Hungry. Needy. And everything she'd been missing. Georgia's hands gripped his biceps, fingernails digging into the cotton-covered skin.

Seconds, minutes, hours…she had no idea how much time had ticked by, but far sooner than she wanted he pulled away from her with a final nip to her bottom lip.

"You left before I was finished." His breathing was almost as labored as hers as he panted out the words. "And I personally think this should happen."

His eyes fixed behind her and his cocky grin slipped easily into place. He released Georgia's waist, and she staggered back a few steps. Wyatt touched the brim of his hat. "Evenin', Paige."

"Nice to see ya, Wyatt," Paige called out to his retreating back as he left, closing the door behind him with a soft click.

Georgia walked back to the couch in a trance,

trying desperately to wrap her mind around what just happened. Even more, deciding whether she was offended or elated. Not up for debate was the fact he left her insanely turned on with that same insatiable lust they had as teenagers. And miserable in the knowledge she'd be going to bed alone that night, just as deprived as she had been when they were younger and Wyatt had insisted they were never "ready," whatever that may mean.

Her best friend, her very best friend in the whole entire world, her ally, her person tilted her head back and laughed. "That was so much more entertaining than either movie."

She grabbed a handful of popcorn and threw it at her friend. "You're not helping." A rock settled into the pit of Georgia's stomach and stole the smile from her face. "I can't do this again."

Paige sighed and clicked the button to restart the movie she'd paused when the doorbell had chimed. "You're going to have to start trusting someone again. I get that he screwed up before, but at the end of the day…he's still Wyatt. Might not be a bad place to start." She grinned wickedly before settling deeper into the couch. "Or you could just use him for that hot bod of his. Asshole really did manage to get more gorgeous over time."

Georgia attempted to return her attention to the screen, but her best friend's words echoed through her brain.

He's still Wyatt.

Yeah, that was exactly the problem.

Chapter Six

Wyatt

Thirteen Years Earlier

"Uh, yeah, whatever."

He figured that was a good enough response. Hoped it would be enough to silence the chatty blonde seated beside him.

Wyatt had no idea why, but the new girl sitting with his buddy's little sister across the cafeteria had caught his attention. Well, he knew why he noticed her. How could he not? In a school filled with unabashedly cookie-cutter kids, she stood out like a show pony at a barrel race. From her heavily rimmed eyes to her jet-black lips and all the way down to the dark combat boots, she was one of a kind.

And the only attention she ever paid him in the past two months was to sneer in his general direction.

He adjusted himself on the uncomfortable bench. Girls didn't ignore him, and they sure as hell didn't give him dirty looks. Well, not until he broke up with them. Then things could get hairy.

This girl, though, this girl had been completely unimpressed with Wyatt from day one. She'd never tried to catch his eyes and seemed to purposefully go out of her way to avoid him. She wouldn't be some easy conquest. She'd be more difficult to win over than the bronc that threw him at five seconds last week.

If there was one thing Wyatt Carlisle loved, it was a challenge.

When he caught her with her back leaning against her locker at the end of the day, her attention focused on the open textbook in her arms, he pushed his hat down further and sauntered over. "Well, hey there, darlin'." He embellished his drawl; the girls always liked that. "I don't think we've been properly introduced."

Bright hazel eyes cut him a sideways glare. "Nope." She popped the P at the end of the word. "And we really don't need to be." She pushed off the locker and started down the nearly empty hallway.

He stared after her for a few minutes before jogging a little to catch up with her. "You're a prickly filly, aren't ya?"

She heaved a deep sigh as she pushed the front door open. "Listen, I get it. I've been here long enough to know everyone falls all over the Rhinestone Cowboy in all of his charming glory. I am so super happy that you're more popular than John Wayne, but I'm not going to be here long enough to need to bask in your shining glow."

Sarcasm and false enthusiasm dripped from her voice. Wyatt was torn between being insulted or amused as hell. This girl was pretty damn funny.

He followed her down the concrete sidewalk, curving to the right and onto the main road. "Hey now, Dark Angel, you don't need to be cuttin' a man off at the knees like that. Just askin' your name."

She hitched her backpack higher on her shoulder and turned to face him. "Dark Angel? Is that supposed to be some sort of joke?" She shook her head and narrowed her gaze. "And don't think for one minute I'm buying that fake accent. There isn't a single person in this entire backwoods area that talks like you."

Wyatt's brows drew together. Okay, now she wasn't funny; she was just difficult. "What else am I supposed to call you when you dress like Dracula's long-lost prom date and you won't tell me your name?" The excessive drawl melted away, leaving only a light accent in its place. "And do ya think you could stop insulting everyone and everything around you for five minutes?"

"Don't be mad at me, Rhinestone Cowboy." She poked him in the chest with one inky-tipped finger. "The only thing funny about this city, this state, hell, my life right now is you. From the hat to the clothes to the clearly deluded rodeo persona, you're the only thing I've got worth laughing at."

She spun on one clunky black heel and walked away, leaving him speechless.

***

Georgia

Georgia quickly crossed the street and along the path through the park. She couldn't stay in the house. She couldn't look at her dad's bleak expression or her grandmother's mask of cheerfulness and hope. Not for one more minute. Not today.

She'd find that small bench nestled in the back under the large oak tree, away from most prying eyes, and allow herself one hour to wallow and cry. One hour to expend all the tears that bubbled under the surface. One hour to drop the badass goth persona she put on like steel reinforced armor every day just to make it through.

Then she'd reapply the wide swaths of eyeliner and walk back home like nothing had ever happened.

It was her routine once or twice a week for the past two months and it worked like a charm. Then tomorrow she could be the supportive daughter she needed to be at home and the moody, sarcastic teenager that kept everyone at a distance at school and she could make it through a few more days.

She found her sacred refuge quickly enough, a relieved exhale escaping her lips as it did every time she found it empty. She sat sideways on the bench, her legs pulled tightly against her chest, as her gaze raked across the heavily wooded area surrounding her.

If she were truly honest with herself, Asheville wasn't that bad. No matter how beautiful she silently found the mountains, lakes, and forests her grandparents would take her to in an effort to sell her on the locale…it wasn't home.

It wasn't Tampa with the easy access

to…everything. It wasn't near the ocean. She didn't wake up in the morning greeted with the tangy scent of the salty sea air.

She rested her forehead against her fishnet stocking-clad knees. She finally gave herself permission to release the tears she fought so hard every day to hide. To let go of a little more of the hope of a miracle for her mom. To forget a few more of the dreams…

"Well, well, if it isn't the Dark Angel in all her emo misery."

Nausea hit her as soon as the deep, husky voice registered in her brain. She wanted to run. She wanted to deck him. She wanted to stop freaking crying before he caught sight of one single tear.

Georgia kept her head bent down, her auburn hair shielding her face from him. "Don't you have some blonde bimbo to grace with your presence? You know, one who wears her Levi's so tight they cut off circulation to her head so she actually finds you interesting."

His footsteps stopped far closer to her right side than she wanted. Georgia closed her eyes, silently pleading with him to turn and walk away.

Instead he flopped heavily down on the bench beside her feet. She quickly spun her head to the left to keep him from seeing her face. "Ya know, Angel, I'm not sure if you're funny or just plain mean."

Georgia scoffed, her throat catching on the sound. No, her internal scream reverberated through her entire being—no, don't cry in front of a stupid freaking cowboy. "Why don't you save your pea-sized brain the agony of trying to figure it out and just get lost?"

"Why the hell do you have to be such a raging bitch?"

She whipped her head around to face him, forgetting for a moment that her eyes were still undoubtedly red, her makeup was running, and her tears were anything but in check. "If your mom was dying, you might not be blissfully charming either. Asshole."

His eyes wide, he reached out a hand and gently touched her cheek and brushed away a tear. "Damn, I'm sorry, Angel. I-I didn't know."

Animosity? Sarcasm? Bitterness? Bring it on, she could handle it all. But the kindness in the sapphire depths was more than Georgia could stand. The dam she worked so hard to reinforce every day broke in front of Wyatt Carlisle, of all people. She hiccuped on a sob, and before she knew it, she found herself folded into his strong arms, crying out her pain into his shoulder.

Her arms slid around his neck of their own accord as wave after wave of fear and despair crashed over her. One roughened hand began to stroke down her hair, and she tightened her hold on him.

Him.

Wyatt.

The stupid freaking cowboy.

The one person who seemed to annoy her on a daily basis just by existing was the only person to offer the kind of sympathy and comfort she needed. The only person who wasn't struggling as much as her. She swallowed and pulled away, wiping her eyes with her palms. "I-I'm sorry. I don't...I never..."

"It's all right, Angel." He offered a small smile, not a trace of his trademark arrogance or intentionally deepened southern accent in sight. "It's only you and me here."

She tucked a strand of hair behind her ear and dropped her head. "My dad...my grandparents...they spend all their time being cheerful to my mom's face, but I see them. When they turn away, when they walk out of her room. A piece of each of them is dying with her. So I-I just never cry in front of them. I want them to believe I'm okay."

Wyatt hooked a finger under her chin. "It's okay to not be okay sometimes."

Georgia couldn't help the upturn of her lips. "Yeah, I guess."

"You should do that more often. You've got one hell of a smile."

Heat rose in her cheeks and she jumped off the bench. "Thanks for, ya know, not...I mean...just..." She sighed heavily. "Just, thanks."

He tipped the brim of his ever-present hat slightly, and every ounce of the Rhinestone Cowboy persona slipped back into place. "Anytime, Angel."

She spun on her heels and walked a few feet away before she paused and turned back. "Georgia."

Confusion colored his face and he shook his head slightly. "Georgia?"

"My name is Georgia." She all but sprinted out of the park, across the street, and far from the stupid freaking cowboy.

Chapter Seven

Wyatt

Present Day

Wyatt stood a few feet outside of the conference room door, staying as silent and inconspicuous as possible. A smile tugged at his lips as Gigi directed people with ease and confidence.

She was brilliant. She was commanding. She was stunning.

He was so damn proud of her he thought his chest would burst. She'd always had a quiet strength about her—and a smart mouth that made him want her like no one else—but this side of Gigi was nothing short of awe-inspiring.

Just then her eyes lifted from the boards spread out on the long oak table and caught him staring at her. Her down-turned mouth curled up and she motioned for him to come in.

As soon as he crossed the threshold, she schooled her features. The smile left the mouth that had been haunting his memory for days, fixing into a straight line. Her shoulders squared and her all too perceptive gaze swung around the room. Wyatt had to stifle a chuckle when he saw each employee all but stand at attention. Damn, his Gigi was impressive.

"Mr. Carlisle, please come in and have a seat." The corners of her lips twitched and her hazel eyes sparkled as she sat on the opposite side of the long table.

Wyatt didn't bother to hide his grin at her faux professionalism. Hell, it was pretty damn hot; he had no reason to complain. "Thank you, Ms. Marsh." He tilted the brim of his hat in her direction and took the chair opposite her.

Her minions took their seats, flanking each side of her, their expressions an open mixture of reverence and fear. And he understood both. His Gigi had always been a force to be reckoned with.

As she launched into her speech, Wyatt fought to keep his eyes on the design boards and the digital images on the tablet in front of him. He couldn't allow his gaze to linger on the hint of cleavage visible at the V of the soft pink camisole she wore beneath her suit jacket. Or her glistening rosy lips.

He'd grossly underestimated the power of an all-grown-up Gigi. The body he'd tentatively teased as a teenager only taunted him more now with her soft curves. It took nearly all of his power to focus on her words and not kick her staff out of the room to spread her across the oak table and…

Wyatt clenched his jaw and shifted in his seat. Not the time or place.

He zeroed in on the images she was swiping across

the touch screen and frowned. He'd given her his business plan, his layouts, hell, he'd even given her a list of already secured sponsors for the first competition he'd be hosting next year. And yet looking at the designs in front of him, it seemed like she hadn't paid a damn bit of attention to any of it. Bright, neon colors nearly blinded him from half the designs and...was that a cartoon bull?

He never imagined when he set the appointment with Elias Joseph that the "brilliant marketing savant" he raved about was none other than the Dark Angel who haunted his dreams. Wyatt knew he had handled their first meeting poorly, but he hadn't been ready. The plan had been to get his ranch humming and prove to Gigi that he wasn't just a cowboy before the begging and long overdue explanations commenced.

And the house. He wanted her to see the house he'd designed with her in mind. Something she would love.

But whatever twisted fate created the situation where he was working closely with Gigi to build his brand and launch a new and much more fulfilling career was obviously a cursed one. Now here he sat, weighted with the responsibility of complaining— again—about the designs her team set before him. Nearly everything she was showing him missed the mark of what he envisioned, and he had no way to tell her without looking like a total ass.

His phone vibrated in his shirt pocket, and the name flashing across his screen only served to heighten his frustration. Dammit, when would Jim stop calling?

"Ms. Marsh, could we please have a moment alone?" He forced the irritated tone from his voice. He bitterly wondered if she'd even looked at anything in the packet he'd given her.

Gigi's brows drew together, but she flicked her left wrist. "Give me a minute with Mr. Carlisle."

They all obediently filed out the door behind Wyatt's chair. All accept the faux timid little brunette who had already tried his patience when she showed up on his docrstep looking for more than just his approval on sketches. She moved from her seat to round the table and stand far too close for comfort.

"Could I get you anything before I go, Wyatt?" She dropped her voice into what he could only assume she intended to be a sultry tone and bent at the waist. The top three buttons of her blouse were undone, and what he could only assume was the result of a push-up bra was showing off its contents through the gaping opening. If this was meant to be a temptation, she fell about three thousand feet short. And she didn't hold a candle to Gigi. "Coffee? Water?"

He locked his gaze with Gigi, intentionally ignoring the girl to his right. He threw Gigi an "I-told-you-so" look and hoped she could read him as well as she did when they were kids.

"I'll be sure to buzz you if Mr. Carlisle or I need anything, Jenny. Thank you." Her cool, dismissive tone reminded him of the smartass, closed-off teen Gigi that captured his heart, and he couldn't help but smile in spite of his irritation and deep disappointment.

No, he hadn't expected Gigi, but if anyone could catch his vision, it would be her.

When the door clicked behind him, he leaned forward over the table. "Please tell me you didn't actually approve this."

"Well, I certainly don't approve of her obvious flirting with our newest client, hell, any client. That is a 'get your ass handed to you' kind of fireable offense in my world. It will most assuredly be dealt with immediately or she will find herself in need of a new internship. I swear she must have missed business ethics or else attended a subpar program because—"

"I mean these." His hand swept across the table. "These don't even come close to representing my brand and what I want my training facility to look like." He propped an elbow on the arm of his chair and rubbed his temple. The exhaustion of creating the ranch and all the extras that went along with it weighed heavy on his shoulders.

A brief flash of hurt flew across her face before her expression settled into something indecipherable. "I'm sorry, Wyatt. Normally I would have looked them over closer, been more diligent but—" Her teeth sank into her bottom lip, silencing her words.

His every sense went on high alert. "But what, Gigi?"

She shook her head and blinked rapidly. "Nothing."

He tried. He tried so hard to keep his hands to himself, but it never really worked around her. He reached across the table and laced his fingers through hers. "Not nothing."

Gigi opened and closed her mouth several times before she sighed and slumped back in her chair. "Gram is…sick. It was…a rough night, and when I got her calmed down, I was exhausted and just passed out."

Memories of their high school days and the disease

that claimed her mother filtered through his mind. And everything made a lot more sense. "By sick…" He left the question hanging in the air, concerned the very word would still hold the same power over her it had in their adolescent years.

"No." She shook her head violently. "Not cancer." She pressed her palms to her cheeks and slid them down. "Alzheimer's. Some days it's barely noticeable, but others…"

Wyatt could see the invisible mantle of responsibility weighing on her shoulders just as he had when he was younger. And just as it had back then, his mind whirled with ideas. He'd intended to come home and win her back, to prove if she could trust him again he'd do his damnedest to not screw it up, but now…now he was adding another objective to the mission. Bring back the twinkle in her eyes. Maybe… "How about a tour, Gigi?"

The slight jump when he spoke attested to her preoccupation and cemented his decision.

"Of my office?"

He smiled at the curious note in her tone. "No, my training facility. Not like the other day, come out and really see it. Take a full tour." He brushed an invisible piece of lint off his shoulder and winked at her. "With the best damn tour guide in the state of North Carolina, naturally." He leaned forward and grasped her hand again. "Please, Gigi."

Heat radiated from the hazel depths as she tightened her hold on him. "I read every word of your proposal and looked at all the blueprints. It was…impressive."

With a shake of his head, he released her hand and

walked around the table, pulling out the seat beside her. "No, you need to see it. See all of it. You need to come out, ride the property with me, look at what's there, and what they're building. I need you to see what I see." He rested a hand on her knee, and her eyes followed the motion and fixed on their connection.

Gigi's gaze snapped up and locked with his. "I-I can't. That-that…I can't, Wyatt."

He dropped his voice and ditched the accent that always drove her crazy. "Please, Angel."

The avalanche of emotion sweeping over her face started with something that looked almost like fear before settling into resignation. "When?"

His fingers slowly trailed beneath her black skirt, and she sucked in a sharp breath of air. He caressed the satin skin on the inside of her thigh. "Saturday?"

Her hand curled around his forearm, halting his progress. "Yes, but this can't happen."

"I know I screwed up, but I promise if you give me a chance…" He twined his fingers through hers and pulled their joined hands into his lap, his voice tapering off into silence as he cursed himself. This needed to be about her. What she wanted. Not just winning her back, not just gaining her trust, but giving her something else besides the weight of caring for someone she loved. All of that would only come through honesty. "Gigi, there was a reason."

"I don't give a damn about your reason." The icy edge to her tone sliced through Wyatt's heart with clean precision. "You are my client. This. Can't. Happen. Not now, not Saturday. You can't show up at my house and kiss me senseless in the middle of the night and disappear again. We have a strictly business relationship this time around. That's all I have to give you."

At the rattle of the closed door, they both jumped, and Wyatt scooted away from Gigi. That same overly affectionate intern swished in, a large tray cradled in her arms. What was her name again? Janet? Jessica?

"Jenny, what are you doing?"

The pointedly sharp tone of Gigi's voice even made Wyatt nervous. Poor girl was pushing her boss's buttons worse than he did. Yeah, he loved ruffling Gigi's feathers, but he knew where and when to stop. Clearly she did not.

An innocent expression Wyatt would bet was more fake than her lingerie-enhanced cleavage settled on Jenny's face and her pale eyes widened. "I thought Wyatt might have changed his mind about a drink." She set the beverage-laden black, plastic rectangle on the table. "Oh, and you too, Ms. Marsh."

Gigi's lids drifted closed and her nostrils flared once. Twice. Three times before she opened her eyes again. "This is Mr. Carlisle, Jenny. And he already told you he did not want a drink. We are currently discussing how we can better meet his needs as our client, and I would appreciate no additional interruptions."

The younger woman's complexion paled, and she offered a jerky nod before backing out of the room.

Gigi cradled her head in her hands as soon as the click of the latch echoed through the room and she groaned. "Havoc. You create havoc and chaos and insanity, Wyatt Carlisle."

He reached between her arms to grasp her chin and

force her gaze to meet his. "And fun, Gigi. We always had fun. See ya Saturday."

***

Georgia

He couldn't make anything easy.

Georgia grumbled to herself the entire drive to Wyatt's ranch. Not only was she working on a weekend and not only had she finally agreed to spend very loosely labeled "professional" time with Wyatt away from the office, but taking the day away from her grandmother meant carefully arranging for a care provider in her absence. As much as her father did, his own business required he be present at least occasionally, and today was one of those days.

A shard of pain sliced through her chest as she passed beneath the arch signaling her arrival at RA Ranch. The loss of her grandfather two years earlier not only sped up her grandmother's mental decline, it necessitated her return home to give her father some added support to take care of the woman he came to love as much as his own mother. Fortunately it came on the heels of the second most painful breakup of her life and made her almost grateful to leave Tampa, the place she was once so desperate to return to.

She took a deep breath and pocketed her cell phone before exiting the car. He had four hours. That was as long as she could afford to spend away from home; Paige and her dad both had plans. And they'd learned from experience that Gram needed to have supervision. A shudder shook her body. One lightly charred kitchen wall was enough to teach them that lesson.

Rounding the corner into the barn, Georgia wasn't surprised to see Wyatt saddling horses. She knew him well enough, really too well considering how long they'd been apart, to think that he'd take anything but a horse out for their little show and tell.

"What are the saddlebags for?" She quirked the corner of her mouth up a little, certain he'd be surprised she still knew what she was talking about.

He spun around and Georgia fought the urge to jump into his arms. She wasn't a teenager anymore. He wasn't the only guy she'd been with. She'd had half a dozen boyfriends since Wyatt Carlisle's abrupt departure from her life. She blinked slowly at the image of Bruce's wide, dazzling grin barreling through her mind.

She tugged on the blue plaid flannel shirt she'd brought along to keep the sun from burning her skin. Right now she needed its protection from the chills engulfing her spine as Wyatt's blatantly appreciative gaze washed over her. His eyes zeroed in on the glittering dark skull on the front of her black and gray striped tank top and grinned.

"Good afternoon, Gigi." He reached a hand out to pat the tan leather draped over the horse. "We're gonna need to eat, aren't we?"

Georgia pressed her lips together. "This is not a date. We've been over this. Business only."

The cocky grin she loved to loathe slid smoothly into place. "We can call it a business lunch if that makes you feel better, Angel."

She rolled her eyes and bit back a farewell as she

leaned against the wall of the barn. If she could negotiate boardroom deals with aging, chauvinistic men, she could handle one stupid freaking cowboy. "So where's my horse?"

He ran a hand over the draft horse's chestnut-colored coat. "Right here. Jake is strong enough to carry both of us." He dipped his chin and cut her a sideways look filled with desire. "And you always did like wrapping your arms around me. Tight."

Don't sigh. Don't moan. Don't close your eyes, and whatever the hell you do, don't remember. Georgia shook her head after her brief internal coaching exercise. "Nope, I want my own horse."

She crossed the few feet and, completely ignoring Wyatt, focused on the giant beast. Jake lowered his head as she approached, and she leaned her forehead against his. "You are a beautiful boy, aren't you?" Georgia couldn't help the smirk she threw toward Wyatt. "You're right, Cowboy. I think Jake and I will work out just fine. Go saddle up something else for yourself."

His brows drew together and he shook his head. "He's eighteen hands high and weighs over two thousand pounds. I'll get you Sunshine. She's more your speed. Calmer, smaller, and good for a beginner. Something that won't throw ya from six and a half feet."

Jake nuzzled against her shoulder as she stroked his mane, and Georgia laughed. "Sorry, Cowboy, you've been outvoted." She focused in on the horse again. "Yes, Jake, you are a special boy. You'd never hurt me, would you?" The horse snorted and stomped his foot in response. Georgia could have sworn he glared at Wyatt for implying he'd throw her. The disdain radiating off the massive creature was adorable and completely entertaining.

Wyatt stormed off, deeper into the barn, muttering under his breath. After several long moments slamming things around while Georgia resisted the urge to mount the horse and ride away without him to prove she was no beginner, Wyatt emerged with a sleek black horse that sported a matching flowing mane. "Fine. Let's go."

He dropped the reins of the horse he was leading to offer clasped hands for Georgia to use as a makeshift step to climb aboard Jake. She rolled her eyes, lifted her foot into the stirrup, and threw her other leg across the saddle. "Lead on, Cowboy."

Wyatt didn't move from his slightly bent position, fingers still laced together, jaw open. "H-how…how the hell did you do that?"

She pressed her heels into Jake's sides and he started off on a slow trot. "Do you think I quit doing something I loved just because you disappeared? I ride all the time, Wyatt." She lowered her chin and captured his stare. "It hurt like hell when you left, but my life didn't pause at eighteen just because you couldn't be bothered to hang around."

A flash of pain flittered across his face, but she tried to ignore it. The girl who stood on his doorstep crying had a few pent-up zingers to dole out.

He offered a brief nod of resignation before mounting his own horse and beginning the tour. She silenced the small voice inside whining because he really was keeping it business only. That stupid part that wanted to bitch him out for hurting her and then see exactly how thoroughly he could make up for all the pain he caused.

Georgia had prepared herself for Wyatt's overzealous charm—which he did indeed lavish on her—but she hadn't expected the passion in his voice. Not for her, but for his ranch, his training camp, and the future competition.

His hands waved over the barren expanse as he described the main office for the training camp, the indoor arena, the paddock, and the dozens of boxes he'd have filling the various stables to house the horses.

"It will be amazing, Gigi. No one within a hundred miles has anything like this. And the big rodeo is going to be great for tourism. I've already gotten some of the highest-ranking guys to agree to come to the opening and the first competition." A wide grin split his face. "It's gonna be awesome."

When they crested the hill that overlooked another area, he dismounted first and rushed to help her down. Her body slid against his as he lowered her to the ground, and heat coursed through her veins. Her face flushed when he gave her a cocky grin, and she stepped away quickly.

In the distance sat the framework of a house. His house. On the other side of the property, far from all the chaos of the planned facility, he was building a sprawling home with an enormous attached garage and a wraparound porch.

She walked a few feet over to a massive tree and leaned against it as her eyes drank in everything on the ranch in the valley below. "This really is impressive, Wyatt."

The fact that it was everything they'd talked about when they were teenagers stuck in her throat. She couldn't manage to remind him of the dreams they'd shared, too scared he'd forgotten. That knowledge would break her more than his departure, knowing that he didn't remember every moment of them the way she did.

From behind her, he slipped his arms around her waist and pulled her tightly against him. After a few moments, she allowed herself to relax against his broad chest. Just this once, she told herself, just for a moment. "I couldn't wait to bring you here, Gigi."

Her breath caught in her throat. No, she couldn't let herself listen to those words, to read too much into them, to care to believe... "Either me or another convenient, willing, warm body...right, Cowboy?"

Wyatt turned her in his embrace, pressing her against the tree. "Dammit, Gigi, no!" He bent, moving his face just inches from her. "How in the hell could you say that...could you think that? There has never—and I mean never—been anyone like you."

Georgia's hands flew to his face. "How could I say that? Wyatt, you left. You bailed. You promised me we'd go together and then you just disappeared."

He moved one hand from her waist to the back of her head and into her hair. A groan escaped her mouth, and she quickly bit her bottom lip.

"Dammit, Gigi, I had my reasons, and I thought I was doing the right thing, and I was trying...oh hell." He growled and crashed his mouth against hers.

Memories began to flood through her mind as she slid her hands around his neck. Their first kiss. Shy, a little awkward, and far too public with her father and grandparents peeking from behind the curtains.

And their last. When he dropped her off at home and she'd gone to bed, hopeful and happy and certain of their future. The kiss that had haunted her dreams for the past dozen years.

She broke free, swallowing back the lump forming in her throat. This was supposed to be business, and she'd just broken her own damn rule.

But the eighteen year old inside of her who broke down into tears when she learned of his departure had questions that needed answers. Maybe giving him just a little affection would help her unlock those secrets. Eventually. Then she could finally have closure for one part of her life. She offered a tight smile. "You, um, you said something about lunch? Because I'm suddenly starving."

Chapter Eight

Wyatt

Thirteen Years Earlier

Wyatt tugged the heavy duffel bag out of his locker. It really was too big to fit in there, but he didn't have a choice. He had to bring all his gear with him so he could go straight to training when his dad showed up after school. Part of the responsibility of blazing his own trail. Or so his father told him.

He finally yanked it free, hiked it up on his shoulder alongside his backpack, spun on his heel to leave, and...

Jumped three feet in the air.

"Damn, girl, have you ever heard of making your presence known?"

She ducked her head and tucked a strand of auburn hair behind her ear. "Sorry." She mumbled the word and shuffled her clunky combat boots. "I-I just...I just wanted to thank you. For...you know, last week and for not saying anything. Here. To anyone. Or...or whatever."

She was beautiful. Even though she added a thick coat of makeup to pale her skin and darken her eyes, she couldn't hide it. The dazzling hazel irises with tiny flecks of gold were sure as hell captivating. And even when they were coated with thick, matte black, her lips curved into a gorgeous smile. Although that was a rare occurrence.

Yeah, he was falling for the goth girl. Shit, this so wasn't in the plan.

Wyatt glanced around at the empty hallway before hooking a finger under her chin and forcing her eyes to meet his. "I'm sure I don't have any idea what you're talkin' about there, Gigi." He winked before turning to leave.

A dozen steps later, a hand landed on his arm. "What...what the hell did you just call me?"

He grinned down at her incredulous expression. Yeah, she was pretty damn cute, even with all the crap on her face. "I called you Gigi."

She narrowed her gaze, but the corners of her mouth twitched. "Why?"

Wyatt bent down, close to her ear. "Because Georgia just doesn't fit you and Angel is only for when we're alone." His lips grazed her cheek as he stood up, and his chest puffed out when he saw the pink stain peeking out from beneath her makeup.

Gigi folded her arms in front of her. "First of all, I'm not some emaciated animal you can adopt from the shelter and rename whatever you want. My name is Georgia. And second, when did I agree to be alone with you?"

Getting under her skin was quickly becoming his

favorite pastime. "Well, ya haven't. Yet. But you will." He reached for her hand and began walking backwards, tugging her with him. "Hey, you can come with me to training tonight. We won't be alone, my dad's driving but—"

"I-I can't." She firmed her stance and pulled free from his grip, wrapping her arms around herself. "I need to get home. My mom…remember?"

This time Wyatt grabbed both of her hands. "And when was the last time you did something for you, Gigi? Something other than school or helping to take care of your mom?" He dropped his voice to the tone he used on skittish colts, barely more than a whisper, in case anyone stumbled upon them in the hallway. He was fairly certain she'd launch into a tirade if she knew he was handling her the way he would a feisty horse, but the technique worked. "Something completely, totally, and selfishly all about you."

Her mouth opened and closed several times before she finally shook her head. "I haven't. My family needs me."

He nodded. "I bet they do, and I'm pretty damn sure you do an amazing job helping out. But I'm just as sure that you need something too." Wyatt gave her another wink and a grin. "And that something is to see the best freaking bull rider in the state of North Carolina train on Lightning Bolt tonight."

Finally her face relaxed and she smiled. Yeah, she had one hell of a smile. "Exactly how many bull riders are in the state of North Carolina?"

"Well, that's a damn fine question." He slid one hand down her arm and laced his fingers through hers. "But it really doesn't matter, Gigi, because you've got the finest specimen right here."

She laughed. His Dark Angel actually laughed. If he thought her smile was gorgeous, her laugh was breathtaking. He didn't even care that she was laughing at him; he just wanted to make sure he heard that sound a lot more often. Shouldn't be an issue, not for Wyatt Carlisle.

As soon as they got outside, she tugged on his hand and his stomach plummeted. The tension was back on her face. His mind raced to think of something to bring back the small amount of light that had been there before.

"I, um, I should call home. Ask, ya know?"

Yeah, she should. *Dumbass*, he cursed himself silently. His slid his phone out of his back pocket and held it out to her. "Here ya go, Gigi." He reluctantly released her hand and jerked his thumb over to the lamppost a few dozen feet away. "I'll wait over there for you, okay?"

She nodded and offered a little smile before flipping open his phone. He crossed the few feet and leaned up against the cold metal, trying to keep Gigi in his peripheral vision without looking like a total creep. His dad's dark blue truck stopped in front of him while she was still on the phone.

Wyatt pulled open the door and threw his gear onto the front seat. "Hey, Dad..." He shot a quick glance over at Gigi, nodding and smiling into his cell phone. "I kinda asked someone to come with us tonight."

Mike Carlisle followed his son's eyes. His brows shot up in surprise. "I'm guessing that's your mystery guest?"

His head dropped. "Yes, sir, but listen,

she's…going through some stuff. I just…" He sighed heavily before locking his gaze with his father. "She needs someone, I think, and…"

"And you want to be that someone?"

What the hell? His cheeks felt hot? No. No way. Wyatt Carlisle may do a hell of a lot of things, but one thing was for damn sure, he never blushed. "Yes, sir."

The older Carlisle dipped his chin and pinned Wyatt with the same penetrating stare that made him confess to force feeding his younger brother Connor a mud pie when he was seven. "How did you do on your last calculus test?"

A glacier of dread settled in the pit of Wyatt's stomach. He swallowed a few times. Not as well as his parents wanted, not as well as they expected. Par for the course. Even if they never said it, he knew he was a glaring disappointment. Especially when he stood beside Tanner's golden glow. "I got a C."

Michael's mouth pressed into a thin line for a brief moment before the tension drained from his face. He offered a quick, curt nod. "That's an improvement. You're going to keep that up, right?"

He damned sure was going to try, but getting the numbers, letters, and symbols to make sense in his head was harder than any challenge he faced. But he no longer had an option; it was pass or lose training. "Yes, sir."

His father chuckled, and the heavy air dissipated at the sound. "All right, son, if you're ready to let your girlfriend see you get your ass handed to you by Lightning Bolt, who am I to judge?"

"No way, Dad, tonight's the night. I'm gonna ride that bull for the full eight." Girlfriend? Was that what she was?

Just then a small, soft hand linked with his. He looked down and she lifted her shoulder as she handed his phone back to him. "They said it's okay as long as I'm home by ten." Her eyes twinkled beneath the heavy charcoal liner. "I get to watch the Rhinestone Cowboy at work."

Pleasure hummed through his veins and he squeezed her hand. He slammed the front door shut and opened the back one, climbing in right behind her. "All right, Gigi, prepare to be amazed."

Yeah, girlfriend sounded about right.

Five hours, a dinner where Gigi managed to charm the pants off his father, and many more falls than he wanted her to see later, he walked her to her front door. "Did you have fun?"

The smile she pinned him with was dazzling. "You were right, Cowboy. I was amazed. Amazed that one man could fall that many times and still be stupid enough to get back up and try again."

Wyatt tried his damndest not to laugh. "That's not stupid, Gigi. That's tenacity."

She tipped her head back slightly and laughed. "Whatever you wanna call it to make yourself feel better there, Cowboy."

He dipped his head down and caught her lips in an all too brief kiss, fully aware of the knowing eyes of his father trained on them from the truck still idling in the driveway. "Does that mean I can call you mine, Angel? Because that would be the best damn feeling in the world."

Twinkling eyes locked with his and she produced a coin out of nowhere, holding it up in front of his nose.

"Flip ya for it?"

"Flip…you mean for you?" Intrigue and confusion went to war in his brain. What the hell was she doing?

She tossed the piece of silver in the air, grabbed it, and smacked it onto the back of her hand, covering it with the other one. "For us. Heads I'll be your girlfriend, tails—"

"I'll be your boyfriend." No way in hell was he leaving this to chance.

Matte black lips curled into a smile as she spread her fingers, revealing the head of the coin. "Looks like you win, Cowboy."

He snatched the silver disc from the back of her hand and stuck it in his pocket with a wink and a smile. "I like keeping proof of my wins."

***

Georgia

Her eyes went from the massive beast standing beside Wyatt to the cowboy himself and then back again. "You expect me to get on that?"

In a move she never understood, no matter how many times she'd seen him do it over the past month they'd been dating, he threw his head back and laughed without dislodging his hat. "Aww, come on, Gigi. Macy is the smallest horse here that's still strong enough to hold both of us. And gentle as a little dove."

Her eyebrows shot up. "That thing has to weigh ten times what I do."

His eyes washed over her charcoal hoodie, black jeans, and standard clunky boots before languidly trailing back up to her eyes. She wasn't sure if she should feel flattered by his openly admiring gaze or offended. When a slow smile spread over his lips and he hooked a finger in her belt loops to draw her closer, she went willingly and decided to go with flattered.

Wyatt's lips brushed against hers lightly, snaking his arm around her waist. "Trust me, Angel, I won't let anything happen to you." He kissed her again, sealing his whispered promise.

She couldn't help but shiver slightly in his embrace. The irony that the stupid freaking cowboy had not only become her boyfriend, but her ally and champion trickled through her mind again. "If that thing tosses either one of us, you've gotta lose the hat for a week."

A look of horror spread across his face briefly before the cocky smile slipped back into place. She'd never admit how much she loved that smile. "A cowboy ditching his hat is damn near sacrilegious, but I've got faith in my horses, so you're on, Gigi." He snuck another kiss. "But what're you gonna put on the line when I win?"

Georgia flattened her palms against his shirt. "How about I give up the black lipstick for a week?"

He nuzzled into her neck. "No way in hell, Angel. I like when you leave reminders of all the places your lips have touched. I have a better idea."

She leaned back in his arms. "That sounds scary."

"If you survive this, you come home with me every Monday after school and we ride."

Her smile fell and she stepped out away from him. "Wyatt, you know I can't. I already go with you every Friday night for training. I need to check on my mom and give Dad and Grandma a break and—"

He covered her mouth. "And you need to do something you like. I think you'll like riding and I know damn well you like spending time with me." He winked and she couldn't help but smile under his hand. "Two days a week you get to be sixteen and have fun. Two days is all I'm asking."

Georgia swallowed back the tears that threatened. She didn't need this. She didn't need him to care. She didn't need him to force her to look beyond…no, she really didn't need this, but it felt so good. Instead of speaking, she simply nodded.

The smile he gave her, the real Wyatt smile, was worth the compromise. He swung himself up into the saddle easily then pointed to the small set of two wooden steps. "Stand there and then give me your hand, Gigi. Put your left foot in the stirrup and swing your right leg over. I'll do the rest."

Before she knew it, she was seated in the saddle behind him and tramping down her nerves. They would be fine. And even if they weren't, that just meant she'd get to weasel Wyatt out of his hat. She grinned as she wrapped her arms around his torso. Yeah, that'd be worth a sore backside or even a broken arm.

His hand covered hers briefly and they started out at a slow pace. She could practically feel the need to race coursing through his body and smiled a little knowing he was holding back for her. Georgia rested her cheek against his back and tightened her hold.

This stupid freaking cowboy was pretty special.

Chapter Nine

Wyatt

Present Day

Wyatt chuckled slightly and the cutest damn blush spread across her cheeks. He held her hips for a few beats until he was fairly confident she was steady on her feet. "Yeah, I packed a few things."

He strode over to where Jake stood patiently waiting, and he dug in the saddlebag for the blanket and food.

"I'll take that." Gigi took the thick woolen blanket from his arms and crossed a few feet to spread it out over the lush green grass.

He pulled the two water bottles out and slapped the leather flap of the bag closed. He needed to focus on the ranch. On her business partnership. On making sure she understood she was a hell of a lot more than "another convenient, willing, warm body." That stung. And managed to amplify his guilt, something he once thought impossible. Hell, the whole reason he'd been drinking so hard the night he got his first tattoo was to try to erase her memory and the pain of leaving her. Even if he'd done it for what he thought were all the right reasons.

He had to be able to prove to her that he didn't come back just to start the training camp, and he didn't just want her brilliant business brain. He came back for her. Every part of Gigi was ingrained in his memory and taunted the corners of his psyche for far too long.

And he really needed to figure out what the hell caused that look in her eyes every time they got too close to what they had once been. If it was him, well...he had three brothers who would be all too willing to kick his ass just for the hell of it.

His forehead fell against the flank of the horse, bumping the brim of his hat. Of all the people on this planet who could possibly be so intrinsically linked to his future success...it had to be Gigi. Mad, pissy, hurt Gigi.

He had to pull it together. Wyatt straightened and sucked in a deep breath before turning around and crossing the few feet to where Gigi sat on the blanket. He dropped down beside her, emptying the contents of his arms.

She opened the containers of cubed cheese, meat, and fruit. She tore a hunk off the loaf of bread and handed it to him. "Nice spread, Cowboy."

Wyatt searched his brain for something to say. Something neutral. Something safe. He stuffed more food in his mouth in an effort to prevent himself from saying exactly the wrong thing. That was his usual M.O.

"You were right." Her words were soft, her gaze fixed beyond him.

"What?" He shook his head, certain he'd heard her wrong.

Gigi's eyes held his captive. She waved her hand, encompassing the valley spread out before them. "This is so much better than your business proposal. It's everything you ever wanted when..." Her chin dipped and she popped a grape in her mouth. "Although the plan you sent me really was impressive. Ya know, for a stupid freaking cowboy."

The mozzarella and prosciutto lodged in his throat. His chest tingled at the mischief twinkling in her hazel depths as he coughed out the offending food. He reached over and ran his fingers down her side. She dissolved into giggles. Wyatt arched a single brow. "This stupid freaking cowboy still remembers where his Dark Angel is ticklish."

Her mouth fell open and she jumped to her feet, racing back to the waiting steed and hopping on his back. "You can only tickle me if you can catch me."

With that she dug her heels into Jake's side and took off for the barn. Her laughter floated back to him as she rode away.

Wyatt threw the discarded blanket over his waiting horse and quickly climbed into the saddle. He urged the beast to go faster until he got to the barn. And a waiting, solitary Jake with no Gigi in sight. He leapt off the horse's back before it had even stopped.

As soon as he walked through the wide doors of the barn a hand reached out from the left side and grabbed the front of his shirt, pushing him against the wall. Before he could speak, Gigi's mouth was on his.

She released her hold on the material, moving both hands beneath his shirt, her fingers dancing across muscles that immediately tightened in response to her touch. He groaned beneath her lips. He fisted the length of her hair, tilting her head and deepening the kiss, never wanting the moment to end.

That was until Gigi pushed against him and broke away. A single tear streaked down her cheek. "Why did you lie to me?"

Wyatt had known for twelve years that any hope of a future with Gigi would involve answering that question, but he hadn't prepared himself for the hoarse tone in her voice or the downturn of her lips. He hadn't been sure that she would still care so much. He had always hoped but never quite believed.

It was equally heartbreaking and encouraging.

His hand slid around the back of her neck. "I didn't lie, Angel. I wanted you with me."

"Then why did you leave? If you wanted me, why the hell did you leave?" She turned away and wrapped her arms around herself. "I went to your house and I stood on your doorstep like a freaking idiot crying because you bailed." When she faced him again, two large wet paths ran down her face.

In that moment, Wyatt was certain his heart had stopped beating. "Because of your dad."

Gigi swiped her fingers beneath her eyes and shook her head. "Not possible. My dad loved you. He was thrilled when I started dating such a 'fine young man.' Hell, he still talks about you even now. Even knowing…"

Even knowing I broke his daughter's heart, he finished for her silently. Wyatt lifted his hat for a moment, ran his fingers through his hair, and set it back in place. "Do you remember the day before I left?"

She dropped her gaze to the ground. Then the wall to the left. Then the one on the right. "Yeah," she mumbled.

Oh hell no, she wasn't getting out of hearing this— all of this—without making eye contact. He strode over to her, holding her cheek in one hand, forcing her to look at him. The fingers of his other hand dug into her hip. Just in case she had any thought of leaving.

"We were at your grandparents' house. In the backyard with those two ridiculous mutts you decided to rescue."

She smacked him on the chest. "They were not ridiculous mutts. Roscoe and Roxy were the best pets ever." Her declaration was met with a huff and foot stomp from just beyond the barn door. She leaned around Wyatt. "Obviously I wasn't including you in that list, Jake. You aren't just an average pet."

Wyatt rolled his eyes. "Would you stop feeding that beast's already oversized ego and pay attention?"

In spite of the lingering sadness tinging her features, the corners of her mouth quirked up into a grin. "Sorry, Cowboy. Didn't realize you'd get jealous of a horse."

He dropped his forehead against hers. "I overheard your dad that day." Wyatt took a deep breath. "He was talking to your grandparents and telling them that...after losing your mom...he didn't know what he'd do without you. You were the center of his world. I couldn't take you away after that. I couldn't do that to him."

She made a choking sound and held a tight grip on his shirt. "That's why you left?" She slapped his shoulder once. Then twice. "Didn't you think to talk to me? Didn't you think I could make that decision myself?"

Wyatt pushed her away slightly, tightly gripping each side of her face. "I didn't want to leave you with that. You didn't deserve that burden. I made the choice. And I screwed it up, but it was my mistake. Not yours. You never had to sit in some dingy hotel room waiting for me to get back from a competition wondering what the hell you'd done with your life. Angel, I took myself out of the equation so you didn't have to decide."

Silence swarmed, the air around them thickened with the desire that was always present as well as the heavy reality of what had driven him to do the hardest thing in his life: break his own heart to spare his Angel. She would have chosen him. He knew that. Her passion and devotion were too strong for any other option.

Gigi deserved—had always deserved—so much better than the little he could have offered her in the early days of his career.

Her eyes widened and she shook her head. "I wanted to hate you. Hell, sometimes I still want to hate you. I just. .never could." Her hands grabbed the back of his neck, her mouth settling into a firm line.

Before he had a chance to ask the thousands of questions floating through his mind, her lips melded to his. Softer. Caressing him with their touch. The tip of her tongue reached out and licked his bottom lip. Wyatt's knees were seconds from giving out just as she released him.

"Does this mean you'll give me a second chance?" The only one he could voice was the only one that mattered in this moment.

Panic flashed in her eyes for a moment. She erased it with a shake of her head, arched an eyebrow, and dug in her back pocket. "Flip ya for it?"

Wyatt eyed the coin she held between her index and middle finger. "Same stakes as the first time?"

Her saucy grin faded. "Close. Girlfriend is off the table."

Wyatt measured his breaths just as carefully as his words. "Not right away, but—"

She shook her head. "A lot has happened since you bailed, and I have a hell of a lot on my plate. I don't have time for the Rhinestone Cowboy to saunter into my life, play the role of sexy hero, and then bail because it isn't working for him anymore." She snaked an arm around his waist. "But I can't deny that the same chemistry that drove me crazy in high school is still here. And I can't deny that I wondered more often than I'd like to admit if we'd be just as good at sex as we were in every other way."

The damned shadows were back in her eyes, and this time he was certain they weren't caused by him. He'd fight this or any other battle it took to get Gigi back, but he knew her well enough to know this wasn't the time. She never would talk to him about what was bothering her until she was good and ready.

She wanted him at least. And she admitted she didn't hate him. That was a starting point. A pretty damn pathetic one, but a place to work from nonetheless. "So what are you proposing?"

A painfully slow blink was her only response as several seconds ticked by. "Heads, you help me christen my bed. Tails—"

"You help me with mine." He winked when she narrowed her eyes at him.

Gigi flipped the coin in the air, caught it, slapped it on the back of her hand, covering it with the other for a few seconds before revealing the result. "Looks like you win, Cowboy."

***

Georgia

Rich, dark soil filtered through Georgia's gloved hands, and the relaxation that overtook her body from the simple task of working in her father's garden never ceased to surprise her. She pressed the dirt firmly around the last clump of geraniums just as her father trotted out the back door.

"So what's bothering you?" Barry Marsh offered the question and the glass of iced tea in one fluid motion.

Georgia removed her gloves, swiped a forearm across her sweaty brow, and took a long draw of the cold beverage. "Who says anything is wrong? I work on the yard every Saturday."

Her father settled into one of the chairs surrounding the stone fire pit, currently sitting dormant in the hot afternoon sun. "You do and I love that you moved back for a whole host of reasons, the fact you've taken the gardening duties off my plate being high on the list. But you don't show up with a trunk full of flowers and start attacking the ground unless you're dealing with something." He waved a hand to the line of fruit trees dotting the back edge of the small property. "Need I remind you that those happened right after you came home?"

Acrid fluid scorched the back of Georgia's throat as she remembered the anger and tears that she took out on the innocent dirt. Often she daydreamed she was spearing the pointed shovel through the empty cavity that was supposed to house Bruce's heart as she dug the holes. "No. You definitely don't." She flashed a mostly genuine grin and fell into the seat beside him. "But at least you got peaches out of that deal."

Barry laughed, stretching his legs out in front of him and crossing them at the ankles. "Yeah, and your grandmother has done an excellent job putting every one of them to use." His jovial smile faltered. "Well, she did."

The quiet reminder sent them both into a saddened silence. Innocent comments sometimes carried the starkest reality.

"Wyatt's back." The words were barely above a whisper, but she knew he wouldn't miss a syllable.

A small "hrm" from her father broke the silence momentarily before it enveloped them again. Only the rattling of the ice against the crystal pierced the air.

"No comment?" The question nearly exploded from her in desperation. Barry had always been a source of wisdom, insight, and guidance for her. Even more so after they lost her mother. More than anything she needed him to talk some sense into her and tell her to run as far and as fast from the cowboy as possible.

Especially considering the fact her best friend

seemed determined to talk her into falling into bed with Wyatt. So much for loyalty.

"That boy loved you, pumpkin." Her father's gaze was fixed on something far in the distance as he spoke. "You were young, but he loved you in a way I can't imagine ever stopped."

She pushed against her knees as she rose with a snort. "His love didn't have to go away. He did. He disappeared without a call or a note or an explanation and even though it might make sense now—"

"Might?" Dark brows rose to nearly meet his thinning gray hair line.

Georgia sighed, pacing along the brick circle her father had built. "It does. He was eighteen and stupid, but his heart was in the right place. I guess." She popped a fist onto her hip. "Just because I maybe can kind of understand it doesn't mean I have to fall all over him."

A deep chuckle met her begrudging admission. "I wouldn't expect you to. You never did make things easy for him. That boy had an uphill battle for you from day one." He held up a hand, palm out. "Don't get me wrong. I'm proud of you for being feisty and strong-willed and stubborn as a mule, and I am damn sure proud of where it led you. Not many people could juggle the things you do."

Offering support to her father and grandparents as they tended to her mother's decline had felt like the hardest thing in the world at the time. But being half of the primary caregiving team for her grandmother was equal, if not slightly worse. The steady mental decline of the woman who had once been vivacious and sharp took another piece of Georgia's soul each day.

Even so, there was no place she'd rather be.

Oblivious to the conflicting emotions cascading through her, Barry tilted his head and continued. "The fact that even at sixteen he was willing to bend over backwards to be with you...doesn't that tell you anything?"

In spite of the weight of the conversation, a grin tickled the corners of her mouth. She'd always loved sparring with Wyatt. It was one of the best parts of them. She couldn't deny that the same tenacity he showed in the arena served him well within their relationship.

Her heart ached through another beat and the cold reality stole her flash of happiness at the memories she still cherished. "I told you, I'm not into the relationship thing. Wyatt and Bruce did a damn good job of handling that particular desire." She resumed her seat beside her father, leaning her head back against the slatted wood of the deck chair. Warm fingers encircled her hand. "I am not going to tempt that particular beast. At least not while Gram..." An errant tear trailed down her face at the suggestion of her grandmother's decline.

Barry stood, kissed her forehead, and silently headed into the house. At the sliding glass door, he paused. "You can do anything you put your mind to, but only you can decide what's most important here."

The whoosh of the panel closing behind him punctuated his exit. Unspoken, but always understood, was that she would have his unfailing support and confidence. If only she trusted herself as much as he did. As much as she used to.

Chapter Ten

Wyatt

Thirteen Years Earlier

The rain was pounding against the windshield so hard Wyatt could barely see the road even with the wipers on the highest speed. But one thing he could spot easily was the figure clothed in black, head bent against the heavy onslaught of water.

"What the hell?" Wyatt threw the question out to the empty cab of his truck before pulling along the curb. He jumped out and rounded the hood, the rain pouring down his back as it ran off his hat.

He stepped in front of Gigi just in time for her to smack right into him. "Oh, I'm so...Wyatt?" She squinted at him from beneath the hood of her black sweatshirt. "What are you doing here?"

Wyatt shook his head and grabbed her upper arms. "What am I doing here? The better question, Angel, is what the hell are you doing here? You're drenched. And shivering. Get your fine little ass up in that truck.

Now."

Her brows shot up, and she popped a hand onto her hip. "Are you ordering me?"

He clenched his jaw tightly. "Normally I love your smartass little mouth and stubborn personality, but you need to actually listen and get in my truck."

She pressed her matte black lips into a thin line and shot daggers out of her hazel eyes. Finally the fight drained from her shoulders when her teeth began to chatter. "Fine."

Wyatt opened the passenger door for her before running around the front of the truck to get behind the wheel. He started the engine and kicked the heat on high but didn't make a move to drive. "All right, Gigi, would you like to explain to me why the hell you were out there walking in the pouring rain? Are you hoping to catch pneumonia? 'Cause I hate to break it to ya, I don't like hospitals, and I sure as hell don't want to visit you in one."

"Let's get one thing clear here, Cowboy. I don't need to explain myself to you. Just because I'm your girlfriend doesn't mean I need to check in with you before I make a move." She folded her arms across her chest and huffed.

He tried to stay mad at her, but she was too damn cute. "I think it's pretty damn sexy when you call me 'Cowboy' like that, Angel."

That took the last of her stubbornness out of her. The corners of her mouth quirked up. "You know it's supposed to be an insult, right?"

Wyatt turned in his seat slightly and reached out to tuck a wet strand of hair behind her ear. "Coming from you, it sounds like a pick-up line." He winked.

"Luckily, I'm a sure thing."

This time she laughed, and he couldn't resist leaning over to run his lips over her coal-colored ones. She moaned against his mouth, and he wrapped an arm around her soaking waist, sliding her closer to him on the bench seat. Her arms snuck up his chest to rest on his shoulders. Only a few weeks into their relationship and this girl already had a huge piece of his heart.

He finally broke the kiss and rested his forehead against hers. "Why didn't you just call me to come get you, Angel?"

She shrugged a little and lowered her eyes. After a few moments, she lifted them again, and a world of hurt was reflected back to him. "I wanted to save Roxy and Roscoe."

Wyatt knew he had a tendency to be self-centered. Maybe even a bit of an asshole. But he paid close attention to everything his Gigi said and he was pretty damn sure she'd never mentioned these Roxy and Roscoe people ever before. He pulled his head back and raised an eyebrow. "Uh, who?"

She reached down and laced her fingers through his, resting them on the leg of her soaked jeans. "Two dogs. They are at the shelter. Well, they've been there. For a long time. And today…" She sighed heavily. "Wyatt, they are going to be put down, and I can't let that happen."

Oh, his little avenging Angel. Pride coursed through him with her declaration, and he grinned at her. A passionate Gigi was a thing of beauty. And he couldn't help but be the tiniest bit smug that he had a hand in stoking her fire and giving her a purpose other than watching her mother's slow decline. "Aren't you glad your boyfriend is a freaking genius and suggested you volunteer there?"

She narrowed her gaze at him, but the smile still lingered around the corners of her mouth. "Yeah, yeah. Score one for the Rhinestone Cowboy." Every muscle on her face firmed. "We need to save them, Wyatt. We can't let anything happen to them."

He squeezed her hand. Yeah, she loved animals and yeah, when she had a purpose, she went after it head on, but there was something more here that she wasn't talking about. He knew her. It had only been a few months, but he knew her. "Talk to me, Angel." He pulled his arm from around her waist to cup her cheek. "What's going on?"

Gigi made a choking sound, and the tears began to stream down her face faster than the pounding rain against the windshield. "Six months. Maybe a tiny bit more but…"

Wyatt stroked his thumb beneath her eye, wiping away some of the tears. His stomach sank to his toes and he was fairly certain he knew what she was talking about.

He couldn't imagine being Gigi. The very idea of losing either of his parents terrified him, but this was the reality she faced. Never knowing what would await her arrival home each day. "Your mom?"

She nodded and fell against his chest, sobbing against his green plaid flannel shirt. He ran his hands up and down her back, searching his brain for something to say that could possibly make her feel better. Rather than choosing the wrong words, he sat in silence, offering soft touches and soothing sounds and praying it was enough.

Finally she lifted her head and his heart stumbled at the haunted look in her eyes. "The doctors told her today, and there isn't a damn thing I can do about it, Wyatt." She sniffled, and despite the serious conversation, his heart warmed. She was adorable. "But I can save Roxy and Roscoe." She grabbed his hand from the side of her face and clutched it against her chest. "Please help me."

Right now, he'd give her the moon if she asked. "Anything, Angel. I'll do anything for you."

She jumped into his lap, despite the steering wheel, and planted kisses on his cheeks, his neck. Then she turned to straddle his legs, pressing her lips to his and grinding against him, making him moan. Teasing every one of the teenage hormones he barely managed to keep in check in her presence.

But she deserved better than this. There was no way in hell her first time—their first time—would be in the cab of his truck on the side of the road. With fresh tears still lingering in the corners of her eyes. Silencing his screaming body, Wyatt gently pushed her away.

"Dammit all to hell, Angel." Wyatt struggled to stifle the raging heat coursing through his veins. The devastation etched on her face lanced through his heart as she scrambled off his lap. Shit. He had been trying to protect her, but all he'd managed to do was hurt her. He hooked a finger under her chin and made her look in his eyes. "Yes. Hell, yes. One day. Just not today, Angel. I want you more than I've ever wanted anyone or anything in my life, but not right now. Not like this. Not when you're in pain."

Traces of hurt still lingered on her face. "One day soon?"

He groaned and grabbed her hand, kissing her palm then the inside of her wrist. "One day when you're ready. But today we need to go save a couple of mutts from the jaws of death."

She giggled and nestled into his side as he put the truck in gear and pointed it in the direction of the shelter. His nostrils flared as he tried to covertly adjust his jeans. This was going to be the longest and most uncomfortable trip in his entire sixteen years on the planet.

***

Georgia

An unusually light swipe of eyeliner across her upper lid and she was done. Georgia laid a hand on her stomach, willing the swarm of butterflies to calm their frantic rhythm. Her teeth sank into her bare lower lip. The creamy face staring back at her was shocking, but she had decided that—just for tonight—she would drop the goth girl persona. Well, mostly. The black lace tank top and glittering skulls dotting her white skirt still screamed to her inner dark side.

She took a deep inhale that stuttered on release. Wyatt was coming to dinner, and her mother had even put forth the effort—and it really was such an effort— to move from her bed to the table to eat with him. What she could eat.

An ironic sneer curled her upper lip. The stupid freaking cowboy was practically a celebrity in her house. Damned if she'd let him in on that detail and feed his already massive ego. It was all she could do to rein it in with frequent insults. Although they usually backfired and resulted in even more preening.

The doorbell snapped her back to reality, and she raced toward the entrance. Her steps slowed when she reached the living room, and four pairs of eyes landed on her. All of them widened as her parents and grandparents took in her appearance. "I'll, um, get that." She muttered the words and cleared her throat.

She pulled the door open and was brought up short. Her jaw dropped and her eyes roamed the length of her boyfriend dressed…like a normal human. The only hint of the rhinestone cowboy that she loved to mock was the ever-present hat perched on his head.

"Holy hell, Gigi, what happened to you?"

The corners of her mouth turned down. Brown shoes and khaki pants teamed with a dark sapphire button-down shirt and matching tie. A tie. The freaking cowboy was wearing a freaking tie. "Me? What the hell happened to you?" She leaned back to catch her mother's gaze from the sofa in the living room. "Sorry, Mama, I didn't mean to curse."

Wyatt bent down, lips close to her ear. "Gigi, you look gorgeous, but I miss my Dark Angel. With the black lipstick that stains my shirt and my skin." His mouth grazed her jaw as he slowly pulled away.

Her lids met and she sucked in a breath. Her sixteen-year-old body raced with hormones that piqued in Wyatt's presence. He knew how to press every button to ignite the flame of desire in her but then turn down her every offer—her every plea—for relief. Constantly saying the time wasn't right. And she loved him for it.

Georgia laced her fingers through his, tugging him through the front door. Her eyes snapped open, catching his blue ones. "We'll discuss the rest of that later."

She led him into the living room and offered an internal cheer when he immediately snatched his hat off his head. Her grandparents were tolerant of her rebellious foray into gothic style, but they were old school when it came to manners. The stupid freaking cowboy just earned himself some brownie points.

"Daddy, I know you've already met Wyatt." She turned to her mom, nearly completely engulfed in the overstuffed couch, and grandparents seated in recliners next to her. "Mama, Gram, Gramps, this is Wyatt."

Her mother's face softened and she patted the empty spot to her left. "Wyatt, come sit and talk to me."

At the same time, her grandmother rose and grabbed Georgia's hand. "Why don't we go and fix the salad? You can set the table."

Georgia opened her mouth to argue. The table was already set and her grandmother didn't allow her within three feet of the kitchen as a rule, unless she was making a bowl of cereal. That had always been safe...so far. Before she could speak, she noted the pinking of her mother's pale cheeks as Wyatt sat on the cushion and gave the woman a lopsided grin and a wink.

Wordlessly she followed her grandmother into the kitchen and began cutting vegetables, grateful for the open floor plan that allowed her to covertly watch the interactions between her boyfriend and family, but mostly her mother. The chunks of cucumber were rough and uneven, but she paid them little attention.

How had she ever thought Wyatt wasn't special? Within moments of his entrance, the dark cloud that hung over their home lifted. His over-the-top animated retellings of things that had happened during training soon had her father and grandfather doubled over in laughter. And a sparkle came to her mother's normally dull eyes.

The magic spell Wyatt seemed to cast over her family carried through the entire evening. Her fingers found his beneath the tablecloth and gripped tightly. When his confused gaze found hers, she mouthed, "Thank you."

The puzzled expression melted into understanding, and he squeezed her hand with a wink and a barely perceptible nod. He returned his attention to the volleying discussion between her father and grandfather on some sports team she had no interest in. Wyatt slid in a few references to his older brother Tanner and all his athletic accomplishments.

When the conversation moved on to his family, Wyatt visibly perked more. In addition to the unabashed pride he clearly had for Tanner, he sang the praises of his two younger brothers, Connor and Dean. Connor was quite the artist and already had his mind fixed on becoming an architect. And Dean, the baby, was an animal whisperer who had zero plans for any sort of future…but at twelve that really didn't matter. Apparently all the Carlisle boys were golden in one way or another.

Lena Marsh offered a shuddering sigh and threw

her husband a plaintive look before fixing her dim gaze on the boy seated beside Georgia. "Wyatt, this has been the best night I've had in a long time." A soft smile curved her lips as her eyes flicked to Georgia before finding Wyatt again. "And I couldn't be happier to know that my daughter's first boyfriend is as charming and bright as you, but I'm afraid I must get back to bed now."

Within seconds, Barry was at her side and supporting her as she stood. Wyatt leapt to his feet to take her other arm, but she waved him off, gave him a peck on one cheek, a pat on the other, and shuffled down the hall.

Georgia got up and rounded the table, claiming Wyatt's hand and pulling him toward the back door. "We will be right back, Gram. And I'll help you clean up."

The light that had brightened her grandmother's face dimmed at her mother's exit. She shook her head with a tight-lipped smile. "That's okay. Take your time."

Georgia all but dragged Wyatt through the backyard to the large oak tree where the tire swing her grandfather had hung for her mother as a child still resided. She pressed him against the opposite side of the tree, out of the view of any prying eyes from her house.

"Gigi, what—"

His words were devoured by Georgia's mouth as she poured every emotion he'd created by just being Wyatt into the kiss. His hands fell to her hips before sliding around her waist to pull her closer. Unchecked tears streamed down her face.

Wyatt set her away from him slightly, his eyes searching hers in the fading light of the autumn evening. "Angel, what's wrong?"

Georgia shook her head, needing a few extra seconds of silence before she trusted her voice to speak. "Nothing, Cowboy. Absolutely nothing." She tugged on the back of his neck until his forehead rested against hers. "Thank you for being my stupid freaking cowboy, Wyatt."

Chapter Eleven

Wyatt

Present Day

"This is coming along faster than I expected."

His older brother's voice carried up to the hayloft, and Wyatt was grateful to have a decent excuse to abandon the hot work. He climbed down the ladder, landing close enough to Tanner that the cloud of dust from his work boots against the ground coated the bottom of the other man's dress pants.

"Dammit, Wyatt, you're lucky I'm on my way home." Tanner uttered a few more colorful names for his brother as he brushed at the dirt clinging to his slacks.

Home.

Nothing had felt like home to Wyatt for more than a decade. He loved every moment of his career, but with every small reminder of what he was gaining cemented the knowledge that his gut led him down the right road again. A home that was more than fifty percent done. A ranch and training facility to take his passion to the next level. And Gigi.

He grabbed a bottle of water from the cooler near the wide door and tossed another in Tanner's direction. That last one was more of a wild card than a certainty, but Gigi was the one thing in the world worth fighting for. And he sure as hell wasn't going to make the same mistake twice.

"So would you like to clue me in to why you wanted me to stop by or are you playing the role of strong, silent asshole today?" Tanner discarded his suit jacket and tie, tossing them over the railing.

Wyatt rolled his eyes. "Listen, I need…" The final word stuck to his tongue, refusing to exit his mouth. It was foreign and undesirable. "Help."

He hated asking for help, and the fact he created a career and a life he was damn proud of completely on his own was a point of pride for him, but if anyone could understand winning back the trust of the woman you loved, it would be his older brother. She may still think of him as a stupid freaking cowboy, but even he was smart enough to know that bailing the way he did coupled with more than a decade of pure yellow-bellied cowardice that kept him from just picking up the damn phone to call Gigi meant he had to focus on gaining her trust before anything else.

His older brother's brows lifted as he tilted his head back to chug the cold liquid. Finally coming up for air, he recapped the empty bottle and tossed it into the bin a few feet away. "You want my help?"

"Let's not make this into something it isn't." Wyatt moved saddles from one side of the barn to the other for no reason other than he was used to being the one giving his brother shit and didn't really like having the tables turned. The movement made him comfortable and gave him an excuse not to look Tanner in the eyes. "I just need...I need to know how you did it."

Tanner narrowed his gaze in on his younger brother. "Did what?"

"How'd you get Izzy to trust you again?"

The steady ticking as time passed in silence nearly drove Wyatt insane. He and Tanner never gave the other a moment of peace. Even when he was out on the road they would trade barbs through phone calls and texts. Occasionally Wyatt made a point of making a comment in an interview that seemed innocuous enough but he knew would piss off his brother.

Next to riding a bull, he considered it his greatest talent.

But they always had each other's backs. Unquestioningly. And if anyone could help him prove his regret and win back Gigi, it would be Tanner.

"You saw Georgia?" The muted question pierced the thick air. He should have known the great Tanner Carlisle would know exactly who he was talking about without even speaking one syllable of her name.

A second later his ringtone blared, disturbing the atmosphere between the two men. Tanner raised a brow at the intrusion. "That her?"

He snorted at his brother as he picked up his phone from the stall where he'd set it. "Highly unlikely." More like hell would have to freeze over first.

Damn. Jim. Again.

He held up a finger to his brother's rolling eyes as he clicked to answer the call. "Jim, for the fourth time this week, I am not doing any interviews or book deals or reality shows. Stop trying." He ended the call and silenced the phone, irritation with his former manager growing.

Tanner eyed him suspiciously. "Everything okay there?"

"Just my former manager having trouble saying goodbye to the best paycheck he had." Wyatt turned to rest his rear end against a half wall of one of the stalls. "And yeah, I did see Gigi. You'll never believe this, but she works for that Joseph Boots and Apparel company. They're going to be one of the corporate sponsors of my competition, and they're designing all the clothes I can sell here at RA. My first full day back in Asheville, I was having lunch with Georgia Marsh." He scuffed his boot against the ground. "What are the chances?"

Tanner crossed the barn to stand beside his brother, copying his relaxed pose. "And she didn't knee you between the legs?"

Squinting at nothing on the ceiling, Wyatt chuckled. "Brother, if looks could kill, you'd be digging my plot somewhere on the back forty." Even though he silently considered Tanner his best friend, he was a little uncomfortable admitting that Gigi's only interest in him currently outside of JBA was as an experimental roll in the hay. An answer to the "what if" from adolescence. Basically the same thing every super model and actress who didn't need his famous ties wanted, to see how good the cowboy could ride out of the saddle.

None of that was anything Tanner really needed to hear. Calling their prearranged hookup a date sounded so much more palpable. And much closer to what

Wyatt was really after. "But she agreed to a date. One. Already did the picnic thing with her up on the hill so she could have a view of everything."

His brother nodded slowly. "But have you shown her the house?"

An escaped breath relaxed the tension in Wyatt's chest when Tanner didn't ask for any more information on the why of their covert date. "Well, yeah. I told you I took her up—"

Realization dawned and a grin spread across Wyatt's face. One that lasted only a moment. "But it isn't finished. The crew has been focusing on the paddock and buildings..." Back to square one of how to create a special date without repeating everything he'd already done.

The older man chuckled and clapped him on the back. "Think outside of the box, little brother. It's amazing what five hundred dollars' worth of pillows and bedding can do. It can even transform the bed of my truck into a damn oasis." An odd grin curled his lips. "And help bring back my wife's smile."

Wyatt's stomach clenched remembering just how close his brother came to losing everything that mattered most, his wife and his family. Yeah, if anyone could help him figure out how to gain Georgia's trust, it would definitely be Tanner.

***

Georgia

Two of the yellow and green capsules, one beige tablet, and a handful of vitamins went into each square

104

container as Georgia portioned out her grandmother's prescriptions into daily doses for the week. The morning doses at least. She then would have a repeat with similar pills in a separate box for her evening medications.

In the same kitchen, at the same counter where she'd done the exact same task for her mother. It was too familiar.

She tossed two frozen waffles onto a plate and put them in the microwave. One meal she absolutely could not manage to mess up. Well, not too often. There was that one time she ended up with wooden discs after setting the power way too high for far too long. Since then, she stuck to doing twenty-second increments. And being okay with eating less than piping hot food for fear another rotation would result in an inedible, cardboard-like creation.

When the appliance dinged, she arranged them on a plate with bananas and strawberries, a small dish of cottage cheese, and a cup of tepid tea. She cut everything into bite-sized pieces, poured a bit of syrup over the waffles, and placed the well-rounded breakfast on a tray.

Georgia bumped her hip against the partially opened door and carried the meal inside. "Morning, Gram!" The forced cheerfulness in her tone would go completely unnoticed by the older woman, but it made Georgia feel better.

A vacant stare was her only reply, but thankfully, Gram managed to get out of the bed she'd been reclining in while the TV played an old black and white show and crossed over to the firm upholstered chair on the other side of the room. Georgia set up a

TV tray and placed all the dishes on the pressed board surface.

Moving about the room setting out clothes and wiping imaginary dust, she chattered on about the weather, the garden, and anything absurd and ridiculous she could possibly think of for their one-sided conversation. Gram dutifully took her pills and slowly ate her meal in silence, allowing a measure of tension to evaporate from Georgia's shoulders.

She was never sure what her grandmother would be like from day to day, hell, from hour to hour. The times where the disease owned her mind and made her fearful and combative would seem to be the worst, but they weren't. They at least gave a voice to the woman still contained within.

It was the moments like this when Georgia specifically told her grandmother about how beautiful the zinnias—the other woman's favorite flower—looked in full bloom and was only greeted with a long, empty blink that her heartache deepened.

She tried to tease her by threatening to attempt to replicate Gram's practically famous peach pie. The comment would have normally elicited an eye roll or groan or exaggerated plea to avoid the oven at all costs after the cookie baking fiasco that nearly burned the house down when she was twelve and visiting them over the summer.

But today the older woman merely stared, not even making eye contact with her granddaughter.

Georgia sighed and crossed the room, kneeling beside the chair. "Would you like to get dressed and come walk with me in the garden? I added some geraniums the other day." A tight laugh escaped.

"Mostly because I was mad at Wyatt and it seemed like a better idea than all the other options, which would have no doubt ended in me paying hefty fines and possible jail time."

Gram turned her head, and a small spark lit her eyes. "Lena? Oh, honey, you look so good today. How are you feeling?"

Scratch that. The vacancy was only rivaled by the times Gram confused Georgia with her mother.

Her grandmother patted her hand and continued on, oblivious to the pain lancing through Georgia's heart with intense precision. "Wyatt? You mean that boy Georgia is dating? He seems like a fine young man, and he really cares about her. I think they will be all right."

A tear slid down Georgia's cheek accompanied by sardonic laughter. She dropped her head forward against the arm rest of the chair.

He had. He had cared about her. He'd made sure her adolescent self was able to bask in a small glow of happiness during one of the hardest times of her life. Throughout the times she wasn't sure she could breathe, much less function, he offered a silent support she cherished.

Right before he ripped the rug from beneath her feet and left her shattered. She cleared her throat and swiped the moisture beneath her lid. With brisk efficiency, she helped her grandmother change into linen pants and a light top and led her to the garden.

The sun and flowers worked their magic to perk up Gram, even though she still kept calling Georgia by her mother's name and pummeling Georgia's already battered heart in the process.

Chapter Twelve

Georgia

Thirteen Years Earlier

The cuckoo clock for her grandparents and matching fluffy robes for her mom and dad weren't their real Christmas gifts. Georgia shifted in the green satin dress that made her mother's eyes light up when she saw her at the dinner table. This was her true present to her family. Ditching the surly goth girl for one day.

She flattened the pencil against the white paper, shading in the flank of the horse. Tomorrow she and Wyatt had agreed to exchange gifts, and she wanted hers to be perfect. What could she possibly get for a Rhinestone Cowboy that somehow managed to handle every part of her and give her all the things she never knew she needed? The intangible things. Time, attention, and kisses that could set fire to an igloo.

Georgia blew away some of the dust from the page and scrutinized the drawing. This was the best thing she could think of. She'd always loved to draw, and her parents had fostered her gift by supplying her with a never-ending stream of graphite pencils and blank sketchpads.

"What are you drawing, Georgie?" The soft voice of her mother—that seemed to grow frailer by the day—barely reached her over the din of the holiday movie playing on TV.

Setting her pencils on an end table out of the mischievous mouths of Roxy and Roscoe, who had already destroyed more than their fair share of her art supplies, she took her design to her mother, being cautious to sit down gently beside her. "It's for Wyatt." She lifted a shoulder. "I didn't know what to get him."

Hazel eyes that mirrored her own lit up as Lena drank in the sketch. Georgia worried it wasn't her best, but the glow lighting the older woman's sallow complexion gave her hope. "This is beautiful, honey. He'll love it."

Before Georgia could explain that she had bought a silver picture frame that had a border that reminded her of a rope, the doorbell rang through the house. Georgia's brows drew together, and a knowing smile covered her mother's face. Who in the world could possibly be visiting on Christmas night?

"You better go answer that." The whispered encouragement was accompanied with a surprisingly firm squeeze on the arm from her mother's bony hand.

The soft material of her dress swished against her bare legs as she walked to the door, swinging it open wide. Every emotion from surprise to embarrassment to a tinge of panic at being caught off guard raced

109

through her veins like wildfire. Her stupid freaking cowboy stood on the other side with his cocky smirk firmly in place.

"Merry Christmas, Angel."

Eyes wide, she shook her head. "Tomorrow. You were supposed to come over to exchange gifts tomorrow."

Wyatt shrugged and squinted, the grin never leaving his far too kissable lips. "Yeah, but I decided to change the plan." He lifted his chin, gaze fixed on something over her left shoulder. "Good evening, Mr. Marsh. Merry Christmas."

Her father dropped her coat around her shoulders, kissed her cheek, and held a hand out to Wyatt. "Merry Christmas, son. Ten o'clock. Don't forget."

From the opposite side, the handles of a gift bag were pressed into her palm. She turned just in time to catch a wink from her grandmother. It was the one she'd picked out to put Wyatt's gift in, but she'd just now finished the drawing and hadn't had time to put it in the frame. What in the ever-loving hell was going on around her?

He pumped the older man's arm once resolutely and nodded. "I promise, sir. Thanks for letting me steal her away."

With very little input from her brain, Georgia threaded her arms through the sleeves of her coat and followed Wyatt down the walkway. When her ballet slipper-clad toe reached the sidewalk that ran in front of her house, she paused and grabbed his arm. "Wyatt, would you care to tell me what you're doing?"

A more genuine smile curled his lips. The one she couldn't find the strength to resist. "I know we planned to celebrate tomorrow, and if you can, I'd still love to spend the day with you." He cupped her cheek tenderly. "But I wanted you to have this on Christmas. And I'm pretty damn lucky your father agreed."

She shook her head to clear away the cobwebs of confusion. "Wanted me to have what?"

Bright blue eyes twinkled in the streetlight. "Trust me, Angel, just trust me."

He led her down the sidewalk, across the street, and up the hill, stopping beneath the arched entryway to the park. "Close your eyes."

Georgia huffed out a sigh. "Wyatt, no. I don't know what harebrained scheme you have planned but I am absolutely, positively not—"

His lips captured hers, stealing her breath and silencing her argument. A soft moan escaped her mouth, and he deepened the kiss. She twined her arms around his neck, and he tightened his firm embrace.

When the need for oxygen necessitated their separation, he offered a smaller, softer smile. "Please, Angel. Just close your eyes for two minutes. I promise I won't let you fall and I won't let anything hurt you."

Begrudgingly she obeyed and allowed herself to be plunged into darkness as her eyes drifted closed. He gripped her hands in his and slowly led her down the uneven path, whistling Christmas carols as they walked.

Fighting the grin he caused was pointless. "You really are something else, Wyatt Carlisle."

He dropped her hands, turned her to the left, and pulled her spine against his chest. His hot breath tickled her ear as he leaned in close. "Open."

With a smirk, she lifted her lids, and every smartass

remark she'd conjured up died on her lips. The bench she'd claimed as her sanctuary, the first place in this whole town where she'd actually felt safe, and the very same spot where Wyatt discovered her that day so long ago, was adorned with a red velvet ribbon. White lights were strung from the large oak tree hanging overhead, and oversized red and green ornaments hung from bare limbs. Fake snow made a trail from where they stood to the wooden bench where a single present wrapped in bright green paper sat.

Georgia turned in his arms, words failing to come. She could only hope he could read the questions she was certain were etched across her face.

"You gave me a gift the first time I saw you here so I thought it'd be a good idea to return the favor." Crimson stained his cheeks, and he ducked his head. His arms fell from her waist, and he tugged her toward the bench. "Come on, you need to open your present."

Her eyes darted around their surroundings. "This isn't the gift?"

Wyatt chuckled and plopped the package in her lap. "Nope, this is just the arena. That," he pointed to the square box, "is the main event."

She lifted the lid on the green box to reveal…a red one. Georgia ripped off the paper and pried open the flaps to find…another green-wrapped gift. With a half-hearted glare, and plenty of accompanying laughter from Wyatt, she dove into the third package. Inside sat a small white jewelry box. The hinged lid offered a tiny squeak and so did she. Nestled on a bed of soft cotton was a silver cowboy astride a horse, adorned with rhinestones. The delicate pendant hung from a fine chain.

"Now," he lifted the necklace out and fastened it around her neck, "you get to keep your stupid freaking Rhinestone Cowboy close to your heart no matter where you are."

***

Wyatt

The internal standing ovation Wyatt was giving himself for nailing the gift he gave her for their first Christmas together went silent when her expression morphed from emotional awe to...something he couldn't identify. He lifted a hand to cradle her face, but she pulled away. And slid the gift she brought with her behind her back.

Gigi scooted across the bench a little, putting a few inches of distance between them. "I can't believe you did all of this for me."

Wyatt mimicked her movement, closing the space she'd created. "Angel, I'd do anything for you." The corner of his mouth kicked up, and he reached around her body. "Now, would this happen to belong to me?"

She snatched the present from his lax fingers, cradling it close to her chest, and stepped a couple of feet away. "Yes. I mean no. I mean..." Her eyes closed and she expelled a heavy sigh. "It's not ready. Not really."

He rose and stood in front of her, hooking a finger beneath her chin to lift her downturned face. The tissue paper and glossy gift bag crackled between them as he pressed in closer. "Talk to me, Angel."

The pool of unshed tears glistened along her lid margin. "I just finished it, just before you showed up. I didn't have time to put it in the—" Her teeth sank into her lower lip, silencing whatever secret she was about to reveal.

Adorable. When she was spouting off insults with her sassy mouth, she was impressive and sexy as hell. But with her face free of all the heavy makeup and hazel eyes completely open and radiating her vulnerability, she was adorable.

And Wyatt was smart enough, even at seventeen and with more than one head trauma to his name, to be honored that she trusted him enough to let down the iron bars she'd erected against the rest of the world. "And?"

Her perfect Cupid's bow lips turned down, and a shuddering sigh preceded her confession. "And even if it were, it isn't enough. Not when you did all this for me. It must have taken a couple of hours. On Christmas Day and you did all of that for me."

Actually, it had taken four, and he had done it the day before after sweet-talking the parks commissioner into even allowing him in over the holiday. But that was a tidbit she didn't need to know. Not when his gift was backfiring and making her feel worse.

He wrapped his arms around her waist, crushing the paper bag and trapping whatever it was inside between their bodies. "I'm gonna ask again and only want one answer, either yes or no. Is it for me?"

The flecks of gold in her eyes sparkled with fire eyes. "You're such an ass sometimes. Yes, it's for you."

Wyatt winked. "Good to know you can follow

instructions." He laughed when she swatted his bicep in response. "Now, second question, did it make you think of me from the first second you saw it?"

She twisted her lips from one side to the other. "Well, I kind of made it, but yeah. I guess. I mean I was thinking of you the entire time. Kind of had to."

An invisible band closed around his chest and tightened. She'd created something out of thin air specifically for him and didn't feel like it was enough? Swallowing a few times finally bought him the ability to speak past the emotions she'd stirred. "Then it isn't just enough, Angel. It's perfect."

She hesitated for a moment with her hand wrapped around the paper rope of the handles before sliding the flattened bag from between them. "Just...there is part of it that isn't done. It's supposed to go in...something."

Wyatt grinned and laced his fingers through hers, taking the gift with his other hand and leading her back to the bench. They sat down in unison, knees touching. He pulled the crumpled tissue from the top before grabbing the cold metal inside.

Every molecule of oxygen disappeared from his lungs when he turned the frame over. The black and white drawing of him astride his horse wasn't just stunning—although he certainly planned to discuss with her why she'd never told him she was an incredibly gifted artist—it was the most meaningful gift he'd ever been given.

A small giggle escaped the creature sitting beside him that he suddenly found more amazing than ever before. How had he not known his Gigi, his Angel, possessed such a gift?

She shrugged. "I guess my grandma must've put it in the frame whenever I got up to answer the door." Her fingers knotted in her lap and then moved to toy with the hem of her green dress. "So that's, um, kind of it. It isn't anything close to—"

Wyatt poured every word that he couldn't move past his throat into the kiss he used to silence her ridiculous speech. Not enough? This was far more than he deserved and was something he would never let go of. Kind of like the girl he held in his embrace.

He pulled back enough to break their lips apart and leaned his forehead against hers. "It's perfect."

Chapter Thirteen

Wyatt

Present Day

"Do you think that you two could possibly just stop screwing up your relationships so I can have my weekends back?" Dean hefted another box out of the bed of Wyatt's truck. "And so I can stop feeling like some contestant on a weird design show challenge?"

Wyatt smacked the back of his youngest brother's head lightly, the same way he'd been doing since they were kids. "Do you think you could stop bitching and just work? It would go a lot faster if you could manage that." He turned and looked at Tanner, carrying supplies to the front porch. "Is this the kind of shit I used to give you?"

His older brother snorted. "Used to? Try still do. Every damn moment of every damn day."

A sly grin curled Wyatt's lips, and he threw an arm around Dean's shoulders, his tone dripping with sarcasm. "Aw, come on, think of all the lessons you're

117

learning from the masters. One day you'll need us to help you whenever you decide to pull your head out of your ass and decide you're gonna ask Jillian out."

An unusual swath of crimson stained Dean's cheekbones, and he shrugged from beneath Wyatt's faux affectionate embrace with a sharp elbow check to the older man's ribcage. "She's just my friend. Now do you think you could hurry this little decorating challenge up? Some of us have actual lives here."

Tanner unloaded a mountain of fluffy pillows and comforters covered in plastic from the bed of his own truck, a silent testament to Tanner's efforts to win back the wife he nearly lost. The softer side of Wyatt that he rarely let be seen aside from Gigi warmed. Despite all their back and forth jabs and unspoken competitions, seeing his brother and sister-in-law overcome the biggest obstacle of their marriage was not only encouraging for him, but a damn fine sight to behold. If there was a relationship he believed in more than him and Gigi, it was Tanner and Izzy.

"How did Connor manage to skirt this sweet brotherly reunion anyway? His happy little ass should be here too." Dean moved to a new topic to complain about.

Wyatt pushed the tailgate of his truck up with enough force to engage the latch. "Kelsey was dragging him to some bridal show or some such thing." He grinned and adjusted the brim of his hat, elbow resting on the truck bed. "But hey, if you feel like trading places with him, I'm sure he'd be none too happy to be out here in the fresh air and let you listen to discussions on the pros and cons of fresh flowers versus artificial. Or if all brides really should wear white."

Dean paused mid-step and squinted at Wyatt. "I don't know if I am more disturbed by the fact Connor has to endure that or you knowing that much about what happens at bridal shows."

Three hours later, Dean hopped into the seat of his low-riding car and peeled out of Wyatt's driveway without a backwards glance at his brothers.

"Seriously, was I that big of a pain in the ass?" Wyatt handed his brother a bottle of water before taking a long draw from his own.

"As I said before, what do you mean was? You're still a damn thorn in my side."

A rare moment of vulnerability flared in Wyatt. He plopped down on the bumper of his truck. "Do you think there's actually a chance in hell I can come back from this?"

The arm Tanner raised to take a drink froze in midair. Finally he took a small sip before recapping his bottle. He sat beside his brother, staring out at the seemingly endless land stretched before them. "I don't know. Hell, there are days I don't know how I came back from damn near ruining my marriage." He leaned forward, resting his elbows on his knees, the hand holding the water dangling between his legs.

Silence descended over them, and Wyatt's mind replayed old, familiar scenes. He and Gigi holding hands, kissing, the countless hours they spent together in the wake of her loss. Even their fighting and sparring—maybe especially that—made up some of his favorite memories.

"Do you think you did the right thing when you left?"

His brother's quiet question immediately struck at the heart of it all. "I think I made the right decision to leave on my own, but I know damn well I handled it the wrong way." He smacked his hands to his cheeks and scrubbed them up and down. "And she would've forgiven me if I'd managed to pull my head out of my ass long enough to call her. Or write. Or send a damn carrier pigeon."

Tanner nodded up and down slowly, taking another long draw of water. "Yeah, that was probably stupider than the whole leaving with no notice part."

Wyatt groaned and pressed his back into the warm onyx tailgate. "So that's a no then? I'm screwed?"

His brother stood and slid his vibrating phone from his pocket, grinning down at the screen. A few swipes of his fingers across the glass and he shoved it back in his pocket. "You're not screwed unless you want to be. None of that means she can't forgive you and you can't work this out; it just means you're gonna need to work your ass off to do it."

Tanner clapped his brother on his back and headed toward his own truck. "Trust me, brother, it can be done."

***

Georgia

Butterflies created an erratic swarm in Georgia's stomach with the tinkling of the doorbell. She fastened her earring before descending the stairs. He was early.

In one form or another, Wyatt had been part of her life for more than a dozen years. Even though she told herself she was over him and had moved on, she still scanned through his social media sites more often than she'd like to admit.

Even when he wasn't present, his draw was undeniable. Even when she was with someone else. Even when she had a ring on her finger.

Wyatt always hung at the back of her mind and then rushed to the front nearly every night she collapsed into her bed crying. She spent the time she was licking her Bruce-induced wounds, missing her stupid freaking cowboy in a very different way. While Wyatt had shattered her eighteen-year-old heart when he left, she'd known even then that it hadn't been malicious or calculated.

Doubt and fear simmered beneath the confident affect she presented. But when she pulled the door open and her stupid freaking cowboy quirked his mouth into a lopsided grin and he touched the brim of his hat, everything other than the warmth of their history and ever present, unlimited lust vanished.

Her own lips twitched with a barely contained smile. He was ridiculous in the very best possible way. "Can't drop the Rhinestone Cowboy persona even just for one night, can ya?"

Wyatt stepped across her threshold, extending to his full six-foot, four-inch height, and snaked an arm around her waist. Instinctively, her hands flew to his chest and stroked the soft cotton shirt. "You don't want me to, Angel. Not really."

Georgia tilted her head back, and the reality of her situation hit her heart with the force of a chaotic storm. She was in Wyatt's arms again. Exactly where she'd spent the first year after his departure praying to be and the last place in the world she ever expected to find herself again. Wyatt.

But this time, everything was different. She wouldn't allow him access to her heart again. This was going to be simply about the attraction and desire they'd always had. Finding out if it was still there and discovering if they could be as good together as she always suspected.

This was sex and nothing more. She didn't have time for a relationship and sure as hell didn't have the fortitude to survive another disappearing act. Her energy was focused in two places, her family and her work. Wyatt offered a brief reprieve, but that's where it ended.

His grip tightened and he pulled her closer, dipping his head to brush his lips across hers. "You look beautiful, Angel."

She let herself melt into his embrace and surrender to his kiss. Neither things she did easily, but it was Wyatt. She'd be telling the biggest lie of her life if she said she didn't still care for him. She just didn't trust him. Or anyone.

The tender, soft caress of his mouth on hers caused moisture to collect in the corners of her eyes. Her hands traveled up the front of his shirt to lock behind his neck. If they never left this very spot for the entirety of the evening, it would still be perfect.

With a final gentle peck, his lips abandoned hers and she fought against a cry of frustration at the loss. She cleared her throat, unsure of her voice but needing to add a little sarcasm-laced levity to their situation. Because that's what she did and that's who they were. "I didn't realize you were such a fan of hibiscus." Her arm swept down the length of her side, indicating the white sundress with pink flowers printed across it.

"I wasn't talking about your clothes there, Gigi." The hand at her side gripped harder, and the other moved to cup her cheek. "You've always been the most beautiful woman in the world to me."

The heart that had been soaring through the sky at being held by Wyatt—kissed by Wyatt—once again plummeted to the earth, greeting reality with a large crack in its already scarred surface. Images she'd forced herself to look at of Wyatt on the beach with one scantily clad celebrity after another, holding each other close, tumbled through her mind. She disentangled herself from him and stepped past him onto the front porch. "I'm sure the swimsuit model you dated would be devastated to hear that. Close the door, will you?"

She forced her sandal-clad feet into as effortless of a glide as possible, wanting to appear calm and unaffected by the notion of Wyatt with anyone else. The needle prick of her conscience reminded her that she hadn't pined for him all by herself over the years. And she sure as hell hadn't been celibate. Considering the diamond sparkling at the bottom of the bay, she really had no right to—

Just as she reached the passenger door of his truck, his hand closed around her exposed bicep, spun her around, and pushed her into the warm metal of the cab. "Dammit, Gigi, would you stop?" He pressed his forehead to hers, and the heavy cadence of his heart beat against her chest. "Half of those so-called relationships were publicity stunts. That kind of shit is part of your career. You know how it works. Some virginal former Miss Teen Oklahoma wants to break into the entertainment business. Her agent calls mine and suddenly we're dating. She could cling to my status to get some elevation for her career. And I'd have a few months where I appeared to be in a stable committed relationship so I could snag all those companies that are just like Elias's and focused on the personal lives of their spokespeople reflecting well on them."

She swallowed, her breathing a shallow, staccato rhythm. "And the other half?" As soon as the words left her mouth, she wanted to suck them back in. Yes, he had hurt her, but this wasn't a fair battle. It sure as hell wasn't productive.

"They weren't you. No matter who they were, what they looked like, or how much money they made...they weren't my Dark Angel. They weren't my Gigi."

His mouth met hers in another kiss, this time passionate and demanding. Needy and desperate. The hot metal against her back was no match for the heat radiating off Wyatt's body. He sucked on her lower lip, and her knees buckled. She melted into him, and his grip tightened, keeping her both upright and pressed tightly against his body.

When they finally came up for air, his breathing was as labored as hers. "I miss you, Angel. There wasn't a day that went by I didn't think of you and wish..." He shook his head. "I was young and stupid, and I screwed up. I promise I will never do something so stupid again."

She held his jaw with one hand, swallowing once. Twice. She wanted to tell him that he wouldn't ever have the opportunity because they would talk about stuff and handle problems together, like a team...

But those were promises she couldn't make. She had priorities that didn't include letting Wyatt Carlisle into any part of her life other than her bedroom. No matter how desperately she wanted to collapse into him and let him work the same magic he had when they were kids.

"Let's just worry about tonight." Georgia tossed the hair that had fallen forward behind her shoulder. "And tonight I believe we have...plans."

She winked, pushing him away a little so she could climb into the cab of the truck, and exorcised all the dark thoughts with them. For one night, she wanted to enjoy the fact her stupid freaking cowboy had come home.

Chapter Fourteen

Georgia

Twelve Years Earlier

She would not skip. She absolutely, positively would not skip.

That would be the complete antithesis of everything she stood for. But damned if that stupid freaking cowboy didn't make her happy. He made everyone happy. The corners of her coal-colored lips twitched, begging to be released into the full smile that was so hard to contain when she was with him. Or saw him. Or talked about him. Or thought about him.

"Hey, um, where ya going?"

Georgia's gaze landed on Paige, the strawberry blonde who had a locker right next to hers and was the only person other than Wyatt she could stand in this town. She might be best friend material. If she believed in that sort of permanence.

"Looking for Wyatt. We're supposed to be leaving soon for his training." Just like they did every Friday.

The warmth and comfort that came from their small routines, the things in her life she could count on when chaos reigned everywhere else, was better than the fleece-lined coat she wore to shield against the December wind. Florida girls were not cut out for this kind of weather.

Paige nodded, toeing the concrete walk with her sneaker. "I was wondering if maybe you'd want to come over to my house this weekend. Like watch a movie or something?"

Still not willing to admit that her time in North Carolina was going to last a lot longer than she wanted, Georgia had kept Paige at arm's length as much as possible. Their friendship offered a companion for lunch and conversation between classes since her schedule varied from Wyatt's, but she was scared to get too close. To care too much. Things like that didn't work out for Georgia.

The lifelong friends she'd had quickly stopped emailing and messaging soon after she moved. All the promises to stay in touch disappeared.

Even her mom…Georgia swallowed the egg blocking her throat. Maybe not by choice, but even her mom would be gone soon. Nothing lasted. Friends weren't forever. The effort to even try seemed pointless and stupid.

But Paige had been the first person not afraid to approach the goth girl that everyone but Wyatt avoided. That counted for something, right?

"That actually doesn't sound awful." She winced as the words crossed her lips. If Wyatt had been here, he would have groaned, well used to her surly responses.

She was struck speechless when Paige tilted her

head back and laughed. "That sounds about right. I've got an annoying as hell younger brother though, so awful is always on the table."

Georgia bit the inside of her mouth before dissolving into matching giggles. Maybe with people like Wyatt and Paige, this backwoods hick town wouldn't be so bad after all. "I just, uh, have to check with my dad and my grandparents first."

Paige's curls bounced with her nod. She ripped a sheet from the notebook she was carrying in her arms, produced a pen from who knew where, and scribbled something hastily. "Here's my number. Just give me a call. We can order pizza or something."

A blue sedan pulled to the curb and honked. Paige shoved the blue-lined paper at Georgia and offered a small wave. "That's my dad. I gotta run. But call me." She turned and jogged a couple of steps before stopping and spinning back to face Georgia. "Oh, I think I saw him by his locker when I was coming out."

Georgia curled her fingers slightly in both acknowledgement of the Wyatt-shaped lead and a farewell. She frowned at her watch as she trudged back into the school building, nearly void of all students now. Where the hell was that stupid freaking cowboy anyway? They were going to be late. There wasn't one part of her that wanted to miss the chance to see him get thrown onto that round hind end by some mammoth bull.

The familiar tan hat stood out right away. It was hard to miss when it was attached to more than six feet of leanly muscled hotness digging through his locker. As was the petite blonde clinging to his back, her arms snaked around his waist, palms pressed into his chest, and her cheek resting between his shoulder blades. Not a beam of light could pass between them, every plane and curve of their bodies perfectly fitted together.

Without making a sound, she turned on the thick heel of her clunky black boots. She paused just outside the door to release the shaky breath that had been trapped at the sight of her boyfriend—ex-boyfriend—being held by someone else. Someone who was everything she wasn't. Perky, happy, and...normal.

She drew in a lungful of the cold air before heading home. Even if she had allowed them, tears wouldn't come. The pain was too deep. Too fresh. And too damned much.

Every nerve tingled, prickling her skin as she walked. The cars driving past at the slow, residential speed limit went unnoticed, overridden by desolate buzzing in her ears.

She forced a reassuring smile for her father and grandparents as she crossed the threshold and managed a weak excuse of not feeling well to explain her unusual presence on a Friday night. As soon as the door to her bedroom latched behind her, she stripped off her clothes and tugged on shorts and a faded green shirt emblazoned with the logo for the college of her dreams far away in Tampa.

That's what she would focus on, she told herself as she curled under the thick down comforter and hugged her pillow close to her chest. Focus on school and grades and making sure USF wasn't just a dream, it was her reality. No stupid freaking cowboys allowed. And the only bull she would care about from here on out was the iconic bull of USF.

She had a plan. And it was a good one. She only wished the tears that finally broke through the dam she'd so carefully crafted would listen to the plan and obediently retreat.

"Gigi? What's wrong? What happened?"

The tapping on her door matched the drumline in her head, but it was the deep baritone rumble that made her groan. The very last thing she wanted to hear. "Go away. I don't feel good."

"That's what your dad said, Angel, but I just wanted to check on you." His voice dropped to barely above a whisper as he spoke the name he told her was only theirs to share. "I was scared when I couldn't find you after school. Let me come in. Talk to me."

Not scared enough to interrupt his time with Becky.

"I'll be fine. Go to training."

Silence met her words. Wyatt Carlisle couldn't creep anywhere if he tried, so she knew he was still on the other side of the door. Her heart begged her to talk to him. To give him a chance to explain and discover this was a crazy misunderstanding because the light it brought into her dark world was becoming necessary to her sanity.

But her mind…her mind was distrustful of everyone and everything. It encouraged her lips to remain closed and body to remain still.

A thud against the oak barrier between her and Wyatt made her jump. The scrape of something sliding down the length of it drew her brows together.

"I'll wait until you're feeling better, Gigi." His voice dripped with sarcasm, and heat crept up her neck knowing he didn't believe her excuse. "I'll wait right here for you to talk to me."

***

Wyatt

Girls. Seriously, what the hell was wrong with them? Well…this girl in particular. He really didn't have time for this; his training was waiting. He closed his eyes and sucked in a breath. Gigi was like an untamed horse. A comparison he was certain would drive her insane but was nonetheless true. The years of working with horses that ranged from exceedingly docile to feisty and scared had taught him one thing.

"Did you forget that I am an incredibly patient man?"

The walls were thin enough her huffing trickled through, and it was like music to his ears. There was something incredibly enjoyable about getting Gigi all riled up.

Wyatt shifted, trying to get comfortable on the hardwood floor. An unforgiving surface that did nothing to help his still tender backside from last night's half a dozen throws. He adjusted his hat so he could lean his head back against the door. If anyone had told him six months ago he'd be missing out on training to sit outside some girl's bedroom door because she was having some sort of temper tantrum, he'd have laughed in their face.

And he probably still would because this wasn't just some girl; it was Gigi. Somehow his Dark Angel had taken precedence in his life and heart, even more important than his strict training schedule. The one that he hoped would ensure a blockbuster debut to the professional rodeo circuit.

One of the scraggly mutts Gigi had insisted on saving from certain demise wandered over and sat down beside Wyatt, laying her head in the lap of his outstretched legs. He chuckled and scratched behind her left ear, just the way she liked. "Well, hey there, Roxy. It's good to know at least one female in this house—"

His words ended on a sharp yelp as the door supporting his back disappeared and he found himself staring at a very pissed-off Gigi standing over his sprawled form. Her arms were folded across her chest and her painted toes tapped far too close to his head for comfort.

Even so, he couldn't help but grin. "Well, hey there, Gigi. You don't look sick...but it is kinda hard to tell with that makeup on."

She popped a brow up quickly. "Good thing you don't have to deal with that anymore." Her eyes scanned down the empty hallway and vacant rooms beyond it. "You've seen me and now you can get the hell out of here."

Wyatt scrambled to his feet, adjusted his hat, and frowned. "Care to tell me exactly what has gotten into you? You're supposed to come with me on Fridays. You promised."

Sparks of anger flared into a raging blaze in the hazel depths raking over him. Her mouth opened then snapped closed at the clanging of pots in the kitchen. She fisted his shirt and pulled him into her room, closing the door with a soft click of the latch. "My grandma is making dinner, and she doesn't need to hear what an asshole my boyfriend was. And my mom is sleeping, and I am definitely not going to rob her of a moment of rest because you—" White teeth sank into her lower lip and cut off her words.

"Because I what, Gigi? What the hell did I do? Because I really don't know. You were fine earlier, but then you stood me up with no explanation." Wyatt gripped her biceps, desperation choking his voice. "Angel, you need to tell me what the hell happened in the past couple of hours."

Black trails of mascara ran down her cheeks. "I saw you. I get it. I was a charity case because my mom's dying and you felt sorry for me." A hiccup shook her entire body. "You don't have to fake interest in the goth freak anymore. Go back to your platinum blonde bimbos."

Confusion plunged Wyatt's mind into a blinding haze. "I need just a bit more information here, Angel. Because I wouldn't let anyone in the world say half the shit about you that I just heard come out of your mouth. Don't think you're that special. I won't let you say it either."

She lifted her arms, breaking his hold. "You were getting your stuff out of your locker and she was clinging to you like a leech. Sound familiar? If you were done playing boyfriend to me, you could have just said it. You didn't have to prove every cliché true."

A boulder sank to the bottom of Wyatt's gut followed by a long litany of curses. He'd shaken Becky off as soon as he realized it wasn't Gigi behind him, but damn, why the hell did she have to pick that moment to see the exchange?

There was no way to defend himself if she didn't believe him. It looked bad. Hell, it looked like exactly what she thought. All he had to offer for proof was his word. And she'd already made up her mind.

He turned to leave, his aching heart begging him not to walk away. Hand resting on the knob, he paused. Eyes closed, he inhaled deeply before turning around to pull Gigi into a tight embrace and crush her mouth beneath his. A hiccuping sob vibrated against his lips before her arms snaked around his neck.

The needy force driving his desperate kiss softened. His fingers stroked up and down her spine, curving her body into him. With more strength than he ever thought he possessed, Wyatt peeled his lips from hers and pressed his forehead against hers. "I promise you it wasn't what you think. She came up behind me and put her arms around me, and I swear I thought it was you, which is the only reason it lasted for longer than a tenth of a second. As soon as I realized it wasn't, I pushed her away and got the hell out of Dodge. And I have no way to prove it other than to tell you that I love you, Angel. I'd never hurt you like that."

Her swollen, red lids lifted and met his gaze. He silently prayed she would see the truth in his eyes, that she felt it in their kiss. The silence engulfed them in its dark depth, churning and twisting his gut into agonizing knots. He was moments from begging her to trust and believe him just this once when a tiny glimmer of his Dark Angel flickered in the hazel orbs.

"I trust you." She pulled her head back from his.

His hold on her tightened. "Whenever anything happens, we talk about it. Got it, Gigi?"

A smile curled her lips, and her fingers dug into the back of his neck. "You're pretty smart for a stupid freaking cowboy. Now kiss me again before we get caught alone in my room."

Chapter Fifteen

Wyatt

Present Day

"Jake!"

Wyatt rolled his eyes as Gigi jumped from the cab of his truck and briskly crossed to the paddock where the damned traitor of a horse reveled in the attention Gigi was lavishing on him. If Wyatt didn't know better, he could swear the beast smirked at him when she nuzzled into his neck. "Let's just see if your new girlfriend shows up to muck your stall and feed you an apple and carrot every morning."

Her hazel eyes shone up at him when he reached her side. "I didn't realize when we made our agreement you were planning a literal roll in the hay."

He sputtered, words choking his throat and making him cough. "Excuse me?"

"Well, we are supposed to be answering all the questions I have left over from high school." She wound her arms around Wyatt's waist and lined her body with his, every curve and plane fitting together better than he remembered. "Because I always knew we could ignite a forest fire if we tried hard enough."

His traitorous body immediately applauded the idea with a tightening of every muscle. His mind raced with ideas of forgetting everything he'd staged and moving straight to the highlight of the evening. But his heart ached with the reminder that his Angel saw him the same way everyone else did. And he had no one but himself to blame for that fact.

"No, I'm taking you to my house, but I thought we could ride Jake out." He slid the cocky smirk in place that he didn't really feel. "As long as you make sure you ride with me this time. And hold on tight."

Gigi smiled up at him. "I'd love to." She swallowed, and a deep pink stained her cheeks. "Riding with you was one of the things I missed the most after you left. I didn't even look at a horse for two years. I couldn't. You brought that into my life at the exact moment I needed it and it was something special we shared."

Every time he thought he couldn't fall any deeper into the hollow pit that had formed from his regret and self-loathing, he realized he had only been hanging onto a crevice and had much lower to go. "I'm sorry, Ang—"

Soft fingers landed against his mouth, and as much as he was trying to stay levelheaded, his pants tightened a fraction. Damn, he'd missed that touch.

"I didn't tell you that to elicit another apology or make you feel any worse. Tonight isn't supposed to be about that."

What the hell is it about then? Because if you say

137

just sex one more time... He kept his internal screams locked far from Gigi's ears. He had to be patient and understanding and own the fact he created this. Even if it might kill him.

She stroked the soft mane of the beast standing to her right who snorted and stomped in reply, indignant at having been forgotten for so long. "You couldn't have picked a better start, though." She brushed her lips across Wyatt's cheek. "Thanks, Cowboy."

His Dark Angel always had a knack for silencing his overly active brain and rapid-fire mouth. A talent that hadn't faded over the years. The comfortable quiet of old friends and lovers whose connection transcended words fell over them as they set out on Jake at a slow canter. He held the reins in one hand while the other covered hers where they met just below his sternum.

Sooner than he really liked, they reached the base of the hill. He dismounted and lifted her off the saddle. Gigi had never been one to conceal her emotions from him. Whether it was the irritation and disdain she showered on him during her first days at school or the lusty need that quickly consumed much of their adolescent relationship, he always had a pretty damn good idea what was going through that beautiful auburn head.

The transition from confusion to understanding to delight played out across her face in under thirty seconds. "Wyatt..."

He laced his fingers through hers, and they climbed the open stairs, stepping around two-by-fours left behind by the construction crew, ready for placement when they returned on Monday. In the center of a large, open square that would one day be a living room was a pile of pillows, blankets, and a cooler of food. All surrounded by flameless candles and lanterns.

Wide eyes stared up at him, a single line across her forehead the only clue to her uncertainty. "This…looks an awful lot like a date."

It was. In his mind. Because there was nothing "just" when it came to Gigi. She was never just a girl. They were never just dating. And this could never be just sex. Not between them. But he'd play the game she set up for now, and he'd take every chance to show her that they could be more, that they should be more, and that if she trusted him again, he'd never screw it up.

Instead of saying a word of that, he dropped his voice and thickened his manufactured drawl. "Why we need something to keep our stamina up there, Gigi."

She rolled her eyes and tugged on his hand, walking backwards to the massive pile of linens waiting. "I am suddenly starving."

She kicked off her sandals and stood on the comforter. Before Wyatt could offer to open the cooler, she whipped the sundress over her head. The orange, purple, and reds of the setting sun kissed her skin, and her entire body glowed in the fading light. His tongue clung to the roof of his mouth and he was helpless to do anything but gawk at her mostly naked form. He wasn't sure if he was still breathing but couldn't bring himself to care. If this was how he would die, what a way to go. His adorably sassy Angel had grown into a woman that conjured a tempest of love and passion that consumed every part of him. Mentally, emotionally, and definitely physically.

"Well, Cowboy, are you just gonna stand there?"

He pulled his boots off and closed the few feet separating them before his mind could kick in. She let out a shriek mingled with a laugh as he lowered her onto the downy mass. Wyatt quickly swallowed every sound when his mouth landed on hers. His hand slipped inside her bra, kneading, teasing, tweaking the soft skin beneath. He trailed down her neck to kiss along her shoulders, smiling at the soft gasps when he lightly pinched the pebble he'd been toying with.

He reached behind her back, flicking open the clasp and eliciting a groan from Gigi. "Should I be worried that you did that so easily?"

Wyatt laughed as he tossed the satin lingerie to his right, letting his mouth replace his hands and feast on Gigi. He ground against her, the denim material creating a delicious friction. "I've always been damn good at that. It's a gift."

She squirmed beneath him, arching her back as his lips trailed along her abdomen, dipping below her navel, pushing her underwear down as he went. He licked along the heated seam before his tongue skated across the tiny bundle of nerves that caused her to buck against his mouth.

"Dammit, Wyatt! I need you." Her scream ended on a whimper as his fingers joined his mouth, heightening her pleasure.

Two digits became three, and he lifted his head, drinking in the flushed beauty falling apart before him. "Now, Gigi, would you deny a starving man the perfect meal?"

His lips returned to the small nub, sucking lightly as his fingers curled inside her. The cry that erupted echoed through the valley around him, and he made a mental note to soundproof their bedroom. Because it damned sure was going to be theirs.

Her hands frantically grasped at his shirt. "Off. Now. Everything." She pulled him back up until his face was in line with hers. "I need you, Wyatt. I need you right now. All of you."

Never one to deny a lady, and completely incapable of saying no to Gigi even if he wanted to, he scrambled to his feet and shed his clothes and hat, tossing them in the general direction of hers. He fished a condom from his wallet and added that to the pile.

Before he could don the latex barrier, Gigi levered up on her elbows. "Not without the hat, Cowboy."

"Oh, hell." He muttered the curse as he snatched his hat from the floor and jammed it on his head. Once he was sheathed, he returned to stretch his body on top of hers. In one smooth motion, he slid inside. "Better?"

Gigi hitched her legs up on his hips and arched her back, deepening their connection. Her teeth sank into her lower lip, hazel eyes wide with desire. She nodded, and Wyatt banked his body's reaction. Barely.

Need and desire quickly took over, and the slow pace he'd started was abandoned. Gigi met him with each thrust, her moans and gasps driving him.

Her hands flew to his face and her widened eyes and opened mouth as she found her second release transfixed him and brought his own exploding completion as he screamed her name.

With more effort than he thought possible, he rolled off her sweat-slickened body, removed the condom, and hurried to return, pulling her against his side. He tugged on one of the blankets to cover them against the cooling air.

She lifted her head and propped her chin on his chest. "Isn't this the point in the program where you feed me, Cowboy?"

***

Georgia

The steady, rhythmic cadence of the pen bouncing off the desk echoed in Georgia's ears as she reined in her desire to interrupt Wyatt's careful perusal of the design boards she'd called him in to see today. They were good. Really good. Finally with a lot of hands-on guidance from Georgia herself they had managed to craft something she was proud of and excited to show Wyatt. She desperately needed to hear him say that they had hit the nail on the head and delivered exactly what he wanted.

His utter silence was chipping away at that confidence with every tick of the hands on the clock.

Blue eyes sparkled up at her as he lifted his gaze to meet hers. "It was that first trip to the ranch that did it, wasn't it? I was right and you needed a horseback guided tour to figure it all out." He set the images on the smooth, cherry surface separating them, leaned back in his chair, and folded his arms across his chest.

Cocky smirk firmly in place.

"You're an ass." As much as she wanted to, Georgia couldn't resist meeting his smile with one of her own, because dammit, he was right. She hated that fact almost as much as she loved it.

His brows kicked up as he stood and rounded her desk, resting his backside against it. "That might be true…" He bent forward, his mouth right beside her ear, his warm breath causing the familiar fire of need to race through her veins. "But you also love my ass. I seem to recall someone's nails digging into it last night while she screamed my name."

The back of her hand collided with his bicep as she tried to ignore the heat pooling between her legs. She was slightly embarrassed at the speed she had texted him the very next night after the one at his ranch. As well as the next night. And every night after. To his face she kept the façade of "sex only" intact, but only to herself did she admit the truth. It was why she struggled to walk away at the end of the night and leave him to sleep in the small room he'd turned into a makeshift bedroom off the main office of the barn. And why she silenced every voice in her head begging her to invite him to abandon the uncomfortable futon in favor of the queen-sized bed that occupied most of her childhood bedroom with the fluffy down bedding and top-of-the-line mattress.

Georgia shook her head and pushed him away. "Not at work. You are Wyatt Carlisle, owner of RA Ranch, host of the First Annual RA Invitational Rodeo, and my boss's latest shining star. You don't get to add the Rhinestone Cowboy into the mix."

The thread of concern that tugged at the corner of her psyche over the past few days gave another jerk, her internal back and forth debate catching fire once again. Could she really trust him not to disappear again? Were they worth leaving herself vulnerable for a second time?

She chewed on the inside of her cheek as he reclaimed his seat, and her body temperature dropped accordingly. At least one degree. Two, if she was lucky.

What did Wyatt Carlisle, that stupid freaking cowboy, want? His mouth opened to speak just as an alert sounded from his phone. She took the opportunity to unabashedly stare. Did he want something more than their steamy encounters?

Was it at all possible that Wyatt Carlisle was as consumed as she was by every cherished memory now joined with the brand new discovery that the chemistry between them a dozen years ago managed to play out into something even better in reality? And was there a chance in hell he'd understand if she told him that he was placing her in an impossible position?

A deep V formed between his brows as his eyes scanned over the screen. His mouth turned down at the corners, and Georgia's facial muscles contracted in response. Whatever message he'd received had clearly not contained good news. His nostrils flared and relaxed three times in rapid succession. His lips pressed together in a thin, straight line.

Her greedy visual consumption of him morphed into concern. "Wyatt...what's wrong?"

When his gaze finally lifted, a tempestuous storm raged in the sapphire depths, strong enough to rival a category five hurricane. His chest expanded and his lids fell shut. When they lifted again, a calm had settled on his face, but worry refused to release Georgia from its cold, steely grip.

"These are great, Gigi." His hand waved over the design boards she'd all but forgotten. "I'm impressed and I support these going to production." Flat, emotionless, and nearly completely devoid of the embellished southern accent she had always tormented him for, his voice caused a shard of ice to slither down her spine.

Her brows drew up. "But?"

He stood and slid his phone back into his pocket before stepping to her side of the desk again to drop a quick kiss on her cheek. "But I have to go." He turned on the heel of his well-worn brown boots and crossed to the door.

Georgia jumped from her seat, reaching him just as he turned the knob. Her hand landed on his, preventing him from turning it. "Wyatt, what's wrong? What happened? Talk to me."

His Adam's apple bobbed, and his eyes searched hers. He lifted his hands, cupping either side of her face. Within seconds, his mouth was on hers, desperate and fevered. His grip tightened on her jaw, and she curled her fingers around his wrists.

In the way she could only ever manage with Wyatt, they spoke without words. Their communication was found in the physical touches they offered each other. The sensory comfort of an embrace and intimate connection. She sensed the torrent of emotions rolling off of him, helpless to do anything other than offer the caress of her lips and the stroke of her thumb across his thundering pulse.

He broke the kiss but kept his hold on her firm, his

145

forehead joined with hers. A small, tight, but genuine smile spread across his face. The constricting band that held her heart and lungs hostage, unable to function, loosened a fraction.

"I missed you, Angel."

"I missed you too, Cowboy."

Only when the door clicked behind him did reality come crashing around her and drive her into the nearest chair. She'd lost all sense of reason because of Wyatt's touch. Wyatt's kiss. Just because of Wyatt.

And dammit, she was still in love with him.

Chapter Sixteen

Georgia

Twelve Years Earlier

"Are you sure about this?"

Her fingers tangled in his and her thumb stroked the back of his hand as they leaned against the metal railing. The guy that just got thrown from the bull Wyatt was supposed to ride limped out of the arena. With assistance.

No matter how many times she accompanied him to training and no matter how many times she saw him leap back to his feet from a fall, she held her breath and kept her ears piqued for the sound of a siren to take her boyfriend to the ER. It never got easier.

Wyatt's grin widened, and he winked from beneath the brim of his hat. "Why, of course I am, Gigi." He pressed in closer and nuzzled against her neck. "Don't you remember who you're talking to?"

She rolled her eyes. "The best damn bull rider in the state of North Carolina." She stole her arms around his neck, holding him in place while he kissed along the column of her neck up to her ear, nipping at the lobe. "Although you never got back to me with definitive numbers on how many bull riders are currently in this state so I have a better chance of looking at overall statistics."

"Damn, you're hot when you talk all smart and stuff." His breath was hot against her skin, and a flush overtook her entire body.

A booming voice from the opposite side of the dusty circle acted as the bucket of ice water she desperately needed. "Wyatt Carlisle, you'll be up soon. Get over here."

He squeezed her hand and gave her a lingering kiss on the cheek. "Prepare to be amazed, Gigi."

"Oh, I already am, Cowboy," she called out to his retreating back.

Well used to the routine, she jogged over to the concession stand to grab a hot chocolate and small bag of popcorn before taking a seat on the bleachers.

He will be fine.

He will be great.

He is Wyatt.

She repeated the mantra over and over just as she did each week. The hyperactive butterflies churning in her gut didn't seem to understand the words were supposed to calm their erratic beating.

Two thrown riders later, Wyatt was standing on the platform beside the metal railing, securing his gear. Even from a hundred feet away, she caught his eye and smiled. He always looked for her before he climbed on the bull. And he always threw a cocky grin her way and added a wink for good measure.

He repeated the same routine as always, and Georgia murmured the same reassurances under her breath as always. "Nothing can break the stupid freaking cowboy."

Wyatt climbed into the chute and balanced himself on the bars, one foot on the bull's back. "Gotta let him know I'm comin'" had been his explanation for why he did that before he gingerly got into position. Even though she couldn't see it, she knew his feet were balanced on the railing on either side of the monstrous beast with toes pointing forward. He was very particular about that fact and stressed the importance of it to her, even though she couldn't remember exactly why.

He will be fine.

He will be great.

He is Wyatt.

Her chest heaved with each labored breath as he continued his pre-ride ritual, running his gloved hand down the rope to heat the rosin and make it sticky to keep his hand from popping out. She'd initially assumed this was for safety purposes, but Wyatt had laughed at the suggestion.

"Why, hell no, Angel, that's to make sure I don't get disqualified."

After her fifth trip to training with him, she knew more about competitions, horses, bulls, and all the accessories required for a career in the rodeo than she'd ever wanted. And before Wyatt, her interest had been exactly zero.

She watched intently as his posture stiffened and he nodded to the cowboy standing on the plank beside him, rope firmly in hand. Her breath caught in her

149

throat as it always did when the gate swung open wide and he flew out of the chute on the back of an animal strong enough to kill him.

He will be fine.

He will be great.

He is—

Not moving.

Georgia jumped to her feet, hand at her throat. "Get up, Wy. Please get up." Her plea to him was low enough no one around her could hear. She waited exactly half a second longer before scrambling down the bleachers and running to the fence.

Still, he laid motionless, curled on his side. Red flashed in the corner of her eye as the rodeo workers at the other end of the arena tried to get the attention of the hulking beast still bucking wildly around the oval. Three cowboys surrounded Wyatt on each side, and all she could see were his boots. Nauseatingly still.

"Wyatt!" This time she shrieked his name as loudly as she could and was rewarded with a half rotation on the dusty ground.

As soon as the bull was secured and locked away, she climbed between the metal poles and sprinted to his side. She dropped to her knees and cradled his face between her palms, not even registering the bare head now that his helmet and face mask had been removed.

"Talk to me, Cowboy."

His deep groan in response was the most beautiful sound in the world. He squinted up at her. "What the hell just happened?"

"Don't move your head, son." One of the older men surrounding him clasped his shoulder as he uttered the instruction.

All the noise around them suddenly came into laser sharp focus. The sirens she feared rapidly coming closer moments before a backboard slid beneath him.

Him. Wyatt. Her boyfriend.

The EMTs tightened the straps around him and hoisted him into the back of the ambulance. "Sorry, sweetie," one of them said, holding up an arm when she tried to climb in beside him, "only family are allowed to ride along."

Georgia planted her feet wide, nostrils flared, and pressed her matte black lips together in a thin straight line. "That is my boyfriend you're taking, and there is no way in hell he's going alone. We can either do this nicely or I can turn into a raging bitch. Either way doesn't matter to me, but it's going to end the same way. I'm not leaving his side."

A moan from inside the back of the ambulance brought her right up to his side before the EMT was able to respond. She twisted her fingers around his where they were glued to his side. "I'm here, Wy. I'm not going anywhere."

***

Wyatt

Wyatt pushed up on his forearms to readjust on the couch and sucked in a sharp breath of air. Damn, that hurt. Nearly everything did. Especially the ass he wasn't allowed off of. Being still was never his strong suit.

But the tap at the oak framing the entrance from the

front hall brought a grin to his face.

"Hey there, Gigi."

He was starved for the sight of her and drank in every inch from the fishnet stockings that disappeared beneath the black plaid skirt to the onyx skull necklace hanging around her neck. She had been vehement about staying by his side in the hospital until he was discharged, even though that wasn't until past one a.m. after all the x-rays and tests had been run, but once he was settled at home, she vanished and hadn't been back for three days.

"Well, damn, you're a sight for sore eyes. And ribs. And femur."

She stood just far enough in the room that the toes of her clunky black boots touched the edge of the area rug covering the hardwood floor but didn't take a step closer to him. Didn't touch him. Didn't kiss him. "And a lot of other stuff you just don't want to mention, right?"

Her eyes were vacant and her voice monotone. This wasn't his feisty, fiery Angel.

Wyatt pushed his palms into the cushion again and scooted forward slightly. "What's wrong? Is it your mom? Is she okay?"

Hazel eyes rolled to the ceiling. "No, she's not okay. She's dying. And I gotta tell you, one person in my life dying right now is about enough."

He swung his legs to the floor and stood, keeping his weight off the wrapped left ankle, and hobbled over to her. "In case you couldn't tell, Angel, I am basically completely alive. I missed you like hell though, so that could be up for debate."

Gigi pulled her arms away and stepped back from

his attempted embrace. "Alive with a concussion, three fractured ribs, and a severely sprained ankle. All from one freaking fall in a training exercise, Wyatt."

Tears collected in the corners of her eyes and spilled over. His arms ached to hold her, but when she folded her own across her abdomen, he read the signal. Stay. Away. "Look at me, I'm okay. A bump and a bruise here and there, but I'm okay."

"You're okay? Then how come you have to stay home from school for a week to recover? How come you aren't allowed to train for six weeks?" She spread her arms out wide. "If you are just so freaking okay, then why do I wake up from nightmares of you breaking your back o-o-or worse?"

This time he closed the space between them and held her tight against his chest. He could promise her that would never happen, but they both would know it was a lie. His passion held risks that were higher than most careers, but it was the driving force behind every decision he made, and he couldn't give it up.

She sniffled against his shirt, rubbing her wet face across the soft cotton. "I don't want to break up with you, but I don't think I can stand to watch that happen again."

"Whoa, hold on." He held her at arm's length and adjusted his stance slightly as the pain shot up his leg from putting too much weight on the injured ankle. "Who the hell said anything about breaking up? I got hurt and, yeah, I'll admit that it was the worst one I've had so far, and it might not be the worst one I ever have." He leaned forward, leaning his forehead against hers. "But dammit, Gigi, don't leave me."

Twin paths streaked down her cheeks. "Every day I

watch my mom die. A little piece of her disappears every freaking day." She cradled his face between her palms. "I can't sit back and watch while I lose you too. I'm not strong enough."

Panic coursed through his veins with the ferocity of a wildfire, destroying every ounce of self-control he had. Wyatt bent down and pressed his lips to hers, the need to prove he was fine, that every part of him was fine, and that this damned conversation needed to go away driving him to deepen the kiss.

He pulled away only when the need for oxygen burned hotter in his lungs than his need for Gigi. "First of all, Angel, you are a hell of a lot stronger than you give yourself credit for. There is zero chance I'd be able to handle half of what you do every single day." He drew in two deep breaths. "But there is also zero chance this is gonna be over that easy. Nothing is gonna happen that could ever take me away from you."

Her eyes widened and her voice dropped to a whisper. "But you fell."

Wyatt tucked a strand of hair behind her ear. "I've fallen before and I'm sure I'll fall again." The corner of his mouth kicked up in a grin. "That's why it's a damn good thing I have a hard head."

For the first time since she'd arrived, a hint of a smile teased at the corners of her lips. "That's a freaking understatement."

He tugged her closer to his body. "Hey, now, I thought my stubborn tendencies were part of the whole cowboy charm you loved so much."

Gigi snorted, and a measure of the tension wrapped around his chest eased. "Yeah, so charming." Her face settled into a sober mask, and she dropped her gaze. "I was scared, Wyatt. So freaking scared."

One finger hooked beneath her chin and brought her hazel eyes back up to meet his. "And I am so sorry you were, Angel. But I really am fine. Banged up, but fine." He sighed and ran his tongue along the back of his teeth. "Let's be honest, I could get hurt tomorrow just walking down the road. Or driving to school. Angel, nothing in life is guaranteed. Nothing is safe."

He gripped her biceps and held her away from him. "The only thing that is a certainty is that I love you. We might not make sense, but we were meant to be together forever. No matter what it takes to get there, I promise you that us is one thing you can count on."

Gigi groaned and tilted her head back. "I hate it when you make sense." Her hands slid up the front of his tear-soaked shirt, and she straightened, intensity pouring from her eyes and piercing into his soul. "Promise, Cowboy?"

His shoulders relaxed, and he pulled her back into the circle of his arms, unwilling to let her out of touching distance. "On my cowboy honor, no matter what it takes, we will be together one day."

Chapter Seventeen

Wyatt

Present Day

A string of curses ran from one corner of Wyatt's mind to the next. He was short. By a lot. A hell of a lot. He paced the length of the guest room at his brother's house where he'd stayed as little as possible this week now that his nights were filled with Gigi. He ran his fingers through his hair and then locked them behind his neck. Even though sleeping on that damned futon was miserable, having the scent of Gigi lingering on the pillowcase made it feel damn near like heaven.

He couldn't fail. Wouldn't. That wasn't an option. But he damn sure couldn't look into those hazel eyes either. Not until he straightened this shit out. He'd sent her a brief text just before five letting her know he wouldn't be over tonight and that he'd see her tomorrow. That maybe they could try for something better than a quick romp in a tiny room off his barn.

Maybe a hotel. Maybe wine. Maybe roses. Maybe a bubble bath. That was all stuff girls liked. He'd add that to the plan to win her back. Tomorrow.

He'd have this all figured out by tomorrow…right?

Two taps at his door barely proceeded Tanner's entrance. His older brother stood just inside the doorway, feet planted wide, and arms folded across his chest. Silently he stared for a moment before offering a brief nod and softly latching the door shut behind him. "So, what happened?"

That would be a solution. A sure one. And easy as hell. His family had always supported his dreams even though they didn't understand them. Even though his mother had still worried. Even though his own poor decisions had impacted them negatively at times.

No. Not a solution. This was his project. His baby. He would dig up the money from somewhere that wasn't attached to the Carlisle family name. Too much stubborn pride coursed through his veins for him to take that path.

Sometimes that meant he had to bunk with three other guys in a dingy motel room because that was all he'd been able to afford. But he'd treasured his success so much more knowing that he had accomplished it all without his family's money bailing him out.

He didn't mind picking Tanner's business brain. Loathe as he was to admit it, his brother was a genius there and he'd be stupid not to tap into that wealth of knowledge, but financial backing? Hell to the no. And that was what he needed right now. What he'd been so certain he had plenty of.

Wyatt pressed his lips together in a firm line and

shook his head. "Just a few glitches I've got to figure out for the ranch and the competition. No big deal."

Never once had Wyatt envied Tanner's life. Boardroom meetings, business trips, golf course networking lunches...none of that appealed to him in the slightest. But for the past year words like stability, consistency, and family waved in front of him like a red flag before a bull. Tempting him to barrel toward a new prize.

Gigi represented every ounce of a future he had just begun to see in clear focus. One that was currently in danger of being ripped away before he'd ever realized it. How in the hell could he admit to Gigi that he was a failure?

Tanner moved his hands to prop them on his hips, still covered by the black dress pants he'd worn to work today. "Listen, little brother, big or small, I can help you iron out whatever issues you're having. It's kind of my thing, you know. Making executive decisions, crunching numbers, sanding square pegs down so they fit in round holes."

"Yeah, that super, duper MBA is so impressive."

Tanner's face brightened as his wife entered the room behind him, and he quickly snaked an arm around her waist. Wyatt had been so completely consumed in his own issues he hadn't even heard the mechanism as the door opened. Despite the invisible mantle weighing down his shoulders, he grinned, never willing to miss an opportunity to irritate his brother.

"Dammit, Iz, you manage to look hot as hell even after leading...how many of those yoga classes again?" Wyatt threw his sister-in-law a wink big enough Tanner couldn't miss it, his smile widening at his brother's rumbling growl. Easy. Tanner made it too damn easy.

Izzy laughed along, well used to the game Wyatt played. "You might not want to say that too loud, Wyatt. There's someone who—"

Her words were stolen by Gigi's abrupt entrance. "Sorry to interrupt, Tanner, but I think your brother has a bit of explaining to do." She dipped her chin and pinned him with a stare that absolutely shouldn't tighten his jeans but absolutely did. "For several things."

Izzy laced her fingers through her husband's hand and tugged him toward the door. She shot Wyatt a meaningful glance before squeezing Gigi's bicep. "In case I don't see you again tonight, it was really nice finally meeting you, Georgia."

In less than the time it took Wyatt to inhale, Gigi's entire face melted into a serene smile. "Thank you so much for understanding."

Dark eyes darted back and forth between them. "These Carlisle boys...they are something." With that, she softly latched the door, and the room fell into an awkward silence.

Damn, but Gigi was a sight for sore eyes. Every part of him wanted to unload the events of the day, but she'd been so proud that her "stupid freaking cowboy" had managed to pull together a cohesive business plan. How could he admit that he was on the cusp of disaster so soon?

"Would you like to explain this?" She held her smart phone in her hand, his last text to her shining from the screen.

He leaned against the bed post and crossed his ankles. "Well now, Angel, that's called a text. Handy little communication tool to send a message from one person to another without actually speaking to them in case you're catching them at a bad time." He intentionally deepened his accent just to annoy her.

She huffed out an exasperated breath. "While I appreciate your insight about digital communication, Cowboy, I'd prefer it if you could tell me why you suddenly decided you were going to be busy tonight."

His lids slowly met and parted, his mind racing with answers. Deflections. Half-truths. Her sparkling gaze cemented his decision. Withholding information in the name of protecting her had created a scenario that made truth necessary, even if it hurt. He couldn't expect her to trust him again if he wasn't completely transparent.

"Can we go to your place?"

Her teeth sank into her lower lip, and her gaze darted around the room. "I…Gram…" she sighed. "She's been agitated lately. I don't think that's the best idea."

"I swear I won't do anything to upset her. Hell, we can sit outside."

Gigi's pinched expression softened and her lips parted. She closed the distance separating them emotionally just as much as she did physically when one hand landed on his shoulder and the other on his waist. "Is it that bad, Wyatt?"

His arms enfolded around her, and he buried his face in the auburn curtain falling over her left shoulder. "I just…I need you right now."

Her grip tightened infinitesimally. "Do you have

everything?"

Silencing every cell in his body that screamed in protest at the loss, Wyatt freed her from his desperate embrace. He collected the papers strewn across his bed and stuffed them in his black backpack along with a change of clothes. There was no way in hell he was back here tonight. He laced his fingers through hers and squeezed. "Let's go, Angel."

***

Georgia

"Please tell me we aren't going to play the 'everything's fine' game and go back and forth ad nauseum because I am tired, hungry, and just want to find out what crawled up your ass so we can move on to much more fun things."

Wyatt tilted his head back and barked out a laugh. "Damn, Gigi, don't hold back."

Georgia kicked her heels off as she spoke and hung her blazer on the back of one of the stools around the periphery of the island in her kitchen. "Just…be quiet. Gram is sleeping and my dad won't be home until late if she…" Her voice trailed off, unsure she wanted to bring Wyatt into this part of her life where anguish warred with stolen moments she treasured amidst the chaos of unexpected reactions from the older woman.

She crossed the room, pausing just a moment before winding her arms around his waist. "One of the best parts of us was always a lack of bullshit. If two stupid teenagers could figure that out, I certainly hope that mature, educated, intelligent adults could carry on the tradition."

His blue eyes widened as he pulled her closer into the circle of his arms. "Did you just call me mature?"

Not a single boyfriend that dotted her past managed to hold a candle to him in any way. It never was puppy love. She'd known for a long time that at sixteen she'd managed to capture lightning in a bottle for a brief period. The genuine heart buried beneath his rhinestone cowboy persona intertwined with his boundless compassion and undeterrable sense of humor to make Wyatt Carlisle one in a million.

Although at this moment his lame jokes were about to deepen the hole he was digging. "Don't make me take it back." She gripped the cotton covering his back. "I mean it, Wyatt. Your misplaced protection is what landed you in the first vat of hot water that you somehow managed to drag yourself out of. I told you that you only get to play the whole 'looking out for me' card once. You did that when we were eighteen. Your hand is empty now, so you better fess up."

Lashes longer than any man deserved rested against his cheekbones as he sucked in a shaky breath. His lips pressed into a thin line, and he disentangled her hands from his shirt, pulling her toward the living room. "Let's sit down, Angel."

Icy steel fingers of dread curled around Georgia's stomach and held it in their iron grasp as they sat beside each other on the sofa. "Start talking, Cowboy. I don't do well with anticipation."

The corner of his mouth kicked up into a smirk, void of his normal arrogance. "Why, Gigi, if I didn't know better, I'd think you were worried." A quick wink preceded the rapid sobering of his face. "It's not about us, Angel, I promise. Don't think…don't think it's anything like that."

The avalanche of fame-induced scandals that had been blanketing her mind calmed. Momentarily. "This…whatever this is, does it affect you? Does it hurt you?"

He pulled her hands into his and held them on his knee. His nod was barely perceptible as he focused on the spot where their two beings joined into one.

Georgia squeezed her fingers against his hard enough to bring his gaze up to meet hers. "Wyatt, no matter what else happened between us, we were friends." She shot him a saucy grin. "That friendship just happens to have some amazing benefits now that we're adults, but I still want to be your friend. Hell, besides Paige, you were my best friend at the worst time in my life." She took a deep breath. "Even if we can't be…exactly what we were, can't we at least be that?"

His answering silence did nothing to lessen her unease. Maybe the whole sex only thing was sounding better and better to him than he let on.

"I want us more than I've wanted anything."

His words slammed into her with the strength of hurricane force winds. "Us can't happen." She ran her thumb along the back of his hand. "But I'd like to be your friend again."

"You're the reason I came home, Angel. Don't ever doubt that." Wyatt's hand left hers and gripped the back of her head, his fingers tangling in her auburn hair. His forehead fell against hers. "I know I don't deserve it, but I'll work my ass off for another shot at us."

She scooted closer to him, their knees bumping against each other. "If you want me to trust you, let's start with telling me what in the ever-loving hell is going on."

"This first," he murmured seconds before his mouth met hers and clung. The passion-induced desperation that normally drove their every encounter was replaced with a tender kiss that whispered all the words neither was willing to speak out loud. His lips massaged hers gently, reverently.

When oxygen deprivation pulled them apart, the haunted look in his eyes sent a fresh slice of pain through her heart. "Tell me, Wyatt."

"I let you down, Gigi." His hands fell from her body, intensifying the chill his words had created.

He stood and paced the length of the living room, pausing occasionally to take his hat off and run his fingers through his hair before setting it back on his head. Georgia silenced the screams in her head that he needed to just spit it out before he drove her to insanity.

Less than a second separated his deep sigh and his heavy proclamation. "The truth is, I don't really know what's wrong. The consultant working on helping with the launch of RA Ranch and the competition sent me a message while I was at your office that there was a problem with the timeline for the grand opening." He locked his fingers behind his neck and drew his brows together. "There was...something. A miscalculation? An unexpected expense? I don't know right now, but the ending is the same. I'm short. By a lot."

Georgia shook her head, trying to process the

information. "You mean money? Wyatt, I saw your financials. You had everything accounted for with extra built in to allow for any incidentals. I meant it when I said that your business plan was brilliant—"

"It's not." He put his hands on his hips, his face mottled with fury. "It's not a brilliant plan, and I clearly didn't account for any issues because I only have enough money to finish the outbuildings and maybe, if I'm lucky, the house. I'll never be able to finish the spectator area or the eating section or…" Wyatt closed his eyes, and every bit of swagger and strength melted from his body. "There isn't gonna be a rodeo."

Georgia refused to accept that was a possibility. There had to be a solution. An answer. Something they could figure out together. Her mind raced with different avenues they could explore when the heavy thuds of Wyatt's footsteps crossing her hardwood floor broke through. "Where the hell do you think you're going?"

He paused with his hand on the doorknob, lips downward in a slight frown. "You were right, Gigi. I'm a stupid freaking cowboy, and I was delusional to think I could do anything this big. Sorry I dragged you into my mess. Again."

The soft click of the door closing behind him was a gunshot to her heart, and Georgia jumped in response. A single tear ran down her cheek, the anguish Wyatt was dealing with so real and palpable in her own soul. He was watching his dream slip away without a clear answer as to why, and his damned stubborn nature meant he was going through it alone.

Chapter Eighteen

Georgia

Twelve Years Earlier

"So what kind of dramatic scene did Wyatt create to ask you to the Sweetheart Dance?"

The girl who shared locker space beside Georgia had somehow turned into her best friend. Only one, really. All the promises from kids back home had fallen apart a couple of months after she moved. And, largely by Georgia's own design, she hadn't found anything more than a low level of tolerance from the kids in North Carolina. Something she suspected only happened because she was dating the great Wyatt Carlisle.

But it didn't stop her from sticking her tongue out at Paige's faux dreamy tone. "If you want to make fun of Wyatt, well, you know I'm on board there, but couldn't you come up with something better than 'Sweetheart Dance?' I mean, that sounds like something you'd see on one of those black and white movies my grandparents love."

Paige closed her locker door and absently twirled a strawberry blonde curl around her index finger. "First of all, after his stunt at Christmas? Yeah, I totally would've expected something big." She blew a bubble of her bright pink gum and then sucked it back in her mouth. "Second, do you even go to the same school as I do? There have been posters up since we got back from break and nearly daily announcements about buying tickets."

Georgia was thankful for the pale makeup that could camouflage her flaming cheeks. She pointedly ignored anything that she thought would be meant to incite school spirit, which definitely included all the colorful banners and announcements lining the halls. Most mornings she kept her earbuds in, blaring music from her mp3 player to silence the "rah-rah, go team" hype pouring from the speakers in the class.

But the fact the first time she was hearing about what was certain to be a ridiculous showing of teenage stupidity from her best friend rather than her boyfriend was annoying. Frustrating. And maybe just a tiny bit painful.

Didn't he want to go with her? There wasn't a chance in hell she'd actually say yes. It sounded like pure torture, but…he never even asked.

Paige poked an elbow in Georgia's ribs. "Come on, you can tell me. Let me live vicariously through you. Was there a trail of rose petals? Did he have on a white Stetson and get down on one knee and sing some ridiculous old school country song that he changed the wording of to fit the dance?"

The angst gnawing at her gut turned what the

167

lunchroom called a breaded "chicken" sandwich, bringing it precariously close to making a dramatic exit. "He didn't ask me."

An increasing throng of students rushing to the final class of the day stole the words she barely managed to whisper.

Her friend leaned in closer, squinting. "What'd you say, Georgia?"

She refused to cry. Not here, not now, and certainly not with any prying eyes around. Not even Paige. "I said he didn't ask me. Not in a romantic way. Not in a boring way. In no way at all. I didn't even know there was a hell on earth celebration called the Sweetheart Dance until you mentioned it."

The other girl's mouth fell open, and she tugged on her hair, chewing her gum with a nearly annoying fervor. "Shit, I'm sorry, Georgia. I just figured…" She lifted a shoulder and waved a hand helplessly. "I mean, he's been like this ridiculous boyfriend doing all the stuff you'd read about in some sappy, far-fetched novel. I thought for sure he'd jump on this and surprise you with something amazing and special and…Wyatt."

Or at least made me aware this thing even existed. Georgia couldn't admit, even to herself, that a larger part of her than she liked wanted to go. She wanted to have that sappy teen romance movie moment where she showed up at the dance and surprised everyone by looking totally different. And an even bigger part wanted to do that on Wyatt's arm.

"Well, screw him."

Paige's words found a way to penetrate her mind through the myriad of emotions blanketing her psyche, and Georgia's head snapped up. "What?"

Her friend spun her around, urging her toward their final class of the day before the bell sounded and they both wound up in trouble. "I said, 'Screw him.' If he wants to play the stupid boy card, then we're gonna play the badass girls one. We can go to the dance together."

In spite of the nausea still causing her abdomen to clench and cramp, Georgia laughed. Just outside of the classroom door, she turned on the thick heel of her boots and threw an arm around the other girl's shoulders. "You might just be the best friend that ever existed."

When Georgia finally released her, Paige cleared her throat. "Yeah, well, I guess to be fair you probably should talk to him first." She thinned her lips and held up an index finger between them. "But if he does anything other than an appropriate level of groveling and begging, we're just gonna flip him off and go solo. But, ya know, solo together."

As Georgia slid into her seat beside Paige as Mr. Tatum started lecturing on post-civil war U.S. History, a little smile crept over her lips. Somehow living in a small town in North Carolina had almost become bearable.

***

Wyatt

A shuddering breath accompanied the crackling as Wyatt balled the paper and shoved it into the side pocket of his backpack. His locker looked as hollow as he felt without his training bag inside.

"You could have said something."

Wyatt's eyes closed, and he swallowed back a groan. He loved Gigi. As cliché and trite as that may sound for a couple of kids in high school...he did. But right now he could practically taste the sassy attitude dripping from her tone. Any other day he would welcome a little sparring with his Dark Angel.

Any other freaking day.

He screwed up as genuine a smile as possible and turned to face her. "Hey, Gigi, listen, I'm not feeling so hot right now and—"

She popped a hand on her hip. "And I don't really care. If you are my boyfriend, you're going to explain what the hell is going on." Gigi stepped closer, the toes of her heavy black boots nearly colliding with his well-worn brown leather ones. "You're going to tell me why I had to hear about some stupid dance from Paige instead of you."

The ever-present thread of vulnerability that laced through the edges of Gigi's hardened exterior smacked him in the face. Yeah, he knew about the dance. He had every intention of not simply asking Gigi to the dance but making it memorable.

Right up until he couldn't.

"Hey." Her sharp tone cut through the haze of self-deprecation that shrouded him. "Talk to me, Wyatt. Why don't you want to take me to the dance? Were you planning on hiding this forever and...hope I didn't find out? Because that's pretty dumb." She shuffled her feet and dropped her head. "I mean, I guess I figured it out kinda late, so I must be pretty oblivious."

Shit. Wyatt hooked an index finger beneath her chin and rested the opposite hand on her hip. He never understood how she could function on a daily basis when her home was in a constant state of suspension, hanging between life and the inevitable. A day he mentally and emotionally prepared himself for upon waking each morning, determined to be prepared to take care of his Angel to the best of his ability.

"Look at me." Her uncertain hazel eyes collided with his, and his mind and body waged the familiar war of lust versus guilt. He wanted every part of her, but there was no way in hell he'd take their relationship to a place that made her vulnerable. Not when she had so many decks stacked against her. "You're not oblivious. You're focused on things far more important than a stupid dance."

She toyed with one of the buttons on his shirt. "I mean, yeah, it's stupid, but if you wanted to go…" Her words died off with her shrug and averted gaze.

Expletives ricocheted through his mind. He kind of loved that she eschewed all the normal trappings of high school life. One of the best nights of their relationship was when they sat together, huddled under a blanket high in the bleachers while she mocked every player, cheerleader, and booster mom that paraded across the field in front of them. Her smart mouth was a gift. The first and last game they went to. She much preferred spending Friday nights at his training with him, and damned if he didn't too.

But she had to pick the one thing he couldn't offer to be the time she wanted to be a joiner. "You really want to be part of the typical high school experience? Why, Gigi, you shock me." He embellished his drawl, hoping to distract her. He really didn't want to admit his failure.

Small hands trailed up his chest and linked behind his neck. "If it means we get to spend the night together, it will be worth the melodrama of high school revelry." Her saucy grin belied the weighted sigh she expelled. "You really should thank me for being so selfless so you can wow your devoted fans."

Shit. Damn. She wanted to go. She really wanted to go. Stall, he needed to stall and figure out a way to handle this. Maybe if he at least got a tutor, his parents would reconsider and let him... at least for her. "Can we talk about this later, Gigi? I gotta run."

Her arms fell, and she flicked her wrist. "Ah, crap, yeah, I'm sorry, Wy. I didn't realize what time it was. You're gonna be late for training." Thin brows knitted together when she caught sight of his empty locker. "You forgot your gear?"

Two paths spread out before him. Deceit or truth. Neither was particularly exciting, but Gigi sure as hell didn't deserve a lie. Something in between? "I don't have training tonight." He hitched his backpack up on his shoulder. "But I have to get home to take care of the horses and study."

Ebony lips turned down into a frown that was equal parts adorable and damning. "Is something wrong with one of the guys? You never miss training. You lied to your parents about not being sick when you had strep just so you didn't miss. What the hell is going on, Wyatt?"

He slammed the locker closed harder than he needed then winced when Gigi jumped at the bang that reverberated through the empty hallway. "I don't have training and won't for a long time to come. And hell, let's just lay this all out because I'm not going to be going out with you anytime soon either."

If it was possible, her face paled more beneath the makeup, and she wrapped her arms around her abdomen. "Wyatt, I—"

"Congratulations, Gigi, you were right. I am just a stupid freaking cowboy." The ache in his chest begged him to stop talking, but if he was going to be an asshole, he might as well go all the way. Maybe she'd decide to find someone better. She deserved it. "And because I am, I just lost out on training, the dance, and being able to take you on anything resembling a date for the foreseeable future."

He fished the crumpled paper from the side of his backpack and shoved it at her. Gigi fumbled to catch it and unravel the ball. He pushed past her and stalked down the hall toward the freedom the exit offered. Freedom from her hurt expression. Freedom from her certain disappointment.

Wyatt tossed his backpack in the passenger seat of his truck, slammed the door, and threw it into gear, foot far too heavy on the gas pedal. He had to run before he confessed it all. Before he told her that as much as he missed training, the worst part of the punishment was letting her down. Taking away something she loved as much as he did because he was a failure.

His palm collided with the steering wheel, and he pushed the accelerator further down, trying to escape the pain of walking away, of losing out on training for his dream, and most of all, disappointing the girl who owned the organ that ached with each beat. The definition of futility.

Stupid freaking cowboy. Wyatt snorted. No surprise, Gigi got it in one.

Chapter Nineteen

Wyatt

Present Day

Wyatt lifted the hat from his head, ran his fingers through his hair, and pushed it back down with more force than was necessary. He pressed his fingers in the corners of his eyes and rubbed at the gritty sand collecting there. A weighty sigh preceded his push away from the cherry desk that was so massive it took up nearly a third of the space of the small office he'd created off the edge of the biggest barn.

It was a space intended for whoever he deemed worthy of entrusting with the day-to-day operations of the ranch so he could focus on his true passion, the competition. A mythical person who had yet to present themselves in the dozens of interviews he'd conducted. The very same ones that were now on hold like everything else in his life at the moment.

He crossed the room and flopped onto the futon, a pathetic, second-class choice that somehow turned into a five-star hotel quality bed when it was occupied with Gigi. He turned his head and buried his nose into the pillow that still held a trace of her scent.

Groveling was going to become his newest hobby if her responses were any indication. The middle finger emoji she sent most recently instead of an actual reply was his favorite.

Tanner and Wyatt always had a stronger bond than their other brothers, and he was grateful Tanner and Izzy both welcomed him to stay at their house for as long as needed while his own was under construction. Being under the watchful eye of his parents at this stage of life was pretty low on his list of desires right now. Somewhere below taking another ride on Crosshair, one of the nastiest bulls he'd ever encountered, and slightly above having each toenail removed.

Despite their bond, confessing all to his brother—something that was sure to happen as soon as Mr. Fix It caught onto the fact something was off—wasn't an option either. Because Tanner could fix this. Their father could fix this. Both of them would in a heartbeat. Family trumped any and everything for the Carlisles, and Wyatt was grateful most of the time for their unwavering support.

But taking their help would mean Wyatt would be left to be the screw-up who couldn't make it on his own in the real world. The Carlisle brother who wasn't capable of handling a real job that didn't involve taking his shirt off to model jeans or getting his ass handed to him by a fifteen hundred pound angry beast. Yeah, that was a title he was pretty damn sure he didn't want to wear.

His feet dangled over the end of the short mattress, and he tossed his hat on the floor beside him. Darkness enveloped him as his lids closed, numbers ping-ponging through his brain.

"I'm getting really tired of chasing after a stupid freaking cowboy more than a decade after I swore I'd never even think of him again. This is basically the opposite of getting me to trust you again."

Her voice cut through the avalanche of dark thoughts consuming his mind and was a much needed balm to his aching heart and wounded pride. Gigi had a way of fixing him, even when they weren't together. Even when the only way she was present was when he pulled her picture out of his wallet or cued up the one he'd saved after he stalked her social media one drunken night. The same site he visited far more than he would ever admit.

And the one where he saw his Gigi wrapped up with some blond-haired, overly tanned creep for months on end. He'd breathed a sigh of relief when the asshole disappeared. Right around the same time her location changed too. Back home to North Carolina. That had been a damn good day.

He partially opened one eye and drank in the beauty of a furious Gigi. One of his favorite sights. "I'm not too hard to find, Angel. If I'm not with you or Tanner...well, there aren't too many places for me to go."

A string of muttered curses accompanied her fingers raking through her hair. "Insanity. Wyatt Carlisle brings chaos, frustration, and total insanity with him everywhere he goes."

Reflexively, he reached for his discarded hat and

plopped it on his head as he moved into a sitting position before pushing against his knees and standing. "And you bring hunger, desire, and every other thing I need to feel better. What's your point?" He gripped her hips, pulling her close before his hands moved to flatten against her spine and align her body against his.

Her lashes fluttered for a brief second before she shoved him away. "You're missing a huge issue here, Cowboy. You bailed once. When you do it again, it doesn't help your cause; it hurts it. If you're dealing with a problem and we are supposed to be..." The incomplete sentence hung in the air between them. The title he wanted taunting him from its unspoken hiding place. "Friends...then we need to talk. Instead you taking off. Again." She sighed and dropped her forehead against his shoulder. "I need you to talk to me when something's going on, and I really need you to not run."

Pain lanced through Wyatt's chest with her words. It wasn't what he was trying to do. This was one hundred percent self-preservation and injured pride. "Shit, I'm sorry." Apologies were becoming his most repeated phrase. Whether it was desperation to bring something good into his world or sheer stupidity, he never really figured out, but the next words tumbled from his mouth without any input from his brain. "If I promise to stop running, will you promise to give us a real chance?"

The widening of her hazel eyes—not to mention the loss of the comfort her body offered him when she took three steps away—was confirmation he'd said too much.

Gigi wrapped her arms around her abdomen. "I have reasons, Wyatt. I'm not just trying to get revenge on you."

He called himself every kind of asshole he could think of and closed the space between them. His arms pulled her close, and she quickly locked her own around him. "I'm sorry, Angel. I'm just…frustrated as hell right now. I've been staring at every account, every expenditure, every payment, and I can't seem to make sense of it. There's nearly fifty thousand dollars missing that I can't account for."

"What would you say if I told you that I could fix this? At least a temporary band-aid that will give you time to talk to your insurance agent—and an attorney, I might add—without screwing up your timeline." Her brows lifted in a silent challenge.

The corner of his mouth twitched. "I'd say I always knew you were an Angel, but that might be a miracle just slightly out of your grasp."

She rolled her eyes with an exaggerated sigh. "Do you want to know or not? This deal might expire if you're gonna pull the Rhinestone Cowboy routine."

"You always did like giving me options." His brows popped twice.

Gigi moved to dig in the small container sitting on his desk before producing a silver coin. "Flip ya for it? Heads I tell you my plan and you don't give me shit, tails I let you figure this out on your own."

He tilted his head back and laughed, releasing her before rounding his desk and reaching into the drawer. "Now, Angel, this is my life, my career, and my future." *Our future*, he corrected in his head but wasn't sure that was something he was confident

179

enough to speak out loud. "We need something a bit more grown-up than flipping a coin."

She lifted one shoulder. "We've always done pretty well with it in the past."

Wyatt held a pack of cards between his fingertips. "Poker, Angel. Something this serious requires a serious game."

A mischievous grin curled her lips, and every nerve ending on his body took notice. The wicked promises the small gesture offered nearly wiped his mind clear of the looming threat to the future he was so carefully constructing.

"If we are playing poker, let's make it really interesting, Cowboy."

He swallowed his suddenly parched throat three times. "What'd you have in mind there, Gigi?"

She leaned across the desk and plucked the deck from his hand. "Strip poker. Winner gets to decide what our next step for your ranch is and where we end up tonight." Her tongue darted out to run along her bottom lip. "I have a lot of ideas."

The answer was quick, easy, and required absolutely no thought. "Deal me in."

***

Georgia

"Three of a kind." He spread three Jacks on the barrel serving as their makeshift poker table with a cocky smirk. Damn him. The overly confident air that radiated off him was nearly as irresistible as the mischievous twinkle in the deep blue eyes that had haunted her far more than she'd ever admit.

Georgia sighed dramatically, laying down a pair of tens. "Shame I only have two of a kind."

He smacked the wooden surface with a bark of laughter then motioned her to stand from the black leather office chair he'd rolled over to place opposite his seat on the couch. "Hot damn, Gigi, lose that shirt."

Over the course of the past hour, she'd won far more hands than him, and the result was her still retaining possession of her panties, bra, and t-shirt while Wyatt sat across from her in only boxers, jeans, and his hat. Which he'd heatedly argued counted as an article of clothing.

She lifted one brow and countered with a wicked smile of her own. "Not so fast there, Cowboy. See, my pair just so happens to be accompanied by three two's." She laid her remaining cards beside the others. "I believe that's called a full house and means that round goes to me."

When he stood and flicked open the button on his pants, she wasn't sure she should gloat too much. The muted grind as he slowly unzipped the fly shot fire and ice through her veins. His thumbs hooked beneath the waist band and pushed the denim down his legs at a tortuous pace.

His penetrating stare caused her heartrate to kick up a notch, but she couldn't look anywhere but at the length of thigh being revealed inch by excruciating inch. Her tongue darted out to trace along her parched lips. She hadn't even realized what she was doing until his deep groan broke through the haze of lust blanketing the air between them.

"Are you trying to kill me, Gigi?"

He kicked his jeans across the room and flopped back onto the sofa, his head falling back against the exposed wood wall, but not before she caught sight of the thickening bulge straining against the front of his boxer briefs.

A strangled laugh escaped her mouth as Georgia collected the cards and began shuffling them with shaking hands, commanding her body temperature to drop to something back in the double digits. "I was just gonna ask you the same thing, Cowboy."

He pulled the cards from her grasp and began dealing them out. "My turn to deal, Angel."

Never, not if they lived to a hundred, would Wyatt ever understand the power of that single nickname on every part of her. It didn't just ignite her raging libido. That happened simply from sharing the same air space with him. No, it spoke to the tender place in her heart, the one that iced over with the terminal prognosis her mother was given and didn't thaw until a stupid freaking cowboy waltzed into her life.

Georgia shook her head and cleared her throat, picking up the five small rectangles and investing far too much emotional energy in the cards she held in her hand. And promptly swore in her head. It would take a miracle to win. She laid more than half of them down. "Three."

The corner of his mouth curled up, and his eyes bounced from the cards in his hand to the ones she'd set down to her. He plucked a single one and set it on the barrel next to hers. "Just one for me."

She swallowed down a growl as he dealt her three more cards and himself one. Another litany of curses she was certain would make the man sitting across from her chortle with delight ricocheted through her mind as she managed to scrape together exactly two cards that matched. Fours. Dammit.

"Whatcha got there, Gigi?"

Her lids narrowed into slits for a brief second, and his answering laugh was proof enough that her poker face sucked. She lifted her chin at him. "You first."

An exaggerated, and clearly fake, frown accompanied a shake of his head. "Ladies first. My mama raised me to be a gentleman."

Both of her brows lifted. "And would your mama be proud of her darling little boy to know he was up at midnight playing strip poker in his barn?" If she was destined to lose, she could at least stall a little.

Wyatt chuckled and shook his head. "You can't distract me that easily, Angel. Show me what you've got." He leaned in, eyes simmering with lust. "And if you bring up my mama one more time, this night might not end the way I've been planning."

Him? The pulsating need that ached between her legs was begging her to forfeit the game, rip the small patch of fabric that still remained on his body, and satiate her overwhelming desire. Although history had taught her that would last for approximately fifteen minutes before she'd be drowning in need again. Nothing was ever enough. Not with Wyatt.

She laid her pathetic hand on the barrel. "Pair of fours."

He tossed his cards down as he stood, thumbs beneath the elastic waistband of his boxers. "I think this means you win, Angel."

Georgia rose, rounded the barrel, and stood in front

of him, one hand on his bare chest. Right over the tattoo she'd never admit meant the world to her. "You're going to let me help you?"

His grin faded and face sobered. "I came back for you. I planned all of this in Asheville instead of Texas or Colorado for us and for our future." He shook his head and wrapped his arms around her waist and pulled her close, her hips bumping against his. "Dammit, I know I screwed up, but I'm back for good, forever, and I'll do whatever you need to fix this. I wanted to do this on my own, but if there is anyone I'd let help me, it would damn sure be my Dark Angel. She's kinda been bailing my sorry ass out since I was seventeen."

She pushed lightly against his chest, stepped out of his embrace, and peeled her shirt over her head. "Pretty sure this means we both win, Cowboy." She motioned to the cotton barely containing his rapidly growing length. "Lose the boxers and tell me you've got a condom close by."

He fished a foil packet out of the pocket of his discarded jeans and dropped his underwear in the space of a heartbeat. With more confidence than any man should possess, he turned back to her and stole any oxygen that remained in her lungs.

Georgia flattened her palm on his abdomen and pressed lightly. "If I win, that means I'm in charge, Cowboy."

He fell back onto the couch and sucked in a breath as she removed the two remaining pieces of clothes separating them. "I'd never argue with a lady."

Too many days had passed with no contact. After a dozen years apart, seeing him on a damn near daily basis, touching him, tasting him, they were things that had become needs rather than wants. And she didn't have the self-control to draw this out.

She straddled his lap, grinding against him and reveling in his answering groan. His mouth moved to her neck and made a path down the front of her as she leaned over to grab the condom. Her teeth ripped the foil packet open as he landed one of the hardened nubs, his lips wrapping around it, and sucked lightly. His thumbs made circles on her hip bones as she rocked against him.

The brim of his hat bumped her shoulder. Just as he reached up to remove it, she planted a hand on top of it. "Don't you dare, Cowboy."

Her hand dove between them, and she wrapped it around his shaft, stroking up and down a few times until a frustrated growl erupted from his chest. Georgia pressed her mouth against his as she slid the condom on him. She lifted up on her knees slightly before lowering herself onto him.

"I love you, Angel."

All of her intentions to go slow flew right out the window as he filled every part of her. Her lips met his again, and every ounce of desperation bled into the kiss. Desperation for his body. Desperation for relief. And desperation to not confess just how much she still loved him too.

She raced up the mountain of desire and paused at the pinnacle, dangling on the edge of climax. His fingers snaked between their sweat-slickened bodies, and he teased the tiny bundle of nerves with his thumb, making her lose every ounce of control. She moved her hips three more times before he screamed his own release. Their cries mixed, mingled, and filled the small room, echoing off the walls.

Georgia laid her damp forehead on his shoulder, trying to catch her breath. "Listen, Cowboy," she panted the words between gasps, "spending the night on this thing is a non-negotiable point." She sat back up, resting against his slightly trembling thighs. "Hotel? We can get a decent night's sleep and have a mediocre continental breakfast in the morning."

The damned grin curled his lips as his fingertips stroked up and down her spine. "A decent night's sleep and...round two?"

She climbed off his lap, snatched her shirt off the floor, and tossed him his boxers. "I'll flip ya for it, Cowboy. Clearly poker doesn't work out for you."

A light smack collided with her ass when she bent down to retrieve her panties, and she spun on her heel to find herself greeted with an unabashedly grinning cowboy. "I'd say it works out pretty damn well."

Chapter Twenty

Georgia

Twelve Years Earlier

F.

A big, red, glaring F and the retreating back of her boyfriend summoned the well of tears to escape and track down Georgia's cheeks as she trudged home. The chilly air biting her face barely registered compared to the roiling of her stomach and the ache in her heart.

He'd never once said he was struggling. Never hinted that anything was even slightly off, much less this bad. Never asked for help or advice.

Wyatt had simply taken the role of her caregiver in her life. He'd been the one person who focused their attention on her, making her rest, forcing her to relax, and giving her a reason to smile when everything else in her world overwhelmed her.

She hung a left at the end of the road rather than the right that would lead to her house. Her feet headed to the bench in the back of the park on instinct without any input from her brain. In her mind's eye, she could still see all of the decorations Wyatt had set out for her Christmas gift.

He was special. Her stupid freaking cowboy was special. Georgia put her feet onto the bench, pulled her knees up, and rested her forehead on them with a groan. Yeah, calling him that would stop immediately. He was special and smarter than he gave himself credit for.

She bounced her head against her legging-clad kneecaps a few times, begging her brain to offer the right solution. Everything Wyatt did for her was so right from being the ridiculous rhinestone cowboy that made her laugh to taking her mind off the inevitable for a few hours a couple of times a week by going to his training with him.

Even if her heart stopped for several beats with each throw until he hopped to his feet with a cocky grin and wink shot right in her direction.

Georgia lifted her head and stared at the paper in her hand for the tenth time. This time, unlike all the others, she moved her focus from the damning grade to his answers. Her legs fell to the side, and she studied a little closer.

If she were in a cartoon, she was certain a lightbulb would have popped over her at that moment. A grin spread across her face. She folded the crumpled paper with more care than Wyatt had and placed it in her backpack, zipping it closed.

Her heart still ached a little at the memory of his hasty exit. More than his pride was wounded by the confession of his shortcoming. But she could fix this.

For a change, she'd solve his problems for him.

Excitement accelerated her feet as she raced home. Her breath was coming in short pants, and she held up a hand, gripping the table where her grandparents sat with the other, as a silent plea for a moment to suck enough oxygen in her lungs to speak. "Can...can I borrow your car?"

Her grandfather's gray brows drew tightly together. "What's wrong, Georgia?"

She paused for a moment, debating on how much she could and should divulge. Wyatt trusted her, and she'd never violate that. But he held the literal key to getting to her cowboy. Vague half-truth seemed like the best option. "I need to head over to Wyatt's and check on him. I just found out he's so sick he can't go to his training, and I'm worried."

It could be technically considered the whole truth because she was pretty sure that Wyatt was probably beyond nauseated by the loss of even one training session.

Dropping Wyatt's name was probably enough in and of itself, but the speed at which her grandfather plopped the keys in her outstretched palm made her eyes roll to the ceiling. She couldn't blame them for their adoration, even if it drove her slightly crazy.

She spent the twelve minute drive fighting against the increasing pressure her right foot insisted on placing on the gas pedal. Getting a ticket or wrapping the car around a telephone pole would both severely impair her ability to fix her broken cowboy. Well, fix him right after she yelled at him for being such a stubborn jerk and not talking to her sooner. Because that was absolutely happening first.

Her shaking finger pushed the button beside the front door of the big, brick house. She'd been to his home countless times, but this was the first time her stomach quaked, uncertain of the reception she'd receive.

Wyatt's mother answered the door, wiping her hands on a dish towel before slinging it over her shoulder. The smile that curved her lips settled a fraction of Georgia's nerves. "Hey, Georgia, this is a surprise."

She nodded and swallowed. "Yes, I-I, well, Wyatt left before I could finish talking to him, and I was hoping I could see him."

The older woman's mouth transitioned to a frown. "I'm sorry, honey, I don't know if Wyatt told you, but he's grounded right now."

She'd prepared for that. "I know, and I know why, and...I think I can help. Please, I don't want to be disrespectful but..." Her teeth sank into her bottom lip. "Mrs. Carlisle, your son has done so much for me, and I finally have a chance to help him. Please let me."

Tracy Carlisle hesitated for a moment before pursing her lips and offering a curt nod. "He's in the barn."

Georgia gripped the older woman's hand for a moment. "Thank you." She skipped down the steps, jumped back in her car, and slowly rounded the house, following the path to the buildings a few yards away. No surprise she found Wyatt methodically brushing Lemondrop's coat with a focused intensity.

"What the hell am I gonna do, girl?" The soft plea to his horse barely reached her ears but hit her heart with the impact of gale force winds to a palm tree in a hurricane.

She leaned one shoulder against the roughened wood of the doorframe. "Step one is to never walk away from your girlfriend like that without talking."

***

Wyatt

He wanted to race over to her and let her fix every part of him that was hurting. What the hell was that kind of thinking? He was Wyatt freaking Carlisle. He might screw up and he might fail, but he damn sure didn't let anyone else share in that. Not his parents, not his brother, and sure as hell not his girlfriend.

Or maybe ex-girlfriend if she gave him the treatment he deserved.

"What are you doing here?" Adding a gruff tone to his voice was one of the hardest things he'd ever done.

She snorted and pushed off the wall, her clunky black boots creating clouds of dust as she walked over to him. "With that kind of attitude, I'm wondering myself, but I'll give you a pass. This time."

"Listen, Georgia, I'm gonna wind up in even more trouble if my parents catch you out here with me. And I have two younger brothers who would be more than happy to rat me out, so just go before I have to deal with any of that, okay?" The forced edge to his voice was like a dull, rusty blade to his heart. Pushing Gigi away hurt like hell, and calling her Georgia was even worse.

That single change may have done more damage

than any pissy attitude or tone. The paling of her cheeks twisted his gut into a knot. One that only tightened when the white of her complexion became a mottled red.

She stalked forward until the toes of her boots touched his. Gigi jammed her index finger in his left pec, bruising the skin covering his equally battered heart. "You don't get to do this, Wyatt. You don't get to play the role of the lonesome cowboy who has to face his troubled life all on his own. You have parents who would do almost anything for you and a brother who would probably drive home from college every week to help."

Every sentence was punctuated with a forceful poke in his chest. The tears collecting in the corners of her eyes shredded the last of his will power, more than her words. "And you have a ridiculous girlfriend who, for some unknown reason, thinks you're pretty damn special and isn't going to let you sabotage yourself and your future by hiding behind your ridiculous pride. Even when you try to push her away. Even when you call her by her real name."

When she swiped under her eyes with her thumbs, the final brick in the pathetic excuse for a wall he'd tried to erect crumbled. He wound his arms around her waist and pulled her close, drawing from the strength she never knew she gave him. "Dammit all to hell, Angel, I'm sorry."

After several beats, she reached up to link her hands behind his neck. "We take stuff on as a team, Wyatt."

Friends only liked him for his manufactured rodeo star persona. His family carefully veiled their disappointment in Wyatt's life plan to get tossed around by a thousand-pound beast instead of following in Tanner's path of college and preparations to take over the company. His brother had been bred for that role since birth and loved it. For Wyatt, it sounded like a fifty-year sentence in a prison worse than Alcatraz.

Only Gigi had seen through the façade and accepted him completely. She was the first person he believed loved him exactly as he was...and the last one he'd ever want to disappoint.

"Ask me what my GPA is."

Her muffled voice against the front of his shirt compelled him to loosen his hold slightly and lean back to regard her with a frown. "What?"

Gigi's black lips curled into a smirk. "I said, ask me what my GPA is."

His brows drew together and his hands moved from her waist to grip her hips. "Okay, what's your GPA?"

"Three point nine." Her palms slid over his shoulders and down the front of his shirt, patting his chest. "And calculus happens to be one of my best subjects."

A measure of the heavy mantle that had been hanging around his neck lightened. "With a score like that I think it is probably easier to just tell me which subject you aren't a complete star in." He pulled her closer, the planes of their bodies lining up in a way that never ceased to cement the fact in his mind that they were meant to be. "And by not a complete star, I'm assuming you lowered yourself to getting a plain old A in one subject instead of an A plus?"

"I don't think I can tell you that without a promise

of total secrecy. You aren't allowed to breathe a word of this to anyone."

Wyatt released one of her hips and stuck out his pinky in the small space between them. "I promise I will never repeat a word of my Angel's shortcoming to another human soul."

Her brows shot up. "Or horse." She leaned around him to look at the mare standing in the stall behind them. "No offense, Lemondrop."

For the first time in over a week since he'd been forced to confess his grades to his parents and accept the punishment they doled out, Wyatt laughed. "I promise not to tell any man, woman, child, or beast anything you say."

She linked her pinky with his and closed her eyes with a sigh. "Gym." She winced at the single word.

He tried to mask the chuckle that escaped with a cough. "Gym? You mean like climb the rope, run some laps, and pretend to learn a new sport kind of gym?"

Gigi released his finger and lightly slapped his bicep. "Yes. So much joining and team building and," she shuddered, "socializing. And there are so many perky, perfect cheerleaders, I want nothing more than to puke."

Wyatt captured her chin between his thumb and forefinger, his mouth hovering a breath above hers. "I love that you hate school spirit." A soft kiss punctuated his words. "I love that you make fun of team sports." Another swipe of his lips. "And I really love that you have a brilliant mind and a three point freaking nine GPA."

This time when their mouths met, they clung,

moving softly against each other at first before his tongue snaked between her teeth and began running along the length of hers. Her muted moan drove him to deepen the kiss and pull her tight to him.

Seconds then minutes ticked by unnoticed and unconcerned, but oxygen deprivation finally forced them apart. "So," he panted out the single syllable and slipped his cocky grin into place, "does this mean you're gonna be my tutor?"

Chapter Twenty-One

Wyatt

Present Day

The intrusive ringing of Wyatt's cell phone startled him out of the deep sleep he'd fallen into, settled and centered despite the chaos swirling in his world. All thanks to the auburn-haired girl curled against his side groaning her protestation at being disturbed. He fumbled with the phone on the bedside stand and muttered an epithet when his younger brother's name flashed across the screen. "Connor, what the hell do you want at," he squinted at the digital display before putting the phone back to his ear, "two-thirteen in the morning?"

Obviously, inebriated chuckling was his response. "Aww, come on, Wy, you're supposed to be the cool one. Always fun, never serious. Hell, you didn't even pick a real career. Although I gotta say, you got more cash than Tanner, which is pretty damn impressive." Another bark of laughter. "Even Dean managed to drag his ass to college, but not good ole Wyatt. Nope. He took off before the ink dried on his high school diploma."

A drunk brother was exactly what Wyatt didn't need at that moment. He rubbed the gritty sleep from his eyes and, with a soft kiss to the crown of her head, disengaged himself from a slumbering Gigi. Who snored, even though she'd vehemently deny it. She reached for him as he rose out of the bed, and he couldn't pretend that he didn't love her need for him, even half asleep. "I'll be right back, Angel."

He stood as close to the door of the hotel as he could and kept his voice barely above a whisper so Gigi would have a chance of sleeping through what he hoped would be a very short drunk dial. "Listen, Connor, I don't know what the hell your problem is, but calling me to throw insults in the middle of the night isn't exactly endearing. What's crawled up your ass other than cheap whiskey?"

"Not cheap, Wy, I'm drinking top shelf stuff." A glass connected with something hard, and the bang echoed over the phone line. "Three thousand, six-hundred thirty dollars' worth."

He shook his head to desperately try to clear the cobwebs left behind by the deep sleep he'd been so rudely pulled from. "If you drank three thousand dollars' worth of alcohol tonight, I'm driving you directly to the hospital for a liver transplant."

Connor laughed. "Not all tonight, but that's why I'm calling. I need a ride home."

Why had he decided to move home again? And when in the blue hell did he become the responsible brother that was called on to be the designated driver? "Can't Kelsey come pick you up?" A creak from behind drew Wyatt's attention to where Gigi stood beside the bed wearing nothing but one of his shirts.

The deafening silence from the other side of the line was telling enough to wipe away the lusty thoughts that had been swirling in Wyatt's brain. A silence he was far too familiar with. "Where's Kelsey, Connor?"

Since Connor first started dating Kelsey, they'd been as disgustingly attached and starry-eyed as Tanner and Izzy. That same sickening love he'd locked away twelve years ago when he left and was now desperate to find again. Gigi walked over and wrapped her arms around his waist, righting his world with the simple act.

"Gone." The single word was empty. And eerily sober. Followed by a hollow laugh. "But she left the ring, and I just couldn't think of a better way to use the money I got from returning it than to finance a little fun."

Wyatt closed his eyes and tipped his head back with a sigh. "Where are you?" This had just jumped from an innocent night out that got carried away to rescuing his brother from something much more serious. Something he could relate to far too well.

The first few months without Gigi would have been filled with far more debauchery if Wyatt hadn't been scraping together his loose change for basic survival. The early days of his career were financially tight to a level he'd never confessed to his family. They would have swooped in and saved the day, and the last thing he wanted was to keep being the designated Carlisle screw up. He'd had enough of that in school when he never seemed to quite measure up to Tanner in anyone's eyes.

Except Gigi. His hold on her tightened as Connor relayed the address of the dive bar that would be closing in thirty minutes. Gigi wasn't impressed by anyone, ever, but she damn sure knew how to look at him in a way that never made him feel less than ten feet tall. Even when he was failing miserably in school, she didn't pity him and didn't let him feel sorry for himself.

Yeah, she was worth every ounce of the energy it took to put up with her rules and guidelines.

He clicked off the call and pulled Gigi a little closer, pressing his lips against the crown of her head. "There are ten thousand things I would rather do right now than drag my brother's sorry ass out of some bar. And most of those things would involve you and seeing what it would take to sweet talk you out of that shirt."

She leaned back in the circle of his arms. "Everything okay?"

Wyatt's fingers trailed up and down her spine, and he sighed. "Connor's fiancée broke up with him and he's taking it about as well as I did."

Gigi arched a brow. "I think you've taken one too many falls from bulls and had one too many head traumas there, Cowboy. I didn't break up with you."

With a final squeeze, he reluctantly let her go and headed into the chair in the corner of the room to pull on something a little more substantial than the boxers he was sporting. "Yeah, well, you always did call me a stupid freaking cowboy. You were right in more ways than one."

Just as he got his jeans around his waist, two small hands snaked around him from behind, tracking up his abdomen. Her lips pressed between his shoulder blades before her cheek rested against his back. "What can I do to help?"

His palms held hers in place, and his eyes drifted closed. The temperamental side that he controlled with frequent reminders of his dumbass decisions that landed them here in the first place sparked. "Nothing. Helping out with lovesick, drunk family members doesn't fall under the 'friends with benefits' responsibility heading."

Her fingers stilled, and the iceberg his words created between them sent a chill down his spine. That was clearly not the right choice.

"Screw you."

Normally, he'd bring himself under control. Remember that the entire point of moving home was to fix everything he'd broken, not destroy it more. Unfortunately, his mouth failed to get the memo in time. He tugged the shirt over his head and spun around to face her. "That's all I'm good for, isn't it?"

Silence blanketed the space between them. He wanted to take back his words, to apologize, to tell her he didn't mean that and tell her that actually her offer meant more to him than anything had in a long time. But more than all of that he wanted her to argue with him and swear she saw him as more than just a hook-up. That she saw them as more than a hook-up.

Instead, she pursed her lips together in a thin line.

"You better go get Connor before he does something stupid. I need to get home to Gram anyway; her sleep schedule is completely messed up." She waved a hand around the room. "This was a nice idea, but…" She shrugged and collected her clothes, disappearing into the bathroom moments before he shoved his hat on his head, grabbed his keys, and headed out the door.

***

Georgia

For half the morning, Georgia scanned through Wyatt's financial statements. Going line by line with a fine-toothed comb in a so far fruitless attempt at decoding where the funds disappeared to.

Although one name kept popping up over and over on repeat. Integrity Investments. Consistent withdrawals, the same amount every month, never a deposit. When she'd had Wyatt list his expenses, assets, and essentially everything he could think of down to the electricity bill, he hadn't mentioned any investments. He'd listed his 401k—which was handled through a national corporation with a reputable representative that didn't raise any red flags for her—but not a peep about a separate company.

And a small one at that. The best her brief research had offered was a very basic website with many of the links, especially the all important company profile section, "under construction."

Her furrowed brow and the downturn of her lips disappeared with a tap on her partially opened office door and a slow, exaggerated drawl.

"Well, hey there, Gigi. I hear you were looking for me."

She swiped the papers aside, hastily shoving them into the manila folder and tucking it back into the center drawer of her desk. "Hey, yourself, Cowboy." Her eyes darted past him to the members of her design team milling about the open concept floor plan. Open other than her office which very much needed the privacy it afforded. Now. "Close that door please, Mr. Carlisle."

His deep chuckle vibrated through the air and shook the defenses she erected each time he entered her workspace. Wyatt crossed the floor and dropped into the chair across from her, throwing his ankle up on the opposite knee and reclining back in the seat easily. "Only you could possibly make that 'Mr. Carlisle' bullshit sound sexy as hell."

Prickles of heat ignited along each cell in her body with his words, and she tried desperately to find her resolve. "We're in my office where I'm the boss and you're the client. 'Mr. Carlisle' is the only thing that can exist inside these four walls."

The corners of his mouth tightened, and his deep blue eyes narrowed slightly. "Yes, Ms. Marsh. You've mentioned more than once exactly where we stand."

Georgia bit back the sigh that threatened to escape at his tone. She wanted to give him the all clear. To tell him that the Cowboy could be reinstated in every way because that's exactly what she wanted. Last night when she finally got her grandmother settled back in bed after a particularly confusing round of "who are you and where is my husband," she let her tears soak her pillow, wishing for nothing more than to have Wyatt's arms around her getting her through the second painful loss. A much more insidious one than her mother's cancer had been.

She was certain surviving her mother's death would have been harder if Wyatt hadn't been there comforting her, supporting her, and making her take the next breath when she simply didn't want to. But if he shot to that level of importance in her life again and disappeared...she wasn't so sure she'd bounce back again.

"Before we send these to mass production and make more than you know what to do with, I want to make sure you approve of the styles, final logo design and placement, and material."

She set the stack of merchandise on the desk between them. When he reached up to grab a shirt off the top, she moved her hand forward to rest on top of his. Their gazes locked, and she hoped her eyes managed to convey all the things words failed to do. That she was grateful he was back and they were together in whatever way they could be. That she was trying, even if he didn't think so. That she still loved him and never really stopped.

At least some of her silent pleas must have resonated as the corner of the mouth that spent almost every night wreaking havoc on her body and scrambling her brain kicked up in a familiar and irresistible smirk. He gave her fingers a quick squeeze before they both settled into their roles, focused solely on business.

As solely as she was able to manage as the musky scent that was inherently Wyatt swirled around her. His long digits stroked across the roughened material of the tote bags, and he made a comment she couldn't manage to register as her brain merrily skipped down the X-rated path of memories they'd created over the past few weeks.

"These are great, Gigi—" He rolled his eyes heavenward. "I mean Ms. Marsh. You already know I loved your concept and design, but this execution is…"

Her recently contoured brows lifted. "Great?"

Wyatt scrubbed his hands down his face and slumped back in his chair. "Yeah, they are. But as things stand right now, I'm barely—and I really do mean barely—going to be able to fund the completion of the competition arena and boarding buildings." His cheeks puffed out before a heavy sigh escaped. "I can't finish the house. How the hell am I supposed to be able to stock merchandise?"

She swallowed; the first threads of the idea she was about to suggest had begun to tickle the periphery of her mind the day after Wyatt had finally confessed to the financial issues he'd fallen into. First she wanted to take time to see if a simple miscalculation was to blame. Even though she was positive the fault didn't lie with Wyatt not being prepared for an eventuality— his plan had covered nearly every possible roadblock and obstacle—she also was just as certain she wasn't going to be able to solve the mystery in time to meet all his deadlines and keep him on schedule.

Her alternate idea would be ideal if only Wyatt could set his stubborn pride aside long enough to listen. "About that…"

Intense sapphire eyes pinned her with highly focused attention. He rested his elbows on his knees and leaned forward. "Did you find something to explain what the hell happened to my money?"

"No, well, not yet. I think I'm getting close, but nothing definitive yet." It wasn't a lie; her gut was screaming at her that the key was hidden somewhere within the enigma that was Integrity Investments. "But I have an alternative."

Even the vigorous shake of his head couldn't dislodge the hat perched there. "I already told you I'm not going to borrow the money from my dad or Tanner or bring Carlisle International in as any sort of investor. No."

Georgia dipped her chin. "Don't comment, Cowboy. Just listen."

A ghost of a smile, laced with a trace of arrogance, curled his lips. "Breaking your 'no flirting in the office' rule there, Gigi."

Her lids shuddered as she rolled her eyes to the ceiling. "My point is I have an idea that doesn't involve any member of your family participating other than buying a corndog at the rodeo."

Wyatt chuckled and linked his fingers together, dangling his hands between his knees. "All right, white flag waved. Go ahead."

"Before you argue or gripe or storm out, promise you'll listen to my entire proposal." At his amused nod, she continued. "You're already working with Elias personally and JBA as a whole. As it stands right now, he plays a minor role. You've proven that you still have an uncanny ability to charm the pants off every man, woman, and child within a seventy-mile radius with that ridiculous rhinestone cowboy persona and intentionally embellished southern accent."

He leaned back in his chair again, propping his ankle on his knee, his bobbing foot the only indication he was anything less than at ease. "Thanks for the compliment there, Gigi."

She affected the sternest face she could and pointed an accusatory finger his way, her twitching lips the only tell that she wasn't as immune to him as she'd like to believe. "You were supposed to stay quiet."

Wyatt mimicked zipping his lips and tossed the imaginary key over his left shoulder with a blinding grin.

Focus, she instructed her wayward brain. "If you increase Elias's role within RA Ranch as a whole rather than just having him as a sponsor for the competition, you'd be able to complete all the business-related buildings and have enough of a bankroll leftover to stock merchandise, hire a food truck, and function with something resembling a staff at least until after the competition." She shrugged. "If it's successful enough, you might be able to repay the investment in full and go your separate ways."

His foot stilled. The rise and fall of his chest slowed. But his eyes never left hers. "Did he already approve this?"

"I was waiting until we talked, but…" She sighed and pinched the bridge of her nose. "But the man talks about you like you're his long-lost son. I wouldn't be shocked if he said he wanted you to join him for Christmas dinner."

The silence that stretched between them grated her every raw nerve. Georgia uncrossed and recrossed her legs at least a dozen times as the painful, deafening quiet engulfed them in its agonizing gaping maw.

Finally, he stood, fished in his pocket for something, and dropped a coin on the desk in front of her. "Flip ya for it?"

She blinked up at him. "Heads you talk to him and take whatever help he offers, tails you... what?"

"Heads I will talk to Elias with an open mind and tails..." He hooked a finger beneath her chin, his thumb stroking across the cleft in the middle. "Tails you let me take you on a real date."

Georgia nodded, unable to find the words to agree. When the shining disc landed face up, her brain battled against the aching disappointment clawing at her heart and claimed control of her mouth. "We could always do both."

Chapter
Twenty-Two

Georgia

Twelve Years Earlier

Just as she closed her locker door, arms encircled her waist and had her off her feet, swinging through the air, before Georgia could even find the words to yelp out a protest. Or kick her faceless assailant in the crotch. Fortunately the spicy musk scent that would forever be ingrained on her mind registered quickly. "What the hell, Wyatt?"

His deep laughter vibrated against her back and sent a chill racing down its length. "Well, take a look for yourself, Angel."

Georgia's eyes filled with tears as she scanned down the paper he shoved in her hand. Five weeks of dogged studying practically every day at her house after school, creative rewards for each improving test score, and stolen kisses when her grandmother's back was turned or her grandfather took the dogs for a walk had finally paid off. "You got a C."

She spun in the circle of his arms just in time to catch the crimson stain across his cheekbones as he dipped his chin. Her heart ached. This ridiculous cowboy was sexy when he was cocky and obnoxious, but ever since he confessed to his struggle with his classes, his unexpected vulnerability wormed its way deeper in her heart. She couldn't control the emotional response to seeing his hard work pay off.

He lifted a shoulder without meeting her gaze. "It isn't an A, but it's enough to get my restrictions lifted and get back to training and—"

Her mouth swallowed the rest of his words as her lips melded with his. She poured every ounce of pride and love into the action, words unable to encompass the depth. Her tongue snaked between his teeth, stroking along the length of his.

Wyatt groaned against her mouth, pressing his palm into the small of her back, lining the planes and the curves of their bodies together like jigsaw puzzle pieces.

"I'm proud of you." She barely managed to pant out the words between labored breaths. She cradled his face between her palms. "I don't care that it isn't an A, Wyatt. You worked your ass off and studied so hard, and I am so damn proud of you."

A genuine, ego-free smile curled his lips. "Yeah? You are?"

Her fingers linked behind his neck. "Yeah. I am."

"So not too bad for a stupid freaking cowboy then?" He leaned his head down until his forehead bumped hers.

Georgia fought valiantly the heat creeping up her neck. "I'm sorry, Wy. I never meant it. Not like that. I think you're a lot of things, but I've never really thought that you were stupid." She swallowed, closing her eyes briefly before meeting his stare. "I promise I'll never say that again."

The corner of his mouth kicked up. "Actually, I think it's pretty damn accurate, and I hope you say it a lot more often."

Her hands reached up to his face, her thumbs stroking down in front of his ears and her fingers curled around his head. "You aren't stupid. You're smart and determined and focused and passionate. You definitely aren't stupid."

"But I am, Gigi." His lips brushed against hers. "I'm stupid crazy about you. I'm stupid excited to spend time with you. And I am stupid in love with you."

Their mouths met again in a soft kiss, saving Georgia from answering. Not that finding words was a possibility for her at all. That cowboy left her speechless.

He set her back slightly and pulled away. "You know the best part about getting released from the Carlisle Penitentiary?"

She twisted her mouth to side and quirked a brow. "That you get back to training before they add some new, big, bad bull you've just been dying to have hand your ass to you?"

"Yes, that too." He stroked a hand over her hair, cupping the back of her head and tugging her close again. "But the best part is getting to take my girlfriend on a real date again."

***

Wyatt

Wyatt laced his fingers through Gigi's and rested their joined hands on her abdomen. She wiggled a little on the thin blanket covering the rocky ground, pressing her spine into his stomach. He fought back a groan and willed his mind to imagine any number of disgusting things to stop the Gigi-induced blaze of fire from shooting below his belt buckle. His cowboy hat-clad head hit the trunk of the tree he was reclining against.

Her thumb stroked the length of his in soft lines. A completely innocent gesture that was completely driving him insane. For weeks she had been dropping not-so-subtle hints that she was ready to have sex. Wyatt had done his best to avoid the topic every time it was broached. But that was getting harder and harder with each passing day.

Literally and metaphorically.

"Is it because of the makeup?"

Her soft question pulled him from the angst he'd been drowning in. "Is what because of the makeup, Angel?"

She sat upright and turned in between the space of his legs. "Do I wear too much makeup? Like, is it too dark and distracting and unattractive? Is that why you don't want to...do...anything? With me?"

The icy heat of desire that had been coursing through his veins died out as the impact of her words hit him with more force that a throw from Lightning. "Gigi, I must have fallen asleep and missed a large part of this conversation, because I swear I don't know what you're talking about."

She tucked her feet under her ebony leggings and fidgeted with the frayed cuff of her slate-colored hoodie. "I'm ready, Wyatt. I keep telling you that. I want to be with you, but every time I try to talk to you, you change the subject or have to go and promise me we will talk about it later." With a huff, she rolled her eyes to the clear, blue winter sky before dropping her head. "I love you and I want to show you that in every way, but I don't think you do. So I just wondered if maybe...maybe you didn't like my makeup. Or my hair. Or my clothes. Or anything and maybe that was why."

Wyatt turned his legs and lifted onto his knees. He gripped her chin between his thumb and forefinger. "There is not one part of that statement that is true, Angel." His lids shuttered closed, and he inhaled deeply, searching his adolescent brain for the right words. "Dammit, Gigi, I want you. I want every part of you. I want to find all of your ticklish spots and discover every place that makes you sigh."

As he was speaking, her hands slowly crept up his arms and locked behind his neck. Her pupils dilated, a flare of desire sparking in their depths. She put pressure on the back of his head and rotated her hips as she lay back on the thin material covering the ground, pulling him with her. "You do?"

He rolled his pelvis forward, grinding into the apex of her thighs. "What do you think, Angel?"

She moaned and brought his mouth to hers. His

arms tightened around her as she used her tongue, her lips, and her teeth to torture him further. When he rocked forward again, she groaned and hooked her legs around his. The whimper in her throat was both his reward and punishment as his jeans constricted even more, the denim creating a painful barrier.

Always one to give as good as she got, she rubbed her core against him and they sucked in their breaths in unison at the delicious friction. His fingers crept under her fleece top, gliding up her smooth stomach to cup one of the firm, satin-covered globes.

A rock dug into the back of his hand and brought him crashing back to earth from the heady sensations that had consumed his mind and eradicated all logical thought. Dammit, that was not how this was supposed to go. He broke the kiss and called himself every kind of ass for her crestfallen expression.

He cupped her cheek. "Angel, look at me." Time stretched out interminably, each nanosecond carrying the weight of an hour, before she opened her stricken eyes to meet his. "I mean it. I mean every word." His hips rolled forward again to prove his desire. "Nearly every part of me screams when I have to put the brakes on because I don't just want you, Angel. I need you so freaking bad."

"Then why, Wyatt?" A stray drop leaked from the hazel eyes sparkling from the sheen of its unshed companions. His thumb swiped it away, his heart fracturing at the sight.

"Because there is one part that thinks you deserve better. That wants to give you perfect." His hand found hers and held it over the left side of his chest. "It's the part of me that says your name with every beat, Angel. I love you too much to let your first time—our first time—be some hurried, bumbling mess. We weren't meant to be like everyone else. We were meant to be different."

Gigi nodded, and Wyatt rolled onto his back, holding her tight against his side. He recited the statistics of every rider from last week's competition in his head, willing the mundane to drown out his need. When Gigi's hand went slack in his and the cutest damn snore puffed out of her nose, he smiled and slid his hat over his face.

Chapter Twenty-Three

Wyatt

Present Day

"Hell, son, this sounds like it's more of a gift for me than it is for you."

Wyatt couldn't help but smile at the older man on the other side of the massive mahogany desk as he rose and extended a hand across the smooth surface to offer a shake. "I'm not sure that's exactly true, sir, but I appreciate it."

Elias stood and pumped his arm. "I would. A rodeo in this area reminds me of home and just so happens to be damn good for my business."

"Where is home, sir?" He fought against the urge to run down the hall, make a left, and grab Gigi to show her just how well her brilliant plan worked out. Elias Joseph had jumped at the idea of partnering with

RA Ranch and hadn't even blinked when Wyatt quoted a six-digit figure.

He hated selling a part of his dream off. When the first nugget of the idea came to him, the same night he got the tattoo and was missing his Angel so hard he could barely remember to breathe, he swore he would do this on his own. Although the pain of having someone else as part of his dream wasn't insignificant, he'd willingly endure it to avoid the complete failure glaring him in the face.

A hearty chuckle was the response. "Why isn't it obvious from this," he pointed toward his mouth, "damn accent that hasn't faded in the thirty years I've lived here? I'm from Texas, son. Small town just outside of Austin." He dipped his chin, his smile dropping slightly. "It was a great place. I'd always planned on raising my kids there."

Wyatt's brows pulled together, and he shoved his hands in his pockets. "Why didn't you? What made you move to North Carolina?"

The nostalgic expression was wiped from the older man's face, and a twinkle lit his cornflower eyes. "Love, son. I fell in love with a beautiful girl with long blonde hair and legs that went on for days...who refused to live in Texas any longer than she needed to graduate from Texas A & M. So I packed up, left my family, and moved eleven hundred miles away for her." He threw Wyatt a broad grin. "And I don't regret one moment of it. The love of a good woman is worth jumpin' through almost any hoop."

Wyatt's mouth opened and closed a few times before he squinted up at the other man. "You gave up everything?"

Elias nodded, the smile not fading. "I did, and I'd do it all over again in a heartbeat." His arm swept wide, encompassing his office. "My business was barely makin' it in Texas, but here I've built a thriving corporation. I visited my family twice a year in the beginning, more now, but here I have three kids, two grandkids, and another on the way. Sometimes you gotta pick what your definition of important is."

The words melted a fraction of Wyatt's frustration. Working to win her back was something he'd banked on doing. Something he knew she deserved. But the waiting…that was killing him.

Gigi, though, she was worth it. She was his definition of important.

He shook the older man's hand and let his heart lead him into the office of the woman who occupied damn near every thought he had. Her eyes snapped up from the papers spread across her desk. The immediate flash of desire was exactly what he needed to see.

"So?" Her brows lifted nearly to her hairline.

Wyatt clicked the door closed behind him, dropped his head, and fought to control the grin struggling to surface. He shuffled his boots against the low pile gray carpeting. "Well…"

Gigi jumped from her chair, rounded the desk, and grabbed his face. "Wyatt, it's okay, I don't know how—"

His sullen expression dissolved into laughter. "He said yes, Angel."

Hazel eyes widened into saucers. "Yes? He said yes? To the entire amount?"

"Yes to the entire amount," he confirmed with a

confident nod, far less troubled by the fact he was letting someone else have a say and a portion of his ranch than he expected. The dazzling excitement reflected back at him silenced every doubt.

Until her lips pursed together tightly and her lids narrowed. Her hands moved from his face to his bicep, where she swatted him once. Twice. And then a third time when his chuckles renewed and amplified into deep guffaws. "You are such an asshole."

He caught her wrist before she could land another blow and pulled her tight against him. "Don't damage the merchandise there, Angel. I might need to grab a few modeling gigs to keep a roof over our heads."

She stared at him silently for a moment but didn't disagree. Instead she swiped her lips across his and stole his ability to think or breathe. "Until then, you might want to get out of here. I don't have the luxury of working for myself or getting paid to show off my body."

Wyatt took a step back and gave her a long, sweeping appraisal, index finger tapping his chin. "That could be arranged. As long as you're only showing off for me, that is."

Gigi smacked his arm again and waved him toward the door. "Go. Now. Before you dig yourself into another hole somehow."

"Don't forget, Angel, we have a date tonight."

She took her seat behind her desk with a heavy sigh. "How could I possibly forget? You've been texting me gloating reminders for three days."

He winked, one hand resting on the doorknob. "Just makin' sure you're payin' attention there, Gigi."

Her eyes rolled toward the ceiling at his

intentionally embellished accent, and he laughed as he shut the door behind him.

The damn near permanent grin was still in place thirty minutes later as he sat across from his brother, making faces while Tanner spewed numbers to someone on the other end. Sitting in this many offices in one day was about to make his skin itchy. He missed the fresh air, even if it was hot and sticky in the summer sun.

"What the hell do you want?" Tanner grumbled as he replaced the phone in its cradle.

Wyatt slapped a hand over his heart and plastered an exaggeratedly pained expression on his face. "Is this really the kind of reception you give your favorite brother?"

The older man snorted. "I don't know, let's invite Dean down here and find out." Tanner folded his hands together on the flat calendar covering his desk and leaned forward. "Really, what do you want, Wyatt? Belle has some sort of couple's yoga thing she wants to try out with me before she offers it as a class and...I am definitely not missing my wife going all ultra-bendy on me for your sorry ass."

A sly grin spread across Wyatt's face. "Your hot, bendy wife is exactly why I'm here." Too easy. His brother made it too damn easy, and Wyatt chuckled at Tanner's mottled expression and flared nostrils. "What I mean by that is...I need some more advice. Gigi agreed to a date. A real one. If you could manage to get Izzy to forgive you for being a complete asshole, maybe I could use an idea or two for Gigi and she'd forget that I was half of one."

"Don't sell yourself short, brother. You are the full

deal yourself." Tanner leaned back in his chair, resting his elbows on the arms, and steepled his fingers in front of his chin. "Where were you planning on taking her?"

Wyatt held his hands up, helplessly. "That's why I'm groveling at the feet of the master for some advice."

"Well, hell," Tanner muttered. "Okay, here's what you do."

***

Georgia

"You didn't answer me, Cowboy." Georgia folded her arms across the navy and yellow sundress she wore, hoping it would fit in with whatever plan Wyatt had formulated for their date. "Where are we going?"

He grinned, his eyes leaving the road long enough to give her a wink before returning to pay attention to the traffic in front of them. "Can't you ever just go along with what I say?"

Georgia tilted her head from side to side, squinting. "I could, but what would be the fun in that? Face it, Wy, I didn't make life easy for you when we were younger. Why would I want to start now?"

Wyatt's hand slid across the console separating them and teased her arms free, lacing his fingers through hers. "I know you don't trust me yet but…just trust me?"

Her heart leapt in her chest and applauded the idea. In a turn of events that shocked her, he owned his actions. He'd apologized repeatedly and profusely.

The cocky rhinestone cowboy let his guard down and was humble. Only for her.

He wasn't Bruce. He wouldn't lead her on, promise her a future complete with a diamond ring, and then surprise her with the revelation that he had a wife and kids. An admission that came only when she called him in tears, devastated over her grandmother's diagnosis and rapid decline. At the moment when she needed him most, when she needed him for more than a rendezvous at her place or as a plus one to an event, he bailed and left her on her own.

But Wyatt also wasn't Wyatt anymore. That realization had been harder to swallow, but he was trying, and she had to give him some credit. He agreed to the impossible "sex only" edict she made even though she knew he wanted to fight for more. When she confessed to missing dinner because she'd slipped straight out of her marketing director skin and into her caregiver role, he'd shown up on her doorstep with a shredded chicken burrito with extra cheese, light on the lettuce, and guacamole on the side. Exactly how she liked it. But he'd simply dropped it off, given her a kiss on the cheek and walked away.

He was acting much more like the boy she fell in love with than the one who left. Half of her heart still hid behind the betrayal-induced barrier she'd created while the other begged her to give him the second chance he was working for. The conflicting ache that had been present since she'd first stepped into the conference room and saw him sitting there intensified.

He was the best parts of Wyatt from before but improved. The childish decisions were replaced with a quiet maturity that both surprised and tempted her

Wyatt as a teen had been driven and focused, but this version of him was…responsible. And harder to resist than she ever imagined.

The welling of emotions at the realization made her hand squeeze his and her heart follow suit when he cut a sideways grin over to her. This Wyatt might be able to not just be everything he had been before, but also help carry some of the heavy weight she shouldered.

And she might be ready to give him that chance.

The might in the equation disappeared when the truck pulled to a stop. All the breath in her lungs vanished, and her jaw dropped to the floorboard. When her mouth finally was able to move, no words came out, and her eyes darted between the scene in front of her and the man sitting at her side.

A very not cocky, not Rhinestone Cowboy smile spread across his face. "I'm gonna guess that means you like it?"

She scrambled out of the truck and stood in front of the bench—their bench—that was completely covered in Christmas decorations. Twinkling lights were snaked around the oak trees on either side, and glittering ornaments hung from the branch with a long length of fishing line.

None of it was exactly the same as it had been before, but it was all incredibly similar. Just like the single tear that managed to escape from her eye. Just like them. Footsteps stopped just behind her, and she turned, brows raised in silent question.

He lifted a shoulder. "Ever heard of Christmas in July?"

She nodded wordlessly as he led her to the bench. And then promptly dissolved into laughter as he produced their dinner: greasy cheeseburgers with a side of bacon and cheese fries. The exact same meal from the exact same diner that they'd gone to when she accompanied him on his first training session.

Finally the word that had been ricocheting through her mind escaped her lips. "How?"

"Well…" He drew out the single syllable to the length of five. "I might have called in some favors. Tanner owed me. Big time."

She waved a hand around at the completely out of place and yet completely perfect winter decorations surrounding them as a bead of sweat trickled down her spine in the oppressive heat despite the fading sun. "You did good, Cowboy."

An unlikely red stained his cheeks, and he dipped his head. "They, um, they finished my house today. The furniture is getting delivered tomorrow. I…" He regarded her through lashes longer than any man deserved. "I know you have to stay with your Gram, I know you can't spend the night, but do you think you'd want to come over tomorrow? Scope it all out."

His words cut off so abruptly that Georgia was certain he was going to say more. When only silence filled the space between them, she cleared her throat.

"I just have to check with my dad. Or Paige. See if one of them can stay with her." She covered the hand resting on his knee with hers. "How…how did you finish it? Where did you find the money?"

Sapphire eyes disappeared behind closed lids for a moment. "I came back for you, Gigi. And whatever happened, whatever screwed up, I'm not going to let that steal the opportunity from us." He held his hands up. "Not that I'm saying you've agreed to anything—"

She cradled his face between her palms, and he immediately gripped her hips in response. "Just tell me, Cowboy. Although if the answer is that you were modeling in your underwear again, we may need to have a talk."

He laughed and shook his head as much as he could in her grasp. "No, I…" he winced, "I got a mortgage. I'm like a responsible adult or some such shit."

Her mouth crashed into his just as he finished speaking. She moved closer until she was almost sitting in his lap. His tongue teased along her lower lip, and she opened to the silent request. Hands and fingers grasped at the other in a mixture of lust, need, and a reconnection deeper than the physical that came so easily.

The short, perfunctory ringtone of her phone separated them long before she was ready to end the kiss. She pressed a hand to her chest and took a few deep breaths before sliding the device from the pocket of her dress. As soon as she saw the display, the fire Wyatt had ignited in her veins turned to ice. Every nerve ending buzzed seconds before turning numb.

A shaking finger connected the call, and she brought the phone to her ear. "What's wrong?"

Paige's moderated professional tone did nothing to ease her worries. "Now, Georgia, don't panic."

"What's wrong, Paige?"

Her best friend sighed. "Gram had an accident and she's on the way to the hospital, but—"

"I'll be there in fifteen minutes."

She ended the call without waiting on a response from Paige. Georgia clicked the phone off and caught

Wyatt's stare.

He cut off her words before they were even formed. "I'll get you there in less than ten."

Chapter Twenty-Four

Wyatt

Twelve Years Earlier

"I can't."

Wyatt rolled his eyes, his forehead falling against his forearm where it rested on the frame of Georgia's bedroom door. "Is there ever gonna be a day where you just say, 'Sure, Wyatt, let's do whatever you want' without fighting me? I'll wait for it. Just give me a date to look forward to."

She pulled her lips inward and clamped them between her teeth. "The twelfth of never work for you, Cowboy?"

He quirked up the corner of his mouth, internally reveling in the rose color blossoming on her cheeks. Nearly a year after they started dating, he found himself more attuned with her highs, lows, and in

226

betweens. "Please, Angel." He cooed the words and reached for her hand, curling his fingers around hers and holding it against his heart. "It's your birthday weekend. Your parents gave their blessing. And your mom said she's feeling good today. I promise."

Her arms folded across her chest and her mouth settled into a firm line. "My birthday was last Saturday, remember? You were here, cake, balloons...ringing any bells?"

"Yeah, but I didn't get to plan that. Today is all mine, so it's your real birthday weekend."

Even though he tried, he couldn't understand the hell she lived through stuck in a permanent state of limbo, suspended between life and death. He knew she was terrified leaving her house because one day she might come back and her mom—

"Sure, Wyatt, let's do whatever you want."

He blinked his disbelief. "That was almost too easy, Gigi. I'm scared to think about what it'll cost me, but I'll take it as a gift for now." He tugged her to him and brushed his lips along hers. "Thank you, Angel."

Wyatt dropped her hand long enough to grab her light sweater and hold it out for her to slip on before lacing his fingers with hers again and leading her out to his truck. He opened the passenger door for her, but she hesitated before climbing in.

Her brows drew together. "Are you taking me out to dinner?" Gigi's gaze traveled over his body. "I'm not really dressed for anything, ya know, fancy or whatever."

Wyatt snaked his arm around her waist, pulling her tightly against him. His mouth hovered over hers.

227

"Angel, you look as beautiful as ever, but don't worry your pretty little head. You are wearing the perfect outfit."

Before she could respond, he landed a much more heated kiss than the chaste one he'd offered in her house. She moaned and reached up to hold onto the nape of his neck, her grip tightening as he deepened the kiss. Magic swirled around them, dissolving reality, time, and every other intrusion.

"I love kissing you," he whispered when they finally separated.

She captured her lower lip between her teeth and smiled. "Me too."

Wyatt groaned and dropped his forehead against hers. "Get in the truck, Angel. Please. Before you totally derail my plans for tonight."

Her brows lifted. "Plans? Wyatt Carlisle made plans?"

"One day," he growled the words as he helped her climb inside the cab. "One day you won't give me grief."

Buckle clicked into place, she pressed a hand to her chest. "Aw, that's so cute. But no, I won't ever stop. You'd miss it and you know it."

He shook his head, closed her door, and rounded the hood of the truck, jumping in beside her before he answered. "Damn straight I would. I love my fiery Angel."

They fell into their normal pattern of easy conversation on everything from normal teenage school angst to Georgia and Wyatt's future careers and, most importantly, how they'd manage to meld her college with his touring schedule. Never once had ending them been part of the plan. What they'd found was so much more than clichéd teenage puppy love that would result in certain heartbreak; she was certain of it. Wyatt assured her almost every day that they could make it work because they were meant to be different from everyone else.

When he made a hard left onto his family's long driveway, Georgia squeezed his hand. "Wyatt, if I'm not dressed for a restaurant, what the hell makes you think I'm decent for dinner with your family?"

He chuckled as he sped along the gravel road, bearing to the left to bypass the house. His gaze traveled over the black plaid skirt, fishnet stockings, and black boots she wore. "Don't worry, Angel, my family is completely disallowed from tonight's celebration." He threw her a wink. "The only thing they are providing is location. And food, because I'd prefer to not poison my girlfriend with my cooking."

"You seem awfully proud of yourself over there, Cowboy. I'm expecting to be wowed."

Wyatt smirked and lifted his brows three times in rapid succession. "I'm shooting for better than wowing ya, Angel. I'm aiming for speechless."

Her answering snort soon erupted into full laughter. She doubled over in her seat as he parked in front of the barn on the opposite side from where the horses were penned. "When have I ever been speechless?"

Leaning over to release her buckle, he tucked her to his side. "Want me to demonstrate exactly how well I know how to make you stop talking?"

The pink tip of her tongue darting out to run along her lips nearly unwound every ounce of self-control he barely managed to hang on to in her presence.

229

"Nope, you promised me an epic birthday, and all I see is a dirty barn." She pushed against his chest with one hand and waved toward his door with the other. "Let's go."

He turned to hold his arms out to help her down, and she jumped into his waiting embrace. Wyatt held her close, her feet dangling above the ground. "I love you, Angel."

She slid down the front of him as his grip loosened, and she smiled. "I love you too, Cowboy."

His shaking fingers intertwined through hers. He led her to the closed door that normally housed the overflow bales of hay for the horses. An unsteady hand covered her eyes at the same time the wooden plank whooshed open.

Wyatt stepped to her side and leaned in slightly to whisper in her ear, "Happy birthday, Angel."

The barrier fell away shortly before the tears streaked down her cheeks. All the hay had been cleared from the small room and was replaced with a floor full of sand, palm trees, and beach chairs. In the corner, a blinding spotlight beat warm beams down on a kiddy pool full of water. The walls were plastered with posters for every Tampa Bay team that existed.

She turned and held his face between her palms. Her body shook in his arms like a leaf caught in a tornado. "Wyatt…"

A genuine smile curved his mouth. "You're homesick. I know you can't go back to Tampa for your birthday even though that's probably the thing you want the most." He shrugged. "So I brought some of Tampa to you."

***

Georgia

Georgia kicked off her socks and shoes as soon as she released the death grip on his neck and dug her feet into the sand. She closed her eyes and soaked in the bliss of the grainy texture rolling between her toes.

After several long minutes, her lids lifted and she drank in the cowboy standing before her. His posture practically oozed with the cocky swagger he seemed to always possess, but tonight it melded with amusement and love. And sent her libido into overdrive. She crooked a finger at him and beckoned him closer with an inviting grin. Maybe tonight…

"Like it, Angel?" His arms wrapped around her waist, and he buried his nose in her hair.

She pulled back slightly in the circle of his embrace and held his face between her palms. "Like it? Are you kidding me? Wyatt, I…I…" Her mouth captured his. Hard. Passion fueled. Desperate. She broke the kiss, for several minutes only the panting of their breaths filling the space. "I hate you so much."

His grin stayed in place for several beats before his face fell and shoulders sank. "H-h-hate me?"

Georgia's teeth sank into her lower lip. This stupid freaking cowboy drove her insane in every way possible. And she loved every minute. "So much."

Her hands fell away from his cheeks, and she stepped out of his embrace. She found one of the blankets hanging on a tack beside a saddle and spread it across the sand. Georgia laced her fingers through his and pulled him down on top of the thick material.

231

Wyatt's Adam's apple bobbed once. Twice. Three times. "Angel, I—"

She opened her legs, tugging him to lay on top of her body. "You are an amazing boyfriend." Her lips pressed to his right cheek. "You are more thoughtful than any girl deserves." And then on his left cheek. "And it has to be hate because there is no way it is possible to love another person this much."

Finally, their mouths connected. Fire raced through her veins, and every ounce of self-control she ever possessed burned to dust from the raging inferno of their passion. She hoped against every hope that he was paying attention in health class and carried the school issued condom in his wallet. It was her birthday weekend after all.

The hot June night combined with their rising body temperature, and a drop of perspiration trickled down her spine. She lifted her hips and locked her legs around his waist. The bulge barely contained behind the denim of his jeans was too close and too damn tempting.

She ground into him, and he groaned in response. His hand trailed beneath her shirt and sighed, committing every path his fingers made on her skin. Georgia arched into his touch as he rounded to the front of her body and reached the satin-covered globes, daring to dip behind and stroke across one firm pebble.

"Please," she whimpered after breaking the kiss. "Please, Wyatt. I promise I'm ready." She flexed the muscles of her thighs around him and offered a wicked grin. "And as of one-twenty last Saturday afternoon, I'm eighteen."

232

Since his own birthday two weeks earlier he'd teased he had to keep his hands off her until she was an adult too. Now, Georgia had no problem using his own words against him. "Are you sure, Angel?"

Her every available appendage twined more tightly around him. "I haven't wanted anything more in my life. I love you with my heart, and I love you with my soul…I am ready to love you with my body."

Wyatt captured her mouth again. This time, every movement of his hands and his lips were slow and deliberate, nearly bringing her to tears with the reverential touches. "You won't regret this, Angel," he murmured against her lips. "I promise I will make this so good for you."

He moved from her mouth to her neck, licking, nipping, and sucking his way down the long, graceful column. She surrendered to the tides of pleasure taunting her body the way the ocean did along the shoreline.

So consumed by his every ministration, the intrusive ringing didn't register in her brain for several moments. "Wyatt, my phone."

An ice bath couldn't have been more effective. She looked up at him, the color drained from the face that was reddened from passion less than a second ago. He rolled far enough away to allow her to reach for the phone in her front pocket but kept one hand locked with her while the other rested against the small of her back as soon as she sat up.

The phone had been something specifically to link her with home while she was at school or with Wyatt or volunteering at the shelter. Only her family, Wyatt, and her best friend Paige had the number, and all were instructed it was only for emergencies.

Her stomach seized. Nothing good could come from this.

She searched his face for the comfort and confidence she knew she'd find only in Wyatt. With a shaking finger, she connected the call. "H-h-h-hello."

The space between her stuttered greetings and the first tear had to have been less than two seconds, but every tick of the clock had happened at an excruciatingly slow pace. But her scream, the toss of the phone, and her crumple into his arms made up for it by happening at the speed of lightning.

He stroked her spine in silence and held her in his lap. The stupid freaking cowboy always knew exactly what to say. And what not to.

Grief and gratitude swirled in a conflicted storm inside of her. She buried her face in his neck and gave in to every emotion clambering for ownership.

Finally, after her tears subsided enough she trusted her voice to speak, she lifted her head from his shoulder and met his red-rimmed eyes with ones she was certain matched. "She's gone."

She collapsed against him again, new sobs wracking her body. But the glimmer of thankfulness burned in her gut. If she had to be anywhere other than with her mother at this moment, being held by Wyatt was the best possible choice.

Chapter Twenty-Five

Wyatt

Present Day

Wyatt hated hospitals.

He'd never been a fan at any stage of his life, but even less so after his first bad fall. The only thing he wanted to do then was get up and walk around to wipe the terror from Gigi's face. Her pain had always been too much for him to handle.

Propping an arm on the metal frame encasing the sliding glass door of the emergency room cubicle that held Gigi and her grandmother, he saw the same expression on her face. Only fading when she would turn and lean into the older woman who seemed to drown in the stark white covers of the hospital bed. She tucked a strand of silver hair behind her grandmother's ear and spoke in tones so low he wouldn't know she was speaking if it weren't for the full lips moving.

It certainly wouldn't be apparent based on any reaction from her grandmother. The woman stared sightlessly ahead, not acknowledging anything Gigi said.

He tried to stay away and give them privacy and respect, but when a single tear trailed down her cheek, the final brick of his resolve disappeared. He'd promised he wouldn't run, wouldn't abandon her. Never again. And this was a moment he could prove that.

Slowly he slid the door open just enough to gain entrance. Before he could offer an excuse or explanation, she began crying in earnest. He did the only thing he knew how to do. In three large steps, he closed the space that separated them and pulled her tight against him. She wrapped her one free arm around his waist, the other still clinging to her grandmother's hand, and buried her face in his neck.

The same helpless feeling that consumed him when he held her in much the same way after the loss of her mother took residence in him once again. He searched his brain for the right thing to say and came up empty, so he kept his mouth shut.

Gigi hiccuped a few times and lifted her head. Her eyes searched his, silently pleading for an answer he didn't have. "Where the hell are the doctors and what is taking so freaking long?"

That was his fiery Gigi, and damn, did he love seeing that. Almost as much as he loved being the one she fell apart to. It was a privilege he reminded himself to never take for granted again. He had to be smarter than his eighteen-year-old self. "Do you want me to—"

"No." The single word nearly exploded out of her. "No, please stay here. Paige…Paige is somewhere making sure they do what they need to do. And looking for my dad whenever he gets here." She gripped the back of his shirt. "Please don't go."

Wyatt's head shook without a moment's consideration. "I'm not going anywhere."

She gave a jerky nod before laying her head back down on his shoulder. He stroked his fingers up and down her spine, the movement comforting him just as much as he hoped it would comfort her. His eyes fell on the older woman in the bed, and his own heart clenched. He remembered her grandmother with the same fire and determination that was passed down to Gigi's mom that gave her the will to fight cancer much longer than doctors expected. And the same grit and strength that Gigi possessed to get her through that decline and loss.

And now she's going through it again.

The realization tightened his hold on her, and she pressed impossibly deeper into his embrace. A tenuous peace descended and lasted until the door opened again. Barry Marsh somehow managed not to change much over the past dozen years, perhaps a bit thinner and sporting just a touch more gray at the temples, but otherwise the same rather imposing figure Wyatt respected and mildly feared in his youth.

But his eyes were a mixture of exhaustion and fear. Nearly identical to what they were when he cared for his wife.

Gigi lifted her head and abandoned both Wyatt's

embrace and her grandmother's bedside to launch into her father's open arms. "I shouldn't have left her."

"Whoa, wait." Barry gripped her biceps and held her away from him. "Do you think you could have prevented this? How, by sitting beside her bed and staring at her for hours to run and grab her at the first movement?" He shook his head and pressed his lips together. "She got out of bed for who knows what reason, and Paige was at her side in less than ten seconds when she fell. You couldn't have done any better than that."

"But—"

He dipped his chin and pinned her with a look Wyatt was grateful to not be on the receiving end of. "But nothing. Now, I'm going to go find Paige and the doctors and see what the hell is going on." With that, he kissed her forehead and turned to leave. He paused at the door before turning around to stick a hand out with a weary smile. "Good to see you back, Wyatt. Sorry we had to meet like this."

Wyatt shook the older man's hand with two firm pumps. "Nice to see you again, sir."

Gigi gripped the bedrail and stared at her grandmother. The woman turned her head to where Gigi and Wyatt stood and blinked three times. On the last blink, a smile spread across her face. "Oh, Wyatt, did you come to take Georgie out on a date?"

A strangled sound from Gigi met her question, but Wyatt ignored it and bent slightly over the rail to hold her grandmother's hand. "Yes, ma'am, I did."

Her silver head nodded, and her eyes slowly closed just as a low, barely discernible string of curses left Gigi's mouth.

Wyatt bent his head and put his mouth next to her ear. "Now you don't want your grandmother to hear you talking like that, do you, Angel?"

With one last look at her grandmother's now slumbering form, Gigi turned around and pinned him with a narrow stare. "I spend every day with her. The good ones and the bad ones and she can't remember who I am. You're back for five minutes and she's falling all over the Rhinestone Cowboy again."

He swallowed back the highly inappropriate laugh that wanted to escape, released the older woman's hand, and pulled Gigi to him again. "Sorry 'bout that, Angel."

She rolled her eyes and dropped her forehead on his chest. "I still hate you," she mumbled into the cotton.

This time a small chuckle broke free. "I know. I love you too."

***

Georgia

Georgia wasn't certain if the call from Ryan came at the perfect time or the perfectly wrong time as she sat in the waiting room for the doctor to emerge from the OR to update them on her grandmother. The distraction from the nauseatingly slow tick of the clock was welcome, but she feared the moment she left the room would be the exact one that the surgeon chose to come in.

By the time her phone vibrated for a third time, she finally made up her mind to answer and gave Wyatt's hand a squeeze before stepping into the hall. "Hey, Ryan, what did you find?"

"Holy hell, Georgia, this is a mess." His loud, nasal voice made her wince. "This guy has been getting fleeced for the past decade. I can't believe he never caught on."

Anger rose within her and pulled her spine into a perfectly straight line. "He trusted the people around him. That isn't a crime. Do you know who is behind Integrity Investments?"

She had a suspicion. From the first moment she began reviewing Wyatt's paperwork and statements and accounts, she had a gut instinct she knew exactly who it was, but she hadn't breathed a word, knowing the betrayal Wyatt was certain to feel if her suspicions were right. She needed proof and hoped Ryan would be able to give her that.

"James Adamson." Ryan spoke the name of the man she'd had in her sights from the beginning.

Her molars ground, and she peered through the glass just as the doctor walked in from the opposite direction. "Listen, Ryan, I owe you one for this. A big one, but I've got to go. Thanks."

She clicked off the line and stepped back into the waiting room just as Wyatt rose to his feet.

He held out a hand to bring her to his side. "I was just coming to get you."

Georgia managed a weak smile, her mind and heart being pulled in two vastly different directions. She turned to the doctor, clad in baby blue scrubs. "How did she do?"

Crinkles formed at the corners of the other man's eyes. "Better than many of my much younger patients.

She's in recovery, and as soon as she's stable, they're going to take her back to her room and you can meet her there." His face sobered. "But she's also eighty-two with a brand new hip. She's going to require in-patient physical therapy for a period of time and then some more once she's discharged home. With her mental status, this will require a great deal of care and time."

The doctor ran through a few more comments on the different facilities and physical therapists that he worked closely with before leaving them alone in the waiting room once more.

Georgia's father turned to her just as the door closed. "I can do mornings and we can get home healthcare to cover afternoons if you can manage the evenings so I can schedule clients and dinners." The flexibility that came along with her father owning his own modestly successful insurance agency had been a luxury both with her mother and grandmother. "I can take the time she's in rehab to move things around to set up a firmer schedule."

She nodded and ran her tongue along the roof of her mouth. Dates, meetings, and already scheduled commitments running through her mind. The majority were in the near enough future nothing would be impacted, but—

"I can help too."

So lost in her own thoughts she'd nearly forgotten his presence until his voice cut through the litany of things she mentally tallied. "That's not necessary. We have this covered."

As soon as she turned back to her father, Wyatt's hand closed around her shoulder, pivoting her back to face him. "I'm here and I want to help."

Her nostrils flared, and unexpected anger welled in her chest. She and her father had been doing just fine for the past year and half without the freaking Rhinestone Cowboy showing up with misplaced intentions, and they'd handle this setback just as well without him. She needed consistency and reliability, and those were words that weren't in Wyatt Carlisle's vocabulary, no matter how desperately she wished they were and no matter how much she wanted to take him up on the offer.

And the fact she couldn't only served to amplify the burning resentment racing along her veins.

Barry picked that moment to take a step back from Wyatt and Georgia, his eyes darting back and forth between them. "I'm going down to the cafeteria to get a bite to eat. Want anything?"

Georgia folded her arms across her aching chest and shook her head. "No thanks, Dad. I'm good."

"Yeah, me too." Wyatt's brow furrowed, but his lips stayed pressed firmly together until the door shut behind her father's back. "What the hell, Gigi? I'm trying to be here for you. I'm trying to prove that I'm not going anywhere and I can handle…whatever you need. I know I screwed up, and I've apologized in ten different ways, but I can't show you that you can trust me if you won't give me the chance."

"I'm done giving chances." She held both hands up, palms facing him. "I gave you a chance when I was eighteen, and you walked away. The first man I managed to trust enough to have a relationship with longer than six months decided that hiding a wife and kids from me was a good idea until two weeks after he proposed, when I needed his support when Gram was diagnosed."

She ran her fingers through her hair and paced in front of the row of linked chairs in the thankfully empty waiting room. "And just when I start letting you back in, you did it again."

His face turned to a sickly shade of green. "Did what again?"

Georgia ran her tongue along her suddenly parched lips and allowed all the hurt and anger she'd bottled up for a dozen years to pour out. "You took me away from my responsibilities and my family to spend time with you. You made everything all about you, and because I wasn't there, Gram fell and needed surgery. Just like you did with my mom."

The corners of her eyes burned with unshed tears. "By the way, it was your manager, Jim. He embezzled hundreds of thousands from you. You need a good attorney."

His jaw dropped, but she pushed past him, fleeing the room and the building before he could say a word. Her fingers flew across the glass screen of her smartphone as she descended to the ground floor in the elevator. Within seconds, Paige responded to her plea with confirmation she'd pick her up in five minutes.

She stood on the far side of the hospital waiting for her best friend and hiding from the view of the front entrance so Wyatt couldn't spot her on his way out. She didn't have time in her life for a part-time boyfriend or strength in her heart to recover if he disappeared again.

Chapter Twenty-Six

Wyatt

Twelve Years Earlier

Her lids had only been shut for a precious few moments when the doorbell chimed again and she jumped beneath his arm. Another condolence. Another offer of help. Another casserole. The table overflowed with them. Southern manners at their shining best. Gigi's grandmother flitted about the kitchen, looking for containers and muttering about not having enough room to store the plethora of food, all in between crying jags. His heart ached for the family he'd come to love almost as much as his own, but he focused all his attention on the one nestled against his ribcage.

Gigi blinked up at him, her hazel eyes clouded with confusion briefly before reality sank in once more. He hated seeing her remember over and over the loss that

244

shook her world. "It's okay, you can go back to sleep Just more food."

Her chin quivered, and she leaned impossibly closer to his side on the sofa. "I don't think I can sleep anymore."

In any other scenario, he would have rolled his eyes. At any other time, he would have told her that fifteen-minute cat naps didn't constitute sleep. But he banked every drop of his swagger and somewhat pushy personality. "Then how about you try to eat something?"

"I'm not hungry."

Wyatt pressed his lips to her forehead. "I didn't ask if you were hungry. I said you should try to eat something."

In the slightly more than twenty-four hours since her mother passed, she'd eaten exactly ten crackers, a third of a bowl of cereal, and one chocolate chip cookie. He'd been counting. Even though grief was clouding her brain and distracting her from anything but the all-consuming pain, his mind was in laser-sharp focus, and he took it as his personal duty to make sure she was as taken care of as possible.

He stood and held out a hand, helping her to her feet. She stood in front of him with dark rims beneath her lids and pale cheeks that were naturally far too close to the pasty color she normally applied.

His arms wound around her waist, and he dropped his forehead to rest against hers. "Please, Angel. Something little, but you need to eat something."

She sighed and closed her eyes. "Fine."

It was a small victory, but one he'd gladly take. He led her to the kitchen and pulled out a chair for her before dancing around her still grumbly and weepy grandmother to warm up a bowl of the beef vegetable soup his mother had sent with him on his brief return home for a quick shower and change before rejoining Gigi.

Both his parents had been less than thrilled with the amount of time their second eldest had spent away from home, especially the nights, but assurances from both Gigi's father and Wyatt himself that they were well monitored and never really alone allowed him a privilege he was grateful for. The chance to take care of his girlfriend.

He set the bowl down in front of her and held a spoon out. "We'll start here."

She pursed her lips and gave him a half-hearted glare before taking the proffered utensil and lifting a spoonful of the hearty soup to her mouth. Wyatt plopped down in a seat beside her and grinned when a small, expected moan escaped her mouth. His mother was a damn good cook.

"This…this is pretty good."

He chuckled as she downed several more bites in rapid succession. Within a few minutes, she tossed her spoon into the empty bowl. She sat back in the chair and folded her hands across her abdomen.

Wyatt quirked a brow. "Dessert?"

She shook her head slowly. "No, I…" Her words trailed off as fresh tears filled her eyes. "Isn't this wrong?"

He reached forward and pulled her hands apart, lacing his fingers through hers. "Isn't what wrong, Angel?"

A fat drop trailed down her cheek. "Being happy.

Enjoying food. Enjoying…anything."

The deep crack his heart carried since he witnessed her unravelling at the news of her mother's passing widened with the statement. He cursed his brain for not having the right answer immediately. Or at all. "I don't know." The truth was all he had. "I've never lost anyone as close to me as you were to your mom. I don't know what's right and what's wrong. But I know your mom loved you, and I'm pretty sure she'd want you to take care of yourself."

She blinked, and he held his breath. Finally she nodded. "Maybe another chocolate chip cookie."

***

Georgia

Empty.
Hollow.
Broken.

Georgia stared sightlessly as the gleaming cherry surface was lowered into the nearly perfect rectangle carved into the dark soil. Her father sat beside her, silent tears streaking down his face. Beside him, her grandfather held her much more vocal grandmother, whose loud sobs echoed through the valley and lanced through Georgia's no longer beating heart.

Dead. She might as well be lying in the coffin beside her mother because she certainly couldn't survive this.

A warm hand encircled hers and drew her attention to the abnormally hat-free head of her boyfriend. She blinked three times. He had been present every day since the call. Unwavering in his support and tender care of her. Their barbs traded for silence, tears, and sleepless nights spent curled around each other with the surprising blessing of her father.

As long as they remained uncomfortably ensconced on the sofa in the living room. A communal room his own grief-induced insomnia often pulled him toward at unspeakable hours.

His eyes lifted from their joined hands and penetrated the dam she'd erected to make it through the day without succumbing to another headache manifested from the countless tears she'd cried. Love and compassion poured from his gaze and shattered the final wall of her resistance. Her entire body shook from the consuming sobs, and she melted into his waiting embrace.

The voice of the minister performing the final portion of the service fell on deaf ears as Georgia allowed her stupid freaking cowboy to shoulder her pain. When they stood to leave, her knees buckled, and she crumpled against him.

Without a moment's hesitation, he hooked an arm beneath her legs and scooped her up, holding her tightly to his chest. The dark cloud of grief held her in an alternate reality, suspended from any awareness of the activity swirling around her. By the time the fog lifted enough for her to find some consciousness of her surroundings, she was sitting squarely on Wyatt's lap in her backyard, Roxy and Roscoe obediently at his feet.

A new emotion overcame her as she looked in his face, and she trembled with its ferocity.

Wyatt pushed a wet strand of hair back from her

face. "Can I get you something, Angel?"

Her molars ground together, and thick, violent rage coursed through her veins. "This is your fault."

His brows knitted together beneath that stupid hat he once again had planted on his head. "What'd you say?"

Georgia jumped off his lap, her breaths coming in short, shallow gasps. "I said," she ground the words out from between clenched teeth, "that this is all your fault."

The color drained from his face, and for a brief moment, hurt flickered in his sapphire depths. His lids closed, and when they opened, the understanding and patience had returned to his steady gaze. "You're not thinking logically right now. I know that deep down you don't mean this."

A mirthless laugh strangled her throat. "Just because my mother is d—" The single word caught in her throat, as if speaking it would somehow make this all more real. "Just because my mother is gone, you think I'm being irrational and ridiculous? Try again, Cowboy."

He stood, and the dogs did with him, nervous glances from the canines darting between them before they both wisely loped away.

"I didn't give your mom cancer. I didn't tell her to stop her treatments. I didn't move you here, even though I am damn glad you did because I can't imagine my life without you." His voice rose with every sentence. He put his hands on his hips and paused, taking a deep breath. "How exactly is this my fault?"

Georgia's eyes narrowed into slits. "I wasn't here

because of you. If your Rhinestone Cowboy persona hadn't taken over and forced your lifestyle on me, I would have been here. I would have held her hand and told her I loved her and had five freaking more minutes with her."

His shoulders dropped, and his head hung down. The ache Georgia had been certain couldn't get any worse after her father called amplified to an impossible degree as her words hit him with the force she'd intended.

But once they started coming out, she couldn't stop them. "You needed fresh meat to fawn all over you at your practice. You needed a new pet project, so you insisted I come to your house so you could teach me to ride." Her finger collided with his solid pec, punctuating each damning statement. "You took over every aspect of my life and disguised it as care and concern for my wellbeing when it was really all about you growing your fan club, wasn't it?"

His jaw clenched and unclenched several times in rapid succession, but he remained silent, not even breathing a refute to her accusations.

"Why don't you just do all of us a favor and get the hell away from my house and out of my life?"

She sprinted through the sliding glass door, past the table overflowing with casserole dishes and baked goods, and didn't stop until she was safely barricaded in her room. Only then did the vicious, cruel words register. Only then did she cover her mouth, appalled at what she'd said. Only then did she allow herself to hate the person she'd just been to the boy who had seen past her prickly exterior to identify her need and attempt to meet it.

And she'd just exiled him from her life.

Two losses within a few days, one completely and wholly on her.

Chapter Twenty-Seven

Wyatt

Present Day

The bright summer sun reflected off the hood of his truck, nearly blinding him even with the barrier of his dark sunglasses firmly in place. The one-story brick building in front of him was barely visible with the light glaring at him, but clear enough to clench his stomach with dread.

Wyatt closed his eyes and called up the same mental images he would conjure to settle himself before taking hold of a bull. The same ones that calmed him, centered him, brought his focus to laser-sharp precision.

Gigi. A filmstrip of her smile, her laugh, her kisses, her touches all played on a familiar loop through his mind. This time the addition of all-grown-up Gigi with her curves, delicate skin, and ability to play his body like a finely tuned instrument added to the high school memories he'd clung to for so many years. The anger he knew he deserved, but it still cut him like a knife. All too soon followed the happy thoughts and was just as quickly banished to the back of his mind.

With a deep breath, he forced his legs into motion and exited his truck. No sooner had his hand landed on the curved silver handle to the law office than a familiar voice hit his ears.

"Damn. You're on time."

Wyatt's head fell back, and he sighed. "Really, Tanner? Can't even trust me to talk to an attorney by myself? Listen. I kinda have a vested interest in not screwing this up, unlike everything else, so you don't need to babysit the Carlisle family asshole today." His hands rested on his denim-clad hips, and he turned to the left to face his older brother. "Don't you have to go cuddle up with my smokin' hot sister-in-law?"

The audible growl from Tanner was almost amusing enough to distract him from the reemergence of knots in his stomach.

"First, you have your own damn girl." Tanner planted his feet wide, and he folded his arms across his chest. "Second, where the hell did you ever get the idea that you're some sort of outcast in our family?"

Wyatt clenched his jaw tightly. This wasn't the time to rehash the myriad of screw-ups that led to that belief—or the fact that he technically didn't have a girl or a damn thing else—as well as the issue facing him now. "It's been pretty clear from day one. I've never measured up to my perfect older brother. Now, if you don't mind, I need to go figure out what my legal options are to try to save my business."

Tanner pulled his forearm back just as Wyatt tried to open the door again. "No, first we're going to handle this once and for all." He dragged his brother to the side as a woman in her forties slipped past them to enter the building.

Not before she tossed Wyatt an appreciative smile and wink. Years of buckle bunnies flirting, suggesting, and sometimes outright demanding his attention and affection had left him numb to almost any non-Gigi female.

"I don't have time for—"

The older man's palm collided with the brick wall to their left and cut off the rest of his words. Wyatt's eyes widened at the uncharacteristic outburst.

"You are damn sure going to make time, little brother." Identical sapphire eyes blazed with a fire Wyatt hadn't seen from his always composed and structured older sibling. "Mom and Dad have never compared us. They never asked you to change, and hell, they supported every single one of your dreams even when they worried you'd kill yourself."

Memories from his childhood and adolescence trickled through his mind. His dad taking him to training damn near every day of the week without fail. Or complaint. His mother packing a second lunch to make sure he was well fed before he got his ass handed to him by some imposing beast.

His brother had a point, but...

"They also made sure every single one of their friends knew when you landed the scholarship that was only awarded to one kid a year. And when you took Wake Forest to the championships. And when you got into grad school." The arrogance Wyatt wrapped around himself to act as a barrier from the self-doubt began to slip. "Academics, sports, business, hell, even Izzy. Everything you do is perfect. You take care of everyone and do everything right."

Silence descended between the two men, and Wyatt's gaze dropped to the toe of his well-worn boots, stabbing against the concrete sidewalk.

"Damn, we need to get you and Georgia on the baby-making wagon soon."

Tanner's amused chuckle snapped Wyatt's head up. "What the hell are you talking about?"

"When you have kids, you'll understand how hard it is to balance everything, but you have to know that they're so proud of you." Tanner shook his head. "They would host parties with all their friends when your competitions were on TV. You know damn well they would crisscross the country to follow you and attend at least half a dozen rodeos a year.

"Wyatt, they are proud of you. I am proud of you. The whole damn family is proud of you. You struck out on your own and made a path for yourself. Just because that's different from me doesn't make it bad and it doesn't make you a disappointment." Closing the distance between them, Tanner awkwardly put his arms around his brother and pulled him in for the kind of hard, brief embrace men had perfected. "And I swear if you tell anyone that I said any of this or that I hugged you, I will deny it about zero point three seconds before I kick your ass."

Wyatt laughed and shoved the other man away. A weight he never really acknowledged lifted. "Deal. Now get the hell out of here and let me save my business." He threw Tanner a wink, unwilling to let the heavy emotion linger. "And tell my hot sister-in-law I said hi."

Three hours, countless pieces of paper, and one highly motivated attorney later, Wyatt found himself wandering down the sidewalk in front of the various businesses and shops. A small blossom of hope began to stir in his chest, and sitting still wasn't an option.

His family loved him and was proud of him. Somehow hearing that from Tanner meant more than all the assurances his parents would certainly offer if they knew how he'd always felt.

His business wasn't safe yet, but together with the attorney they were creating a plan.

And even if Gigi was mad right now, they would get through this. Failure wasn't in his vocabulary. He would prove to her that she could trust him. That started by not going anywhere. Even if she thought that's what she wanted.

Being a pushy asshole was something he was good at. He'd spent too many years creating this mess by staying away to give up after just a few weeks.

Sunlight reflected off a glittering diamond in one of the storefront windows and drew his attention away from the thoughts swirling in his head. A princess-cut center stone flanked on either side by onyx set into a platinum band.

The perfect engagement ring for a Dark Angel.

He bit the inside of his cheek and hesitated for a moment before going inside. It was a risk that could easily backfire, but he damn sure had to try.

***

Georgia

"Did you see that? That was nine seconds on the meanest bull at that event." The deep and largely fake Southern drawl hit her ears before she saw him. "Now, really I only needed eight seconds to win, but...why not show those boys how the real champ does it?"

His laughter mixed with a softer, lighter one, and Georgia blinked as she crossed the threshold into her grandmother's room at the rehabilitation facility. Nearly a week there and, aside from a rough start, the older woman was progressing well enough a meeting had been scheduled for the following day to set up a discharge plan.

Wyatt sat in a chair beside Gram with his tablet in one hand and pointing at the screen with the other, obnoxious cheers coming from the device's speaker. "Now this one wasn't quite as pretty—"

"What the hell are you doing here?" She put a hand on her black pencil skirt-clad hip and pinned him with a glare. Stubborn, arrogant, and pushy. Why did he insist on continuing to be so freaking pushy?

Light sparkled in the older woman's eyes, and she held a hand out to her granddaughter. "Georgie, Wyatt was just showing me some movies from his training. He's going to be quite the professional one day."

He shrugged as Georgia crossed the room and perched on the bed on the opposite side of her grandmother's chair. "She thinks I'm still seventeen." He threw Georgia a wink. "Hell, some days I still think so too."

Her teeth sank into the sensitive flesh of her tongue

until the coppery taste of blood trickled out. If her grandmother hadn't been present...

Instead of the verbal beating he so richly deserved, she smiled and patted Gram's hand. "Yes, he is going to be...something."

Warmth filled her eyes as she looked back and forth between Georgia and Wyatt. "Don't you two listen to anyone who tells you that you can't find the person you're meant to be with when you're young. Why, I met your grandpa when I was just fourteen, and we've been married for fifty-five years now."

A fresh slice of pain lanced through Georgia's heart at the reminder her grandmother lived in the past. This year would have marked their sixty-first wedding anniversary in September if Gramps hadn't passed six years earlier.

She'd long ago learned to stop correcting the older woman and allow her to stay wrapped in the happiness of the past that enveloped her. Even when she confused Georgia with her mother and even when it took another piece of her heart.

The stupid freaking cowboy could never take a hint and grinned at her grandmother's words. "Gram, you are a genius. I keep tellin' Gigi not to listen to any negative Nellies." He winked up at her. "We were meant to be different."

Georgia pressed her lips together and took three long, deep breaths, hoping to calm herself to retain the false shroud of serenity and happiness she presented to her grandmother. With a far brighter smile than she felt, she stood. "I'll keep that in mind, Gram. I just need to talk to Wyatt for one second, but I promise we'll be right back."

Fake grin firmly in place, she all but dragged Wyatt from the room, down the hall, and around the corner where they had a measure of privacy. "I am going to ask one more time, what the hell are you doing here?"

"Visiting Gram. Are you tired? Sick? I mean I woulda thought that answer was pretty obvious there, Gigi."

Cocky, arrogant, son of a—

What was it Tanner's wife did? Teach yoga? Maybe she'd need that to exorcise some of the stress Wyatt created at the base of her skull. "Why?" It was a demand more than a question.

Some of the confidence drained from his face as his entire countenance softened. He reached a hand up but held it a breath away from her cheek before dropping it at his side. "I told you I wasn't going anywhere. I love you, and you can trust me." He stared at her for exactly five heavy thumps of her heart. "I learned my lesson, and I'll never screw up that badly again. You can trust me." He emphasized every syllable of the final four words he repeated.

The stupid freaking cowboy left her speechless and locked in a familiar war between logic and love, common sense and aching longing.

"But I'm also going to respect your space, so I'll go say goodbye to Gram now, but I'm not bailing."

He turned on his heel and walked away, taking half of the wall she'd valiantly tried to build to keep him out with him.

Chapter Twenty-Eight

Wyatt

Twelve Years Earlier

She didn't mean it.

It was a familiar refrain Wyatt had been trying to soothe his battered heart with after Gigi laid into him about all the things he'd done wrong. There wasn't a bull he'd encountered who could drop him as fast as a few choice words from his hurting Angel.

He'd done every bit of that for her. How could she possibly think otherwise? Okay, there may have been a slightly selfish component, because Gigi was beautiful always, but when she smiled? Damn. That was stunning. And her laugh could fix any part of him that ached.

Wyatt shook his head, flicked his turn signal on, and flew up his driveway. He'd certainly get a lecture about his speed if either of his parents or nosy younger siblings caught him, but he didn't care. He was on a mission.

His foot had just touched the landing at the top of the stairs, only a few steps from his bedroom door, when his father's voice brought every muscle to a halt. "What are you doing, son?"

The wooden railing bit into his palm as he tightened his grip. "Just getting changed and then heading back to Gigi's." He winced and turned, regarding his father over his shoulder. "If that's okay."

Mike Carlisle stood in silence for a moment, every bit the classic father, holding a coffee cup in one hand. "How is she?"

Hurt. No, exhausted. No, broken into a million shards of splintered glass that Wyatt had no idea how to put back together. But he damn sure was bent on trying. "Not good. I don't think I should leave her for too long just yet."

He left out the part of her kicking him out and screaming in his face and telling him she basically never wanted to see him again.

She didn't mean it. He had to believe that.

"I want to tell you that you two are far too serious for a couple of high school kids. Especially considering the fact that you plan on leaving right after graduation to start your career and travel all the time…"

Anticipation twitched Wyatt's toes. He needed to get back to Gigi. "I feel like there's a but there."

Matching blue eyes locked on his. "But then I remember how I met your mom, and I see how much you love this girl and how she has changed you." He

261

took a long sip of his coffee then lifted his chin. "Go take care of her and let me know if you need anything."

Without any further comments, Mike turned back into the living room, but the brief conversation played on repeat in Wyatt's mind. He'd never been as good as Tanner. He wasn't as smart and he didn't have that damned golden touch, but in this moment a new appreciation for his family, even if he was certain they didn't understand him, washed over him.

The lingering warmth stayed with him as he drove the five short miles back to Gigi's. His stomach clenched as he parked, but the need to be present, even if mildly unwelcome, overwhelmed his...self. Wyatt knew he could be a cocky bastard, but when it came to Gigi, he was firmly and happily in the backseat to what she needed.

Barry Marsh's pale, hollow face greeted him at the door with a vacant smile. "She won't talk to me."

The fracture in Wyatt's heart deepened. Gigi had a habit of making sure her grandparents and father were okay before dealing with anything herself. The knowledge that she was shutting everyone out wasn't encouraging.

He positioned himself in the same place he'd been before, seated on the floor outside her bedroom door. This time he thought ahead and grabbed a pillow off the couch to cushion his backside, even though all the throws he'd survived should have made him impervious to the uncomfortable hardwood floor.

Just before he took his seat, he'd knocked and let her know he was there. He tilted his hat over his eyes, absentmindedly stroked behind Roxy's left ear, and waited. Even though it may kill him. Not the waiting, he'd wait forever. The distance between them. Not being able to hold her in his arms.

Rustling behind the door snapped him out of a sleep he hadn't realized he'd fallen into, and he stood, ear pressed to the door.

"Wyatt?" Her voice was soft and completely devoid of all anger.

He lifted a hand, holding it against the wooden plank separating them, hoping she could feel him. "Yeah?"

In less than the space of a heartbeat, her door flung open and she launched herself into his arms. Sobs wracked her body as her arms and legs tightened around him to a suffocating level he'd never been more grateful for. "I'm s-s-sorry. I'm so sorry."

Wyatt stroked a hand down the length of her auburn hair. Wordlessly, he carried her back out to the garden, the place he knew she'd find some measure of peace. The echoing clacks from Roxy and Roscoe's nails followed behind. "Shh, Angel. None of that."

Tears soaked the shoulder of his shirt. The heat from the June sun created sticky trails down his spine. None of that mattered as long as he could hold her.

"I love you. I shouldn't have said any of that to you. You've done more for me than anyone and—"

Another gut-wrenching wail swallowed her next words, and Wyatt tightened his grip in response. "Just listen right now, Angel. There is nothing you can say to make me stop loving you. Nothing will ever happen that can make me stop loving you. You stole my heart, and I'm really okay with never getting it back."

***

Georgia

Georgia's eyes fell on the bare space of the floor that would normally be occupied with a brightly lit, colorfully decorated fir tree.

Her grandfather hadn't suggested taking a trip to the Christmas tree farm.

Her grandmother had set a small tree in the center of the dining room table and extoled the virtues of the minute nod to the holiday rather than the typical excessiveness she embraced.

And her father barely strung two words together.

She went along with her grandfather's change in subject anytime Christmas was broached. She agreed with her grandmother even when she was screaming inside that she wanted the little slice of normalcy of the season. She focused on making sure her father ate and drank and continued breathing.

But now it was Christmas Eve and her fractured heart wanted some trapping of the holiday, anything. A wreath, a stocking, hell mistletoe would make her damn near giddy. She wiggled her toes in the ebony tights covering her feet and legs. A crazy desire for the goth girl to want a little holly jolly in her life, but the hunger was there, begging to be fed.

A thundering knock on the door pulled her out of the dark place she only dared share with Wyatt. Before she could get to her feet to answer, it burst open, and a scraggly tree that barely reached his shoulder stood in front of the very boy she'd been thinking of. The one who carried her every burden and dried her every tear.

"Wyatt? What the hell is that?"

A gasp and rustling behind her barely proceeded a clacking tongue. "Georgia Leigh Marsh, watch your tongue…" The words died on her grandmother's lips as the older woman rounded the corner from the kitchen. "Oh my."

Her stupid freaking cowboy tipped the brim of his tan Stetson adorned with a ridiculous red Santa hat on top of it. "Evenin', ma'am. There was this little elf that mentioned you hadn't had much luck finding a tree, so the big guy at the Pole sent me to remedy that situation."

He threw a wink at Georgia as he charmed the pants, and a layer of sadness, off her grandmother. Laughter mingled with tears as the older woman kissed Wyatt's cheek. Her father and grandfather filed in and stopped dead in their tracks at the periphery of the room.

Georgia clamped down on her lower lip, half expecting one or both to demand the exit of any decorations—other than the two-foot tabletop tree that hinted at the holiday—from the house. Or for both of them to turn on their heels and leave in a wake of anguished silence, more on par for their norm.

Her father's gaze darted from her to Wyatt seconds before he embraced her boyfriend in an emotional hug. His whispered, "Thank you," barely reached her, but it managed to stitch another piece of her broken heart together.

Within minutes, the tree was secured in the stand, and everyone began pulling boxes down from the attic, stringing lights and hanging ornaments while her grandmother stirred hot cocoa in a pot on the stove.

They sat on the couch, sipping the warm drink as her father and grandfather debated white versus colored lights and the first spark of life flickered in two of the men she loved the most. All because of the third.

As if he knew she was thinking of him, he leaned in, nuzzling against her ear. "Think I'd be able to steal you away for a little while? I have something that's just for you."

"I think the Rhinestone Cowboy could ask for the moon and the only debate would be which one of my family members would be pulling it to earth for you."

His deep chuckle vibrated her side where they touched. As expected, her request to take a walk with Wyatt was quickly approved as the sudden resurgence of Christmas overtook her household.

"Where are we going, anyway, Cowboy?" She hadn't thought to ask until after she'd collected her coat and they stood on her front step.

Wyatt grinned at her, his broad, blindingly white grin unnerving every part of her. "To our spot, of course."

He didn't need to elaborate further. Her chest burned with the gratitude and overwhelming emotion as they entered the park and walked along the path to the bench, bathed in the same twinkling lights it had been last year.

She turned in to his waiting embrace, melding her body against his, laying her cheek on his chest. "Is this going to become a tradition, Cowboy? Most people do things like gingerbread houses or bake Christmas cookies, ya know, not decorate a park. Simple things.

Normal things."

Wyatt dropped a kiss on her nose before leading her to the bench. "We aren't most people, Angel. We were made to be different. Think about it. Who would ever dream a rhinestone cowboy and a dark angel could possibly be meant to be? And yet...here we are."

Words were impossible in light of his declaration. Every bit of it was true. They made no sense, but despite everything that should indicate they couldn't possibly work, they just did.

His hands gripped her, and she noticed for the first time the slight tremble. "I love you, Angel. And even though we're young, I know I will never love another girl the way I love you. And...dammit, I don't want to. You are it for me."

He released her, digging in his front pocket, and pulled out a small, square white box. When she gasped, he quickly started shaking his head. "No, it's not—I mean, one day it will be, but this isn't—" He sighed and cleared his throat, lifting the lid. "What I'm trying to say is this isn't an engagement ring. I love you more than I ever dreamed possible, but even I know better than that."

She lightly punched his shoulder, desperately needing to add some levity to the situation. "Damn straight you do."

He slid the silver band, adorned with two small, connected hearts in each of their birthstones, a ruby for Georgia and a sapphire for Wyatt. "Good to hear you know what this isn't, but what this is is a promise. A promise that I will always love you. A promise that I will always put your needs before my own. A promise that I will try my best to be the kind of man who deserves you."

Never before had anyone said anything so profound, so meaningful to her.

"Gigi, I want you to wear this to remind you of every one of those promises as well as a seal of all the promises to come. Because I want you in my life today, tomorrow, and forever with every high and low that will bring."

How he expected her to think, much less speak, she had no idea. She simply nodded and wrapped her arms around his neck, climbing into his lap and getting as close to him as possible without...

Her lips found his, and the thought took hold of her brain and body at the same time. She twisted in his lap until she straddled his thighs, grinding into him. He groaned against her mouth, and she slid her tongue inside, her hands tugging up the flannel shirt under his open coat and diving beneath, desperate to touch his skin.

Their bodies rocked in time with each other in slow, symphonic movements, fingers stealing beneath clothes, finding tender, sensitive places. His mouth left hers to trail down her neck, sucking lightly at the base where her pulse throbbed.

"Please," the word escaped her mouth on a sob. "Please, Wyatt. I promise I am ready and I love you and...oh hell, please."

His shallow breathing echoed hers, and she wanted to scream out her frustration at the shake of his head. "And I love you too, Angel. Too damn much to let our first time be here like this. Too much to allow it to be anything rushed." His fingers tangled in her hair.

"When it's right, it will be right in every way."

She groaned and dropped her forehead against his shoulder. "I hate the fact that you insist on everything being perfect and the fact that it makes me love you even more."

Wyatt laughed and pressed his lips to her temple before setting her back and helping her stand. "Now there's a first. I usually nail the role of Carlisle family asshole pretty well."

Georgia stopped on the path out of the park and cupped his face between her palms. "Wyatt, that's a title you created. No one believes that. Not anyone in your family, your adoring fan club," she rolled her eyes, "and certainly not me."

He stared at her for the space of a dozen heartbeats before devouring her mouth in a needy, passionate, desperate kiss. One she was certain she'd remember for the rest of her life.

Chapter Twenty-Nine

Wyatt

Present Day

He scrubbed a hand over his clean-shaven jaw and ran through the list in his mind again as he slowly buttoned his shirt. The first thing he had done was make sure he had furniture. At least the minimum, round table, two chairs, and a couch. A massive TV was mounted on the wall above the fireplace and was far bigger than he needed, but it was his one indulgence.

Well, the TV and the bed.

That was the one piece of furniture where he didn't opt for the cheapest model in the showroom. He did his damndest to pick out one that was similar to the ivory tufted headboard she had at her house, only the next line up with a luxurious mattress and decadent bedding in a shockingly warm teal pattern.

At least that's what the saleswoman at the store had told him. The only thing Wyatt saw when he turned to smooth his hand over the rich material was Gigi tangled in the sheets.

He closed his eyes and took a deep breath. Every day for the past two weeks, he'd arranged with her father to take over the afternoon shift with Gram instead of the home health nurse. He joked with Barry that it was his way of paying him back for working with Wyatt's own insurance agent in filing the necessary claims to rebuild his finances in the wake of the embezzlement issues while he waited on the law to catch up.

Today he would take the same shift he always did, but with one notable exception. Tonight Paige and Barry had both agreed to take the night shift when Gigi got home. Tonight he was going to remind her of the same thing he told her when they were teenagers; it's okay to have something for herself. He patted the bulging right front pocket of his jeans with a slightly shaky hand. Tonight…was everything.

The house was in perfect order. His gaze swept over the living room to make sure he'd stashed his work boots away and cleaned up any mud trails they'd left behind. The lingering scent of the freshly laid wooden floors and final coat of paint had dissipated to a much more tolerable trace than it had been earlier this week.

He climbed into his truck, slid on his dark sunglasses, and threw it into drive. Everything was falling into place despite the hiccups and bumps in the road. He snorted. Jim, the damned rat. His fingers absently traced the circle in his pocket as he drove. Even thoughts of his lying, stealing, manipulative former manager couldn't erase the hope burning in his chest.

Wyatt eased his truck along the curb in front of Gigi's house and took a deep breath and knocked twice before letting himself in. Something he would have never dreamed of when he was a teenager, but something Barry had insisted on when Wyatt took his own place on the rotating shift of caregivers for Gigi's grandmother.

The two men exchanged a brief hello, and Barry updated Wyatt on how the morning had gone and let him know that Gram was taking a nap after her physical therapy. He grabbed his laptop case and headed for the door. "I have two meetings, but Paige is going to be here by five just in case I'm running late."

Wyatt's lips twitched. "That's perfect, sir, thank you."

The older man lifted his brows. "Son, I think it's high time you start calling me Barry."

He laughed and nodded at Gigi's father. Wyatt still called his own dad "sir" and couldn't see that ever changing for either man. "So noted."

The afternoon passed at a snail's pace. Or so he thought because he was certain when he checked the clock five minutes ago it was only three when Paige burst through the door, completely out of breath. "Georgie. Early. Right behind me."

Wyatt laughed and leaned over to give Gram a peck on the cheek before he stood. A gesture she seemed completely impervious to as her eyes stayed fixed straight ahead on the game show playing on TV. Some days were good, some days not so much, but Wyatt was grateful he had a chance to be here for them all. "She has to ruin all my plans."

Paige winked and pushed him toward the door. "Not if you haul that jeans model ass of yours out there. Scoot!"

He rolled his eyes but did as he was told and reveled in the start he gave Gigi when he met her on the front porch.

Her eyes moved from his head to his toes and back again. "Going somewhere, Cowboy?"

"Yep." He tipped the brim of his ever-present hat and held his arm out. "And you're coming with me."

Gigi's face paled, and she shook her head, taking one step back from him, her high heels sinking into the dirt of the front lawn and causing her to curse. "I-I can't, Wyatt. Gram needs me."

He took two steps forward and cradled her face in his hands. "Is there ever gonna be a day where you just say, 'Sure, Wyatt, let's do whatever you want' without fighting me? I'll wait for it. Just give me a date to look forward to."

A smile curled the corners of her glossy red lips, and her mouth parted slightly. Wyatt groaned from the temptation. The entire time he'd spent helping to care for her grandmother, he never once tried to kiss her or touch her, needing to prove he wanted more than just the sex she initially offered.

The inappropriate comments, however, tended to sprinkle many of their interactions.

"Paige is with Gram, and your dad is going to be home soon too. I promise she's fine." He winked. "I covered her in bubble wrap myself."

Her palms fell on the front of his shirt, and she nodded. "Sure, Wyatt, let's do whatever you want."

***

Georgia

"Are you taking me riding, Cowboy?" she playfully teased Wyatt as they pulled alongside the barn.

His brows drew together, and he threw her a bored look. "You ought to know better than to expect a repeat of anything from me by now, Angel." He winked. "Or at least not in the last decade or so." With that, he leapt from the truck, rounded the hood, and opened her door, holding one hand out to her. "Ready, Gigi?"

The two words sounded benign to anyone else, but to Georgia they carried a heavy weight. She'd lain in bed every night this week, eluded by sleep and consumed with thoughts of Wyatt. He'd been better than his word. Not only had he unfailingly shown up daily and seamlessly slid into the role of co-caregiver with Georgia, Barry, and Paige, he'd done so with no fanfare, no arrogance, and without laying a freaking hand on her.

That last point was up for debate on whether she appreciated it or hated it.

Never once had he had other plans; never once had he been late. He'd been there. Exactly as he promised.

Paige was right, he wasn't Bruce. And he wasn't even the Wyatt that had left, even though that boy would always own a large part of her heart.

He was the man who proved himself reliable and trustworthy. And completely deserving of a second chance. A decision she hadn't told him, but one she'd made nonetheless. One she had every intention of telling him tonight until he managed to unwittingly highjack her plans.

She pressed her hand into his and slid from the truck. "I'm more than ready."

Instead of taking her inside the barn, he led her around to the far corner where they stopped. He produced a blindfold out of his back pocket. "Trust me?"

Without a single doubt or moment's hesitation, she breathed out her response. "Yes."

He gingerly placed the material over her eyes and held both her hands in his as they rounded the corner, walked along the side, and turned to the back.

Every molecule of air disappeared from her lungs when he removed the blindfold. A large rectangle was created from railroad ties, and the entire space inside was filled with sand. Two large palm trees were planted at the far corners, and wooden Adirondack chairs sat between them.

His arms wrapped around her from behind. "You give up so much for those you love and do it without a second thought. I want you to have a piece of somewhere you love here, and I want this to be your home."

He turned her to face him within the space of his arms. "And more than anything, I want to be the one person you count on when everything around you is crazy." Wyatt leaned down and pressed his forehead to hers. "I haven't always made the best decisions, Angel, but this time I choose to stand by your side and never leave. I choose us."

Wyatt kissed each wet cheek, and his hands fell from hers to dig in his pocket. He dropped to one knee and held out a breathtaking onyx and diamond ring. "I don't deserve a second chance, but if you can find it in your heart to give me one, I promise I'll spend the rest of my life earning it."

Breathing was difficult, and words were impossible. His actions over the past several weeks had slowly stitched her heart back together in ways she hadn't realized until this moment. Until it beat so strongly for him, speaking his name with every thump against her ribcage.

"Georgia Lee Marsh, will you marry me?"

Chapter Thirty

Wyatt

Twelve Years Earlier

Wyatt read the text for the fifth time.

Gigi: I want to visit my mom, but I don't want to go alone.

He answered the only possible response.

Wyatt: When?

Not once in the months since her mother had passed had Gigi expressed the slightest interest in visiting her mother's grave. Her grandmother practically lived there, going every day and spending at least three hours with her only child, even in the bitter cold of February. Wyatt suspected that was a factor in Gigi's decision to ignore the entire concept.

But what did he know? He'd led a charmed, damn

near perfect life compared to the agony his Dark Angel dealt with for far too many years. The closest loss of his life had been an uncle, three years earlier, from a tragic accident. Shock had settled into grief that dipped into an awkward ache at the sight of his mother cradling his aunt closely, offering comfort despite her own pain of losing her only brother.

His alert dinged again, pulling him back to the reality of helping his girlfriend navigate the choppy water of grief as best she could.

Gigi: Today. Now. Will you go with me?

The last thing she needed to do was ask. There was zero chance he'd be anywhere other than holding her hand, holding her, as she took this momentous step toward finding a new normal in the wake of the overwhelming loss.

Wyatt blinked slowly three times when Georgia opened the front door, her face stripped of the pale foundation and dark kohl eyeliner. The black lipstick traded for a pale gloss. Her clothing of choice still a nod to the goth girl that owned his heart with black sweatpants and a gray sweatshirt with a glittering black skull on the front.

"You sure about this, Angel?"

A single tear tracked down her cheek, and she shook her head. "Not in the slightest, but it's now or never. We graduate in three and a half months, and then we're going off to chase a dream." Her smile was small and didn't quite reach her eyes. "It's now or never."

She slipped a chilled hand in his and pulled the

door behind her closed. The walk from her house to the cemetery was largely in silence. Several times his eyes landed on her bent auburn head, and he struggled to catch his breath. Her petite five-foot four-inch frame housed a level of strength he couldn't imagine.

He squeezed her hand because...he couldn't not. His body, his heart...it couldn't help but respond to the call of his Gigi.

At the brick entryway, she hesitated. Wyatt tightened his grip. "We don't have to do this today. We can come back tomorrow. Or next week." Images of how shattered Gigi had been in the days and weeks following her mother's funeral added a note of desperation to his voice that he struggled to bank.

She squared her shoulders and looked up at him. "I can do this, just..."

His fingertips grazed her jaw as her words died on her lips. "Just what, Angel?"

Vulnerability reflected back at him in her wide-eyed gaze. "Just don't leave me."

Her words sliced through his heart with precision. He moved to stand in front of her and cradled her face between his palms. "I'm not going anywhere, Angel. I told you before, you and I are a forever thing. Most couples that fall in love in high school break up, but not us. We were meant to be different and break every stereotype."

Gigi's lips twitched. "Except for that whole rhinestone cowboy thing, right? Because you seem hell bent on fulfilling that role."

He grinned and joined his lips with hers because...what else could he do when his Dark Angel stole his ability to form words?

She gripped his wrists where he held her face and stroked her thumbs along his pulse point. It was wrong and he almost hated himself, but even with the weight of where they were surrounding him, his body responded to her feather-light touch. With more strength than he knew he possessed, he brushed his lips across hers one final time before breaking the kiss.

If he had any hope of being the support she needed without his hormones making him look like a total jackass, he had to focus. There was no chance that could happen when she was melting his brain with her lips.

They walked along the path winding between headstones and footplates. Even though she'd never made the trek here before, Gigi walked resolutely toward her mother's resting place like she'd done it every day. Each step purposeful and determined. Wyatt was helpless to do more than keep the tight grip on her hand and pray she'd let him hold her if she fell apart.

Her cadence slowed when they were less than ten feet away. The fingers laced with his began to tremble seconds before the vibration consumed her entire body. He dropped her hand and wound his arms around her waist, tugging her close to his side.

Wyatt pressed his lips to her temple as they stood a short distance from the blue marble etched with her mother's name and a brief dedication.

Unaccounted for minutes ticked past in silence before her soft voice cut through the cold winter air. "Did I tell you I wrote that?"

He blinked down at her upturned face, surprisingly

free of tears. "Wrote what?"

She nodded to the headstone. "That poem. I wrote it for her for Mother's Day and…" Her head dropped. "And she told Dad that she wanted that verse put there. I-I was mad at first. When he told me. I wrote that to tell her how much I loved her and would always love her. It didn't belong in an empty soulless place like this."

His brain struggled to find words, to make words. What the hell was he supposed to say to that? "And now?"

Gigi tilted her head and fixed her gaze straight ahead for a moment before turning back to him. "Now I'm glad a part of me will be there to honor her forever."

Once again they were cocooned in a blanket of silence, but unlike before, this was a calm, peaceful quiet. He moved to stand behind her, pulling her close to his chest.

"Thanks for coming with me, Cowboy."

Shock radiated out to consume his entire being. Did she really just thank him? Didn't she know there was nowhere else he could imagine being if she needed him other than right by her side?

But he swallowed down every word and, instead, dropped a kiss on her auburn crown. "Thanks for wanting me to come with you."

***

Georgia

"Whatcha lookin' at there, Gigi?"

281

She squinted up into the bright late spring sun as Wyatt approached and grinned. "I printed out some information on different colleges offering distance learning options."

Wyatt thumbed through the papers she had spread out across the picnic table as he straddled the bench seat beside her. "I don't see USF here."

The wave of regret that washed over her every time she thought about parting with her dream college hit once again, and her smile faltered slightly. "They don't offer online classes for marketing, so I am looking at some other options."

He tilted her head and regarded her in silence so long she looked away and began shuffling the papers, trying to fit them in the folder. Heat inched up the back of her neck completely unrelated to the warm sun and completed related to the intent stare from the cowboy on her left.

"But USF is your dream."

She swallowed down the disappointment surfacing at the accuracy of his words and smiled. "Dreams can change."

His brows knitted together, concern etching into his features. Georgia had come to terms, as much as she could, with the knowledge that she had to choose between Wyatt and the college she always intended to make her alma mater. The decision hadn't been as easy as she let him think, but in the end she believed more in the power of their relationship, and every promise he'd ever uttered, than she did in anything else.

Georgia pushed the folder away and turned on the bench, angling her leg up in front of her. She leaned forward and brushed her lips across his a couple of times before he groaned, tangled his fingers in her hair, and pulled her close for the deep, soul-rendering kiss she'd come to expect from him. The one she knew would never be found in another.

She slid her palms up the front of his shirt and laced them behind his neck. His tongue snaked inside her mouth, and she was helpless to silence the whimper. Or prevent her body from scooting closer to his.

The boisterous voice of one of the football players several yards away was enough to bring them both back to their reality and the knowledge they were very much in public. And very much at risk of being caught by one of the faculty members.

Her cheeks warmed as they broke the kiss. "And besides," she continued as though her brain hadn't been turned to mush by the rhinestone cowboy that commanded her heart as much as he did her body, "I've managed to log enough AP classes I will basically start as a sophomore almost anywhere I go."

They discussed a few options, but the slight V that had formed between Wyatt's brows when she first mentioned picking a different college never fully disappeared. The bell rang, summoning them in opposite directions. With a much briefer parting kiss than their earlier one, and promises to meet at the end of the school day to go to his training session, she headed to her fourth period class, falling in step beside Paige easily.

"You two make me nauseous." Paige stuck her finger in her mouth and pretended to gag.

Georgia laughed and bumped her shoulder against

her friend. "Don't blame us because Evan turned out to be a grade A asshole. I'm still willing to knee him in the b—"

Paige clapped a hand over her mouth. "If I take you up on that, you need to make sure it looks like an accident. No discussions ahead of time."

They were laughing as they found their seats in the classroom. Georgia reached into her backpack to pull out her binder and managed to deposit the folder containing all the college research onto the floor.

Paige began gathering the papers and handing them back to her. "What's all this?"

Georgia shrugged and concentrated on neatly stacking all the papers, giving her a very good reason to avoid eye contact with her best friend. "Just some of the best colleges for a marketing degree."

"Why are you college shopping? I thought that was a done deal, written in stone. It has always been USF or bust for you."

Every time she revisited the decision, she felt less and less sure she was making the right one. "Yeah, but things change. If I want to be with Wyatt, I need to be able to travel. USF doesn't offer marketing as an option for distance education."

Just as Paige began to protest, Mr. Martin called the class to order and began to drone in his monotone voice about literature at the turn of the century.

Throughout the class, she fought the same gnawing at her gut that questioned the path she'd chosen.

Chapter Thirty-One

Wyatt

Present Day

Her silence made the granola bar he'd managed to devour moments before she walked through the door pitch and roll in his stomach. He wanted to believe she'd say yes—or preferably "hell, yes"—but nothing was a guarantee. And Gigi was nothing if not stubborn.

She also had every damn reason under the sun to shoot him down and make him spend a dozen years groveling to make up for the past twelve he'd been a complete idiot. It was bad enough to leave the way he did, but when his yellow-bellied ass didn't call for days, then weeks, then months, then years, it became too late.

If she gave him the chance, he'd happily spend the

next fifty years making it up to her, but hopefully with his ring firmly in place on her left hand.

She pressed her fingers against her mouth and her shoulders shook with sobs, propelling him to his feet. "Hell, Angel, I'm sorry if this is too soon—" What he thought were sobs were giggles that turned into peals of laughter. His brows drew together and lips turned down. "Okay, I am officially confused."

"Oh, yes, of course I'll marry you, but…how in the hell did you manage to find a black engagement ring?"

Wyatt blinked once. Twice. And a third time for good measure. He held up the hand with the ring still pinched between his thumb and forefinger. "Wait, did you…say yes?"

She held his face between her palms and smiled the same radiant smile that bowled his heart over when he was sixteen and hadn't failed to do it every time he'd seen it since then. "Yes, I said yes."

He slid the ring on her finger moments before he locked his arm around her waist and picked her up, spinning her in a circle.

She said yes.

He set her down and sealed his lips with hers, desperate for the taste of Gigi once again. She softly moaned against his mouth, and his knees nearly buckled from the impact. He didn't regret keeping a small distance from her while he focused on rebuilding the part of them he'd damaged so deeply, but he damn sure wasn't going to waste the gift he was being given now.

His hands dropped to grip each of her hips, and he pulled her against him. The barely perceptible groan gave him the entrance he needed, and his tongue snaked along the length of hers, taunting and teasing the way they always did.

Gigi fingers dug into the back of his neck, keeping his mouth joined firmly with hers and not allowing an atom of space between them. Not that he had a single complaint.

"The house…" he managed to gasp out when the need for oxygen required them to break apart. "The house is done. I have furniture, well, some anyway. But I have a bed. One I think you'll like. It's just like yours—"

"And how do you know what my bed looks like? I've upgraded since high school, you know."

He winked and pressed against her with a grin. "I know and I may have taken a peek or two while Gram napped in the afternoons." He trailed his mouth along her jaw, nipped at her earlobe, and ran down the column of her neck. "I needed to make sure I got something my Dark Angel would like."

She moaned and arched into his touch. "But your house is damn near a mile away."

Wyatt leaned back. "So what do you propose instead?" He gestured toward the sand. "No offense, Gigi, but I don't think I'd like to get sand in certain crevices, if you know what I mean."

A saucy smile curled her lips. "How about a roll in the hay instead?"

He smirked and reached into the front pocket where he always kept the same coin he'd flipped more than a dozen years ago on the front step of her house. "Flip ya for it."

Gigi's eyes followed the silver disc as it flew into

the air, his hand caught it, and he smacked it down onto the back of the opposite hand. "Heads we break in that soft, comfortable, four hundred thread count covered bed at my place."

"Tails I won't have to wait that freaking long."

Wyatt laughed and slid his palm away, revealing the back side of the coin. Gigi gloated as she scurried up the ladder, and Wyatt scrambled to follow behind her, still holding the piece of silver in his hand.

One more secret he had to reveal.

***

Georgia

He held the coin between his thumb and forefinger. "Do you know what this is?"

Georgia rolled her eyes. "Are we really going to do an elementary school math class here, Cowboy?"

The cocky smirk slid easily into place along with every ounce of his excessive Rhinestone Cowboy persona. And Georgia fell a little more in love.

"This, Gigi, is the same one I flipped the first night we kissed." He sauntered closer until he stood right in front of her, tossing the coin in the air before grabbing it and repeating the action.

Everything melted away other than the all-consuming love burning inside her chest. She reached up and gripped the back of his neck. "I love you, Wyatt Carlisle."

His eyes widened, pupils dilating to the size of saucers. "That's the first time you said it. This time around." He chuckled a little and dropped his forehead to hers.

She grinned up at him, allowing every emotion she'd vainly tried to withhold to shine through. "I figured I told you enough times when we were kids, and since nothing changed, you'd know it was still in effect."

The hand that had been stroking up and down her spine stilled. "Nothing changed? You…you never stopped loving me? Not even when what's-his-name was hanging around?"

"His name is Bruce—"

"Yeah, we don't need to ever utter that name again."

She laughed, one hand sliding from around his neck to stroke the front of his shirt. Right above the spot where the tattoo she very much intended to lick along every line branded his body. "Never, Cowboy. I never stopped loving you."

Georgia had barely finished speaking the words when he captured her mouth with his. Passion and desire fueled the lusty kiss that slowly softened into something more. He lifted her against his body and gently lowered her into a pile of hay.

"I love you, Angel, and I know this is basically every cowboy's wet dream, but are you sure this is where you want to do this?" His lips moved along her jaw to her neck, nipping at the sensitive flesh. "I have a ridiculously comfortable bed at my house."

"Later, Cowboy, later." She gasped as his tongue licked the space behind her ear, and he lightly bit her lobe. Her legs wrapped around his waist, and she pushed into him, annoyed at the barriers of clothing separating them. "Right now we have a hell of a lot of time to make up for, and I don't want to waste that driving."

He sat back on his heels, took off his hat, and whipped his shirt over his head. "I never argue with a lady."

She grabbed his belt buckle, unfastened it, and slid it through the loops, tossing it across the room. "Then put the damn hat back on your head and get a move on."

Wyatt groaned as he plopped the hat back on his head. He reached down and tugged the camisole free from her slacks, hissing as her white lace strapless bra was exposed. "Am I gonna have to wear this hat every time we have sex?"

Georgia flicked open the button on her pants and slid the zipper down with a muted hiss. "Maybe not every time, but let's hold off on making that decision for a while, hmm?"

He ran his hands from her shoulders, over the lacy lingerie, and down the front of her body until he landed on the waistband of her pants. A slight tug and she lifted her hips to allow him to pull them free and join the rest of their clothes across the room.

She moved her legs back around him, but he captured her right heel before she could lock them into place. His thumb stroked along her Achilles tendon, a spot she'd never thought erogenous before but now drove her insane.

Wyatt grazed his lips along her calf, his teeth sinking into the skin behind her knee. He hooked her ankle over his shoulder and bent down, rubbing the hard bulge of denim against her heated core.

Georgia groaned, and he laughed in response, his

mouth brushing over hers.

"Do you like that, Gigi?"

She growled in response, gripping his shoulders tightly. "I'd like for my fiancé to get his fine ass naked and show me that he hasn't forgotten how to take a good ride in his...lengthy retirement."

He stilled over her for half a second before erupting into laughter. "You are the only woman who could drive every part of me crazy at the same time."

Allowing her eyes to feast on him as he stood to remove his jeans and boxers, she reached behind her and unhooked her bra before sliding her underwear down and kicking them free. "I take that as a compliment of the highest order."

Wyatt dropped between her open thighs, his lips finding hers immediately. "I love you, Angel."

She gripped his neck and pulled him back slightly to lock eyes with him. "And I love you too, Cowboy."

He kissed a path from her mouth to one puckered nub as his finger pinched and teased the other before he switched sides. Georgia arched into him, every nerve tingling, her body responding to him in the way it only ever did for Wyatt.

His thumbs moved to caress her hipbones as his mouth continued down her abdomen, his tongue dipping inside her navel. As his lips brushed her heated core, her head shot up, and she almost exploded at the sight of that ridiculous cowboy hat planted between her thighs.

All of the oxygen shot from her mouth as his tongue ran up the seam. She fell back on the cushion of hay, panting as his hands and lips wreaked havoc on her body, teasing and tormenting her until she barely clung to the edge of sanity.

With a final suck on the tiny bundle of aching nerves, begging for undivided attention, Georgia's hold released and she was launched from the pinnacle into a sea of exquisite pleasure. Wave after wave crashed over her with his continued ministrations until she tugged him back up her body. "Condom?"

He held a foil packet between his thumb and forefinger with a cocky grin. "Got it covered. Well, not yet, but I will." He winked and ripped the package.

She levered up on her elbows and frowned at him. "Where the hell did you pull that thing from? Do you have a secret stash somewhere?"

Wyatt chuckled as he sheathed himself and returned to her, nuzzling into the nape of her neck. "A man's belt buckle is an important thing, Gigi. Especially when it has a handy compartment to keep emergency necessities."

"Only you, Cowboy." She lifted her hips and pushed against his hard length as she tried to catch her breath.

Wyatt raised up onto his elbows and stared at her for a long moment before he rocked his hips forward and slid inside, filling her physically. "Thank you for loving me enough to give me a second chance."

And just like that, her stupid freaking cowboy managed to fill her heart just as much as his body had.

He moved slowly at first, sealing his words with every stroke inside of her, but the passion that always consumed them quickly took over, and within moments, another burst of stars exploded in front of Georgia's vision. She was swept up in a fresh current of ecstasy when Wyatt growled his own release close to her ear.

Several long seconds later, he peeled himself from her and fell beside her on his back with a deep chuckle.

Georgia reached over and pinched his arm. "Hey, maybe all those buckle bunnies let you get away with this kind of behavior, but it's typically frowned upon for you to laugh after you're done making love to your future wife."

He turned onto his side and propped his head up with his hand, his elbow resting just above her shoulder. "Sorry, Angel, but you gotta admit, it's pretty damn funny."

"What's that, Cowboy? I wasn't timing you. Did you manage to last a full eight seconds?"

His expression sobered, and he held up one finger. "First, that isn't funny. You are more than welcome to run a clock next time, and I guarantee you'll be sufficiently impressed with my endurance abilities." He picked a piece of straw from her hair and stuck it in his mouth. "What is funny is, after all my high school fantasies, I finally got an actual roll in the hay."

Georgia winked and pulled the stem from his mouth and brought his lips down to hers. "Happy to be of service, Cowboy."

Epilogue

Three Months Later

"Hey, big brother! I can't believe you're actually hitched!" Connor slung his arm around Wyatt's shoulders in an awkward and unsteady embrace.

Wyatt sighed and disengaged from the younger man. "Dammit, Connor, couldn't you keep your shit together just for one day? Especially considering the fact it's my wedding day."

Matching blue eyes, the one trait every brother had inherited from their father, narrowed at him as Connor straightened to his full height. "I'm fine. I keep telling you that. This is a party. People are supposed to be happy. Damn, what happened to you? You were supposed to be the fun brother."

Before Wyatt could give him the appropriate ass beating—either physically or verbally, whichever came first—that he so richly deserved, Dean grabbed Connor's swaying form. "Go make out with your wife or whatever the hell you old married people do. I've got this one."

Soft hands encircled his bicep and shoulder from behind, and a delicate chin rested on his shoulder. "We'll figure out what to do with him."

Wyatt turned and pulled his newly minted bride flush against his body. He captured her left hand and kissed the diamond and onyx ring he'd slipped on her finger in the early morning hours a few days after they'd reconciled. "He does have one thing going for him. That whole making out with my wife thing sounds like a pretty damn good idea."

He pulled her behind the large tree adorned with mason jars filled with candles hanging from the limbs on crystal strings. Where to have their wedding hadn't been in question for a moment, especially not once Wyatt finally disclosed that RA Ranch was, in fact, the Rhinestone Angel Ranch. Meant for them from the beginning.

"Aren't there things we are supposed to be doing like cutting the cake or entertaining guests or…" The words died on her lips as he pressed her against the tree, and his lips descended to her neck, making a trail of fire down to her shoulder.

Wyatt pulled back and clucked his tongue. "What do I keep telling you, Angel? Who cares what we are supposed to do? We were meant to be different."

The End

Acknowledgements

For my Double A Team, the reason I do everything, including breathe.

For Ginger who has inspired my character Georgia with her state name and love of USF. The Iconic Bull plays an epic role here.

As always to my beloved hashtags and the brilliant ladies attached to them.

My #RChat lovelies, you are the reason I have a single book, much less a series. Your endless support and the lessons you've taught me have shaped my writing life. I could not have done this without you.

My #BoardmanBitches Evie & Hannah, I can never thank you enough for living close enough to make the real life struggles bearable.

My #MDO darlings Evie, Marit, and Meka, our inappropriate jokes, half (or more than half) naked men, and adult toy discussions give me life.

As always, I have to end with all the gratitude for the person—MY person—who refused to allow me to quit, told me breaks were okay, and shined a light to help me find my way out of several bouts of writer's block. Evie, I can never thank you enough for being you, for being here, and for being mine.

About the Author

Books, coffee, and chocolate make up both the heart and body mass that is better known as Amelia Foster. She has been a lifelong lover of the written word, both as a reader and an author, and completed her first manuscript at the ripe old age of five complete with illustrations. Sadly, her art was a medium that never improved over time although thankfully her writing has.

From sweet to salacious the only requirement Amelia has in books she reads–and definitely in the ones she crafts–is an excessively satisfying happily ever after…and then a little bit more.

Facebook:
https://www.facebook.com/amelia.foster.1213986

Twitter:
https://twitter.com/afosterauthor

WordPress:
https://ameliafosterauthor.wordpress.com/

Instagram:
https://www.instagram.com/ameliafosterauthor/

Pinterest:
https://www.pinterest.com/ameliafosterauthor/

Join our Reader Group on Facebook and don't miss out on meeting our authors and entering epic giveaways!

Limitless Reading

Where reading a book
is your first step to becoming
limitless...

LIMITLESS PUBLISHING *Reader Group*

Join today! *"Where reading a book is your first step to becoming limitless..."*